"Will remind readers what chattering teeth sound like." —*Kirkus Reviews*

"Voracious readers of horror will delightfully consume the contents of Bates's World's Scariest Places books."
—*Publishers Weekly*

"Creatively creepy and sure to scare." —*The Japan Times*

"Jeremy Bates writes like a deviant angel I'm glad doesn't live on my shoulder."
—Christian Galacar, author of GILCHRIST

"Thriller fans and readers of Stephen King, Joe Lansdale, and other masters of the art will find much to love."
—*Midwest Book Review*

"An ice-cold thriller full of mystery, suspense, fear."
—David Moody, author of HATER and AUTUMN

"A page-turner in the true sense of the word."
—*HorrorAddicts*

"Will make your skin crawl." —*Scream Magazine*

"Told with an authoritative voice full of heart and insight."
—Richard Thomas, Bram Stoker nominated author

"Grabs and doesn't let go until the end." —*Writer's Digest*

BY JEREMY BATES

Suicide Forest ◆ *The Catacombs* ◆ *Helltown* ◆ *Island of the Dolls* ◆ *Mountain of the Dead* ◆ *Hotel Chelsea* ◆ *Mosquito Man* ◆ *The Sleep Experiment* ◆ *The Man from Taured* ◆ *Merfolk* ◆ *The Dancing Plague 1 & 2* ◆ *White Lies* ◆ *The Taste of Fear* ◆ *Black Canyon* ◆ *Run* ◆ *Rewind* ◆ *Neighbors* ◆ *Six Bullets* ◆ *Box of Bones* ◆ *The Mailman* ◆ *Re-Roll* ◆ *New America: Utopia Calling* ◆ *Dark Hearts* ◆ *Bad People*

FREE BOOK

For a limited time, visit www.jeremybatesbooks.com to receive a free copy of the critically acclaimed short novel *Black Canyon*, winner of Crime Writers of Canada The Lou Allin Memorial Award.

HELLTOWN

World's Scariest Places 3

Jeremy Bates

HELLTOWN

PROLOGUE

"Abby doesn't need a man anymore.
The Devil is her lover now!"
Abby (1974)

Inside the mold-infested abandoned house a brass Chinese gong reverberated dully, followed by liturgical music minced with electronically produced effects. The door at the far end of the room opened and a large woman emerged clothed in the customary habit and wimple of a nun. She held a cased ceremonial sword in one hand, a black candle in the other. The deacon and sub-deacon, both clad in floor-length robes, black and hooded, appeared next. The high priest came last. Unlike the others, his face was visible, the top of his head covered with a skin-tight cowl sprouting horns made of animal bones. He wore a black cassock and matching gabardine cape with scarlet lining. His eyes were dark, shimmering, though his long bushy beard was far from Mephisthophelean.

The procession congregated a few feet in front of the altar, the high priest in the middle, the mock-nun and deacon to his left, the sub-deacon to his right. They all bowed deeply, then looked down at the naked woman who lay atop the holy table. Her body was at right angles to its length, her arms outstretched crucifix-style, her legs spread wide, each limb secured in place with ropes anchored to iron eyelets on the floor. Her pale white skin contrasted sharply with her brightly made-up face and ebony hair. The number of the beast, 666, was scrawled in blood across her bare breasts. On the wall above her, painted in red, was the Sigil of Baphomet: a goat's head in an inverted pentagram within a circle. A large upside -down cross hung directly before the face so that an eye peered ahead from either side of it.

The organist switched to *The Hymn to Satan*, a perversion of Bach's *Jesu Meine Freude*. The deacon rang a deeply toned bell nine times. Then the high priest raised his hands, palms downward, and said: "*In Nomine Magni Dei Nostri Satanas, introibo ad altare Domini Inferi.*"

The black mass had begun.

The car in the driveway was the first in a string of bad omens for Darla Evans. It wasn't a pickup truck or even the rusted Ford Thunderbird that Mark's friend Henry Roberts drove. It was a little red Volkswagen Beetle. It occupied most of the small driveway, so Darla pulled up to the curb, bumper to bumper with Mark's aging Camaro. She got out and retrieved her suitcase from the Golf's trunk, breathing in the crisp autumn air.

Seeing her recently purchased home, Darla felt a burst of nostalgia, even though she'd only been away in Akron at the career fair for two days. The house was a quaint turn of the century, three bedrooms, two baths, with a large backyard—a perfect place to start a family.

As Darla wheeled her suitcase up the front walk, her hand absently touching her barely noticeable baby bump, she glanced at the Bug. She wondered who it belonged to. Not the construction guys. They wouldn't be caught dead in anything so dainty. Someone to do with the wedding? Darla and Mark's mother Jennifer were taking care of most of the preparations, but Mark had been tasked with organizing the photographer.

Darla didn't bother fishing her keys from her handbag. Mark never locked up when he was home. Sure enough, the front door eased open, and she stepped into the small foyer. Stairs on the left climbed to the second floor; the living room opened to the right. The entranceway to the latter was sealed with transparent plastic. Through it she could see a jumble of masonry, a few scattered tools, and a gray coating of dust on the floor, marred with a zigzag of booted footprints. She and Mark were refinishing the original redbrick fireplace mantelpiece, which dated back to the 1920s.

Mark's loafers rested at the base of the cast-iron radiator, next to a pair of black pointed-toe sling-backs with high heels. A work associate? Darla wondered. She tilted her head, expecting to hear their conversation. She heard nothing. She thought about calling out, announcing that she'd returned from the career fair early, but given the silence she decided Mark and his guest were likely out on the back patio.

She left her suitcase standing upright and followed the hallway to the kitchen. She frowned at the two empty fishbowl wine glasses on the counter, next to an empty bottle of Merlot. Confusion stirred within her and, hovering beneath that, like a dark shadow, alarm. She told herself a perfectly innocent explanation existed as to why Mark would be sharing wine with someone who wore pumps and drove a red Bug. Of course there was. She and Mark had the ideal relationship. Everyone said so. They'd just bought the house, were expecting a baby. There was no room in that scenario for what the whisperings in her head suggested. She felt ashamed to be considering such a thing.

She continued to the rear of the kitchen and looked through the sliding glass doors. Plastic patio set, old barbeque, sagging shed—nobody anywhere in the yard. Darla thought about calling out again, but this time she kept quiet for a different reason. *Because you might disturb them? Because they might have time to—to do what? Get themselves decent?* She returned the way she'd come, her head suddenly airy, her stomach nauseous.

Back in the foyer Darla stood at the bottom of the stairs, hesitating. She thought she heard a faint something, maybe someone speaking at a low volume. She started up the steps. Ten to the landing, right turn, six more. Carpeted, they didn't creak. The plan was to toss the carpet and restore the original hardwood hidden beneath.

When she reached the second floor, she confirmed what she'd thought she'd heard. Voices, murmurings, coming from the master bedroom. She started in that direction, floating now, disconnected from herself. It was as though her body had flooded itself with a cocktail of potent chemicals to numb her from the inevitable pain lurking very close. She knew that men and women cheated on each other. It was a fact of life in a monogamous society. She just never imagined Mark doing it to *her.*

It can't be him in there, she thought irrationally. *It has to be someone else.*

Halfway through the third segment of the black mass, the Canon, the sub-deacon fetched a chamber pot from the shadows and presented it to the nun, who urinated into it, smiling beatifically, while the organist played a low-pitched, rumbling hymn. The high priest said, "In the name of Mary she maketh the font resound with the waters of mercy. She giveth the showers of blessing and poureth forth the tears of her shame. She suffereth long, and her humiliation is great, and she doth pour upon the earth with the joy of her mortification. Her cup runneth over, and her water is sublime. *Ave Maria ad micturiendum festinant.*"

When the nun finished urinating, the sub-deacon retrieved the font and held it before the high priest, who dipped a phallus-shaped aspergillum into the fluid. He turned to the four cardinal compass points, shaking the aspergillum three times at each. "In the name of Satan, we bless thee with this, the symbol of the seed of life. In the name of Lucifer, we bless thee with this, the symbol of the seed of life. In the name of Belial, we bless thee with this, the symbol of the seed of life. In the name of Leviathan, we bless thee with this, the symbol of the seed of life." He raised the phallic aspergillum breast-high in an attitude of offering to the Baphomet, kissed it, and placed it back on the altar. Then he uttered the purported last words of Jesus Christ upon the cross: "*Shemhamforash!*"

"Hail Satan!" the assemblage replied.

◆ ◆ ◆

Darla stopped on the other side of the bedroom door. She could hear a woman's voice purring, the words punctuated with throaty laughter. She wanted to turn around, leave, pretend this wasn't happening, but she couldn't do that. Steeling herself, she opened the door—and everything inside her collapsed at once. Her lungs, so it was hard to breathe. Her nervous system, so she became numb. Her heart, slit in half, emptied, hollow.

Mark lay on his back on the queen bed, his well-toned body naked except for a pair of blue briefs. A tanned peroxide blonde straddled him, groin to groin. She wore nothing but a black frilly thong. In one hand she held a pink feather duster, in the other, a red candle, which she was using to drip scalding wax onto Mark's chest.

Mark turned his head toward Darla as if sensing her presence. Seeing her, he threw the woman off him and sat bolt upright. "Jesus!" he said, and for a moment he appeared furious, as if outraged that Darla would have the gall to walk in on him while he was getting it on. Very quickly, however, he adopted a suitably ashamed and worried countenance.

"Wha...?" The woman turned and saw Darla. Her eyes widened in surprise.

"Get out," Darla told her evenly, venomously.

"Hey, sorry, we should have gone somewhere else—"

"Get out!" she screamed.

"Okay, okay, like chill out." Her casual tone was infuriating. She would walk away today and likely gossip about what happened with her friends. It wasn't her life abruptly in shambles.

Darla marched over and grabbed the slut by the blow-dried hair and yanked her off the bed. The woman yelped.

"Hey, Dar, hold on," Mark said. "Take it easy. Let's talk."

Ignoring him, Darla dragged the woman—bent over, shrieking, bare breasts flopping—across the room, shoved her into the hallway, slammed the door shut.

Then she whirled on Mark. She wanted to hurl every curse word she knew at him. But she could articulate nothing. She bit her bottom lip to keep it from trembling.

"Listen, Dar," he said, scratching the back of his head, "it's not what you—"

"Don't give me that! Don't you *dare* give me that!"

He closed his mouth and seemed at a loss for what to say next.

"How long?" she said.

He got off the bed, pulled on his acid-wash jeans.

"How long?" she demanded.

Banging at the door. "Mark! I need my clothes."

Mark started toward Darla, thought better of it, kept his distance. "A few weeks," he said.

"Who is she?"

"It doesn't matter."

"*Who is she?*"

He shrugged. "Someone from the ski resort."

"Hey!" the woman persisted. "I'll go. I just need my clothes."

"Let me send her off," he said, "and we'll talk."

"Get out."

"What?"

"Get out of this house."

"Dar, you're not thinking straight. Let me get rid of her—"

"Get the hell out of this house, Mark, or I swear to God I'm going to hit you."

"Dar—"

"Go!"

He frowned, angry again, undecided. Then he scooped up his yellow Polo shirt with the embroidered logo of his auto repair business, a black bra, and a red tartan dress. He left his socks, inside out, on the floor. On his way to the door he stopped in front of Darla and tried to touch her on the shoulder. She slapped him across the cheek. He recoiled in shock. More anger, then weary resignation. He left the bedroom.

"Hey, thanks," the blonde said, taking her dress. "And sorry about this—"

"Not now," Mark snapped.

Darla remained where she was, arms folded across her chest, beginning to shake. The front door opened and closed. A car started. Then another. Moments later the sound of the engines faded, and she was alone.

The high priest removed the black veil that covered the chalice and paten. He lifted the latter in both hands, on which rested a wafer of turnip, and said, "Blessed be the bread and wine of death. Blessed a thousand times more than the flesh and blood of life, for you have not been harvested by human hands nor did any human creature mill and grind you. It was our Lord Satan who took you to the mill of the grave so that you should thus become the bread and blood of revelation and revulsion." His voice became harsher, more guttural. "I spit upon you, I cast you down, because you preach punishment and shame to those who would emancipate themselves and repudiate the slavery of the church!" He inserted the host into the woman's labia, removed it, and raised it to the Baphomet. "Vanish into nothingness, thou fool of fools, thou vile and abhorred pretender to the majesty of Satan, the true god of gods! Vanish into the void of thy empty Heaven, for thou wert never, nor shalt thou ever be!" He dropped the host into a small bowl and pulverized it with a pestle. He mixed what remained with charcoal and incense and set it aflame with a white candle. While it burned he picked up the Chalice of Ecstasy, which was filled not with blood or semen but his drink of choice, Kentucky bourbon. He raised it to the Baphomet and drank deeply. He replaced the chalice on the altar, covered it and the paten with the veil, then bowed and gave the blessing of Satan, extending his left hand in the Sign of the Horns: the two outermost fingers, representing the goat, pointing upward in defiance of Heaven, the two innermost pointing down in denial of the Holy Trinity. "*Shemhamforash!*"

"Hail, Satan!"

Darla returned to the Golf with her unpacked suitcase and drove. She couldn't stand to be in the house any longer. Every room reminded her of Mark. The kitchen where they'd spent so many mornings in their housecoats making each other breakfast, the den where they'd snuggled up on the sofa together in the evenings to watch TV. Certainly not the bedroom. God, the tramp had been in her *bed*. How could Mark have allowed that? How could he violate the sanctity of the place where they'd conceived the baby that was growing inside her?

With this acid in her head, Darla tooled aimlessly around Boston Mills. She felt lost and confused as if half her identity had been torn away from her—and in a sense she supposed it had. She'd been with Mark for ten years, ever since he'd asked her to their high school prom. He'd been the only stable fixture in her adult life.

Despair filled her. The house was Mark's. He'd paid the down deposit with his savings, and the bank loan was in his name. So she couldn't stay there. She was homeless. Not only that, she had less than a hundred dollars in her bank account, no job, and a baby on the way. There had been a couple of jobs at the career fair she'd thought she might do okay at, but even if she was hired for one tomorrow, she likely wouldn't start for a few weeks, and she wouldn't be paid for another few weeks after that.

Family, she thought. She still had family. Her parents had moved to Florida several years before, and her older brother was teaching English in Japan or South Korea or China—somewhere too distant to think about. But her sister, Leanne, was only forty minutes away in Cleveland. Darla could crash there for a bit, maybe even look for work in Cleveland.

Then again, that meant Darla would have to deal with Leanne's husband, Ray. He was a smug white-collar bank manager who'd always thought of Darla and Mark as uneducated country bumpkins. No, she couldn't show up on his doorstep pregnant and single and broke. It would be humiliating.

Darla began running through a mental list of her friends —and realized she didn't even know who her friends were anymore. They would have to take sides, wouldn't they? How many would choose her over Mark? Likely not many. It didn't matter that Mark was a cheating slime ball. He'd been the extrovert in their relationship, she the introvert. He had an easy way with people she didn't. He'd come out of this scandal unscathed, while she would end up ostracized, an outcast in the very town where she had grown up.

Suzy, she thought. Yes, Suzy. She was single, had just been through a brutal divorce herself. She would sympathize with Darla's predicament. She'd make some strong coffee, they'd sit down, she'd listen to Darla bawl, she wouldn't judge or take sides.

Suzy lived ten minutes away in Sagamore Hills. It would be fastest to travel north on Riverview Road, then east along West

Highland. But Darla decided to detour through Cuyahoga Valley National Park. It would give her a bit more time to get herself together.

She crossed over the Cuyahoga River, then turned left onto Stanford Road. Soon the trees of the national park closed around her—oak, ash, maple, walnut, hickory—and she began to feel calmer. Nature had a way of doing that to her, as she supposed it did for most people. Also, she enjoyed the isolation the park offered, the idea of being on her own. She felt free. *And now I am free*, she thought defiantly. *Mark's gone, out of my life. And maybe that's for the best. Better to find out about his cheating ways now than later on. I'm still young, only twenty-six. I'll meet someone new, start over again…*

Darla had been so preoccupied with her new-life fantasy she didn't realize it was nearly dark. That was the thing with October in Ohio: you had the day, and you had the night, and you had about ten minutes of dusk in between.

She clicked on her headlights—and in the rearview mirror noticed a car behind her do the same. She'd had no idea anyone had even been there.

The car seemed to be accelerating toward her. Darla watched it approach, waiting for it to overtake her. It didn't. Instead it came right up behind her and sat on her tail.

What was the idiot thinking?

Darla was about to pull over to the shoulder, to give the car more room to pass her on the narrow two-lane road, when it rammed her back bumper. She cried out in surprise. The car rammed her again, harder. The steering wheel jerked dangerously in her hands.

The lunatic was trying to run her off the road!

Was he drunk? On drugs?

Heart racing, Darla stomped on the gas, pushing the speedometer needle past fifty, past sixty. The car stuck behind her as the road angled upward steeply. Then the car rammed her once more. This time it remained glued to her ass, *pushing* her. She had to fight the steering wheel to keep it straight, and just as she thought she was going to lose control, the vehicle fell back.

Darla cried out in triumph a moment before the road disappeared in front of her—and she realized her mistake. This stretch of Stanford Road was nicknamed The End of the World because the hill culminated in a brief summit that dropped off sharply on the other side, creating the temporary illusion that you were driving off a cliff—or the end of the world.

Darla had breasted the summit at eighty miles an hour and shot clear into the air.

When the Golf crashed violently back to earth, the front bumper tore free in a fiery display of sparks. The vehicle wrenched to the left, plowed through the smaller shrubbery lining the verge, into the forest, and struck the trunk of a large tree, coming to an abrupt, bone-crushing halt.

With the human sacrifice now at hand, the organist began to play deep, furious chords, while the gong-ringer struck the instrument with the heavy mallet rhythmically, continually. The nun handed the high priest the ceremonial sword. He held it aloft with both hands and recited Lovecraft in a loud, commanding voice, "Oh, friend and companion of the night, thou who rejoiceth in the baying of dogs and spilt blood, who wanderest in the midst of shades among the tombs, who longest for blood and bringest terror to mortals—Gorgo, Mormo, thousand-faced moon—look favorably on our sacrifice and win forgiveness for me and for all those for whom I have offered it. *Tuere nos, Domine Satanus!*"

"Shield us, Lord Satan!" the assemblage cried.

"*Protege nos, Domine Satanus!*" he shouted.

"Protect us, Lord Satan!"

"*Shemhamforash!*"

"Hail Satan! Hail Satan! Hail Satan!"

The high priest sank the sword into the woman's belly.

◆ ◆ ◆

Mark's infidelity, detouring through Cuyahoga Valley National Park, the maniac in the car behind her—these were the first thoughts Darla had entertained, or at least the first ones she could recall, since the crash. But with each passing second she felt herself becoming more lucid, more self-aware. It was as if she'd been in a black abyss deep underwater, and now she was floating upward toward the surface, to the world of the senses. Indeed, she could hear voices, she could smell some kind of incense, she could feel...oh God, the pain! Her body throbbed, nowhere and everywhere at once. Still, she held onto the pain, she wouldn't let it go, because where there was pain there was consciousness.

The surface drifted closer. She could almost reach out and touch it.

Darla's eyes cracked open. She made out several men hovering over her, their faces lost in the shadows of their cowls.

A fireball exploded in her abdomen, far worse than the pain that had lured her from the void, and with wide, glassy eyes she saw that the blade of a sword protruded from her navel, blood pooling around the wound, coloring the surrounding flesh a blackish red.

She screamed.

1987

CHAPTER 1

"Groovy!"
Evil Dead II (1987)

T he headlights punched ghostly tunnels through the shifting fog. Birch trees stripped bare of their fiery Autumn colors and towering evergreens lined the margins of the two-lane rural road. A cold rind of moon hung high in the starless sky, glowing bluish-white behind a raft of eastward-drifting clouds.

Steve slipped on his reading glasses, which he kept on a cord around his neck, and squinted at the roadmap he'd taken from the BMW's glove compartment. "We're on Stanford Road, right?" he said.

"Yup," Jeff said, one hand gripping the leather steering wheel casually. He was eyeing the rearview mirror, either making sure their friends were still following behind them in the other car or admiring his reflection.

Steve wouldn't be surprised if it were the latter. Jeff was about as vain as you could get. And Steve supposed he had the right to be. Not only was he tall, bronzed, and blond, but he was also athletic, successful, and charismatic—the proverbial stud every guy wanted to be, and every girl wanted to date.

Steve himself wasn't bad looking. He kept in shape, had neat brown hair, intelligent brown eyes, and a friendly manner that girls found attractive. However, whenever he was hanging out with Jeff he couldn't help but feel more unremarkable than remarkable, intimidated even.

"I don't see this End of World road anywhere," Steve said, pushing the glasses up the bridge of his nose.

"No duh, genius," Jeff said. "The End of the World's a nickname."

"For Stanford Road?"

"Yup," Jeff said.

"Why's it called The End of the World?" Mandy asked from the backseat. "Does it just end?"

"I'm not walking anywhere," Jenny said. She was seated next to Mandy.

"Will you two give it a rest?" Jeff said, annoyed. "I have everything planned, all right?"

Mandy stuck her head up between the seats to study the map herself. Her wavy red hair smelled of strawberries and brushed Steve's forearm. "Hey, the road *does* just end," she said. "What gives, Jeff? Can you tell us what we're doing out here already?"

"Sit your ass down, Mandy," he told her. "I can't see out the back."

"Noah's still behind you, don't worry."

"Sit down!"

"Jeez," she said and flopped back down. She mumbled something to Jenny, and they giggled. They'd been doing that all car trip: mumbling and giggling with each other like they were schoolgirls. Steve found it hard to comprehend how they could be so comfortable with one another, considering they had met for the first time only a few hours before.

Jeff glared at them in the rearview mirror, but said conversationally to Steve: "You know, legend has it that cutthroats and thieves hang out along this road and rob anyone driving through."

"That's bull," Mandy said. "How do you rob someone in a car?"

"With a giant magnet," Jenny said, pulling her blonde hair

into a ponytail, which she secured with an elastic band. "It drags the car right off the road, like in the cartoons. Pow!"

"Right, just like that," Jeff said. "And you're in med school?"

"So how?" Mandy asked.

"Because the road doesn't just end," Jeff told them. "Part of it was closed down, yeah. But you can still go around the barricade and drive on the closed-down part. You have to go super slow though because it's narrow and twisting. That's how the cutthroats get you. They just slip out of the woods and—" He hit the brakes. Inertia slammed everyone forward against their seatbelts. Mandy and Jenny yelped.

Laughing, Jeff accelerated. Behind them, Noah blared his horn.

"God, Jeff!" Mandy said. "You're such a dick!"

"A small dick I've heard," Jenny added, and the two of them broke into more giggles.

Jeff scowled. "A small dick, huh?" he said. "You've never had any complaints, have you, babe?"

Mandy rolled her eyes.

"Well?" he demanded.

"No, hon," she said. "No complaints."

Mandy turned her attention to the haunting black forest whisking past her window. It really did look like the type of woods that would be home to a ruthless band of cutthroats. The shadowed maple and oak and elm had already shed all of their foliage, leaving their spindly branches denuded and shivering in the soughing wind. They stood interwoven with the larger pine, spruce, and cedar, the great needle-covered boughs sprouting from the trunks like dark wings, masking whatever may lay behind them.

What if Jeff was telling the truth? she wondered. What if when they eventually got to this closed-off road and had to slow down a deranged man—worse, a *pack* of deranged men—

swarmed the car, dragged her out by the hair, and slit her throat?

What if—

No. Mandy banished the "what ifs" from her mind. No cutthroats were living in the forest. She was safe. They were all safe. Jeff was full of it. Not only that, he was full of *himself* too. *You've never had any complaints, have you, babe?* Who said stuff like that? The answer, of course, was Jeff. His ego was so big it couldn't see its shoes on a cloudy day.

Mandy and Jeff had been at a party a short time back, a "model party," or at least that's what everybody called it. It had been hosted by Smirnoff vodka. The models had been hired for the glam factor. There were no Christy Brinkleys or Brook Shields in attendance. The models all hailed from the no-name talent agencies that dotted the backstreets of New York City. They were the D-list hired out for photo shoots in obscure magazines or low-budget cable TV commercials. Not that you'd know this by talking to them. Everyone Mandy had mingled with had a tale about brushing shoulders with Burt Reynolds or Christian Slater—and missing out on their big break by inches because of some unfortunate reason or another.

Anyway, they did have their looks going for them. Mandy knew she was attractive. She'd been told this her entire life. People often said she resembled a red-haired Michelle Pfeiffer, even though Mandy thought her eyes were a little too close together, her nose a bit too pointy. Yet the no-name models made her feel positively average. They were all taller than her, had the flawless, thin bodies of fourteen-year-old boys, although with breasts, and most importantly, they knew how to flaunt their sex appeal.

At the end of the evening, while waiting for a cab, Jeff, tipsy, said, "Did you see that guy? The one with the long hair?"

"They all had long hair," Mandy told him.

"White shirt unbuttoned halfway down his chest."

Mandy had seen him. He'd been gorgeous. "What about him?"

"You think he was good-looking?"

"Ha! You're jealous," she said.

"Hardly. But I'll tell you this much. He's probably the first guy I've ever seen who's better looking than me."

Mandy stared at Jeff, thinking he must be kidding. He wasn't. Up until that point in his twenty-six years of existence, Jeff had seriously considered himself to be the best-looking man on the planet.

Mandy blinked now, and instead of the trees and the blackness beyond the car window, she saw her glass-caught reflection. It was vaguely visible, transparent, ghostlike. It gave her a case of the creeps.

Shivering, she faced forward again. No one had spoken since Jeff had challenged her to find fault with his love-making.

Mandy didn't like prolonged silences, they made her uneasy, and she said, "Complaints, huh?" She wrapped a lock of her hair around a finger. "Do we have time? This could take a while."

"Name one," Jeff said.

She leaned close to Jenny—who she'd been happy to discover shortly after they met shared a similar goofy sense of humor—and whispered: "He has a hairy butt."

"Grody!" Jenny whispered back.

"And he likes to be spanked—it's like spanking a monkey!"

They broke up in laughter, and when Mandy's eyes met Jeff's in the rearview mirror, she stuck out her tongue at him.

"Real mature, Amanda," he muttered.

"Whatever," she said and continued laughing.

Jeff clenched the steering wheel tighter. Mandy could be a real pain in the ass sometimes. He wondered why he put up with her. He was a securities trader clearing a hundred grand a year, for Christ's sake. He could have any woman he wanted. Didn't she realize that?

He needed someone smarter, someone more on his level, someone, well, like Jenny. She wasn't only a long-legged blonde bombshell; she was a medical school student to boot. He visualized the two of them on paper: Wall Street Trader and Cardiovascular Surgeon. It was certainly more impressive than Wall Street Trader and Makeup Artist. And was that all Mandy was going to aspire to in life? How much difference was there between a makeup artist and a carny face painter? He chuckled to himself, considered mentioning this comparison out loud, but decided not to sink to her childish level.

Jeff focused on the road ahead. The occluding fog was as thick as pea soup, as his grandmother had been fond of saying, and he needed to pay attention. The last thing he wanted was to run into a deer or a bear. The 1987 BMW M5 was less than a month old, in pristine condition, and he would like to keep it that way. Did he need the car? No. He took cabs to work every day and rarely left the city. The same went for the prewar Tribeca co-op he'd been renting since last July. It was far too big for just him, he rarely set foot in the two spare bedrooms, but they were good to have to show off when people came over. Success, he had learned, was more than earning a six-figure salary. It was cultivating an image that people envied and respected.

And Mandy wasn't jiving with that image, was she? They'd been together for four years now, and she was still as clueless about business and politics and world events as when he'd met her. What was it she'd said to Congressman Franzen the other week while he'd been discussing with Jeff the recent armistice reached in the Iran-Iraq war? Why don't they call it the Middle *West*? Good God, she was becoming an embarrassment.

Jeff's thoughts turned to Jenny again. He visualized her wearing a white doctor's coat, a stethoscope around her neck, and nothing else. What a fantasy that would be! Of course, that's all it was: a fantasy. Steve was his good friend. He wasn't about to hijack his girlfriend, even though he was sure he could if he wanted to. No, there were plenty of other smart, successful women out there.

Through the mist, a bridge appeared ahead of them.

"Hell yeah!" Jeff cried out. "There she is!" He crunched onto the gravel shoulder just before the bridge and killed the engine.

"What's going on?" Steve asked, looking up from the map and removing his glasses.

"Crybaby bridge!" Jeff announced.

"Are you for real?" Steve said.

"Crybaby bridge?" Mandy said, poking her head up between the seats once more. "Why have I heard of that?"

"It's an urban legend," Steve told her. "A baby gets thrown off a bridge, it dies, you can hear its ghost crying in the middle of the night. Crybaby bridges are all over the country."

"Yeah, but this one's different," Jeff said.

Steve looked at him. "How so?"

He grinned wickedly. "'Cause this crybaby's genuinely haunted."

Steve undid his seatbelt, stuffed the map back into the glove compartment, and got out of the car. The night air was cool and fresh and damp, the way it is after a storm. It accentuated the raw scent of pine and hemlock. Fog swirled around his legs, sinuous, amorphous, reminding him of the dry ice used in horror movies to turn a mundane graveyard into a hellish nightmare crammed full of the shuffling dead. He tilted his head, looking up. Directly above the bridge the canopy had receded to reveal a patch of black sky framing a full moon.

Steve howled. It was a mournful, lupine sound, the effect of which turned out to be surprisingly eerie and realistic.

"Nice one, Wolfman!" Jeff said, tossing his head back and joining in gleefully.

"Boys will be boys," Jenny said, sighing with put-upon melodrama.

Mandy said, "You know they're going to be trying to scare us all night?"

"Let them," Jenny said. "I can handle a werewolf or vampire. I have a black belt in judo."

Steve's lungs faltered. His howl cracked. He looked at Jenny and said, "You have a black belt in judo?"

"I trained with Chinese Buddhist monks."

"Nice try. Judo's Japanese."

"What do Chinese monks practice?" Mandy asked.

"Kung fu," Steve said.

"Well, maybe the Chinese monks that Jenny trained with also practiced judo too."

Jeff's wolf howl sputtered into chuckles. He began shaking his head.

"What?" Mandy said, planting her fists on her hips.

"No comment," he said, shooting Steve a this-is-what-I-deal-with-everyday look.

"Hey," Mandy said. "Shouldn't we put our Halloween costumes on?"

Everyone agreed and went to the BMW's trunk. Steve scrounged through his backpack for the white navy cap he'd brought, found it at the bottom of the bag, and tugged it on over his head.

He heard a zipper unzip behind him. He started to turn around only to be told by Mandy to stop peeking.

"Peeking at what?" he said.

"I'm changing," Mandy said.

"Right there?"

"Hey, bro, stop perving on my girl," Jeff said, eyeing Steve up and down: the white navy cap, the red pullover, the pale trousers. "Who the hell are you supposed to be?"

"Gilligan," Steve said.

Jeff guffawed and turned his attention to Jenny, who was slipping on a pair of cat ears to go with her black eye mask and bowtie. "Come on, help me out," he said to her. "A dog? Wait, a mouse? Hold on—someone who is completely fucking unoriginal?"

"What are you?" Steve asked him.

Jeff shrugged out of his pastel blue blazer and yellow necktie —he had come straight from work to pick Steve and Jenny up out front of NYU's Greenberg Hall—and exchanged them for a black leather jacket. He held his arms out in a ta-da type of way.

"No idea," Steve said.

"Michael Knight! You know, from that *Knight Rider* show." He whistled. "Sexy mama!"

Steve turned to find Mandy adjusting her boobs inside a skintight orange bodysuit with a plunging neckline. Accentuating this were shiny orange boots, yellow tights, and a feisty yellow wig with black highlights. In the center of her chest was the ThunderCats logo: a black silhouette of a cat's head on a red background.

"Cheetara," she said, smiling hopefully.

Noah, Austin, and Cherry were approaching from Noah's green Jeep Wrangler, appearing and disappearing in the swiftly morphing clouds of mist. Austin, carrying an open bottle of beer, was in the lead. He'd shaved the sides of his head and styled the middle strip of hair into a Mohawk a year or so ago. With his satellite ears and angular face, however, he looked more like Stripe from *Gremlins* rather than a punk rocker. A flock of crows, tattooed in black ink, encircled his torso, originating at his navel and ending on the left side of his neck, below his ear. Now only a couple of the birds were visible, seeming to fly up out of the head hole cut into the cardboard box he wore. Condoms were taped all over the box, some taken out of the packages and filled with a gluey substance that surely couldn't be semen.

"You get one guess each," Austin told them, tipping the beer to his lips.

"A homeless bum," Steve said.

"A total jackass," Jeff said.

"Homework," Mandy said.

Austin frowned at her. "Homework?"

"That box is a desk, right?"

"Right—I dressed up as homework."

"Don't keep us in suspense," Jeff said.

"A one-night stand, mate!"

Steve and Jeff broke into fits. After a moment Mandy laughed hesitantly. Then she said "Oh!" and laughed harder.

"Gnarly, hey?" Austin said, smiling proudly. "So, how the fuck is everyone?"

"Not as good as you, apparently," Jeff said.

"This is my first beer. Right, Cher?"

"I've lost count," Cherry said. She was perhaps five feet on tiptoes, though her teased hair gave her a couple more inches. Jeff called her Mighty Mouse, which always ticked her off. She'd grown up in the Philippines but moved to the States to work as a registered nurse a few years ago. She had nutmeg skin, sleepy sloe Asian eyes, a cute freckled nose, and the kind of sultry lips that would look good sucking a lollipop on the cover of *Vogue* magazine, or blowing an air kiss to a sailor shipping off.

Noah joined Steve and took a swig from a bottle of red wine. He was the polar opposite of Austin: wavy dark hair, unassuming good looks, mellow, disciplined. Even more, he was an up-and-coming sculptor. His first exhibit a couple of months back had been well-received by critics, and he'd even sold a few pieces.

"You a boxer?" Steve said to him, referring to the black shoe polish he'd smeared around his left eye. He'd also drawn a large P in black marker on the chest of his white long-sleeved shirt.

"A black-eyed pea, dude." Noah nodded at Austin and Cherry, who had gravitated toward Jeff and the others, and said, "Those two are a nightmare together." He was speaking quietly so only Steve could hear.

"Fun drive?" Steve said.

"How about I drive you and Jenny back? Jeff can deal with them in his car. We almost crashed into an eighteen-wheeler when Austin was getting into that stupid box." He took another swig of wine, glanced about at the trees and vegetation deadened by the mist, and said, "So what's the deal? Why'd we pull over here?"

Steve shrugged. "First stop on the haunted Ohio tour."

"Can't believe we agreed to this."

"Hey, you never know—we might see a ghost."

"Yeah, and Austin will get through the night without

spewing."

"I'd put my money on seeing a ghost."

"He's already had four or five beers in the car."

"Maybe he'll puke *on* a ghost. That'd be something."

Jeff released Austin from a headlock, kicked him in the ass, and hooted with laughter when Austin whimpered. Then Jeff clapped his hands loudly, to get everyone's attention. "Okay, listen up, ladies and dicks," he said, immediately commanding attention the way he could. "This bridge—it's called Crybaby Bridge, and it's the real deal."

"Why do I feel like I'm being sold blue chip stock?" Jenny said.

"Snake oil," Mandy said.

"I'm being one hundred percent legit," Jeff said. "Hundreds of people have verified that this bridge is haunted. *Verified*, pussies. And if you want to—"

"How'd they verify it?" Steve asked.

"With those spectrometers the Ghostbusters use," Noah said.

Jeff darkened. "Will you two twits listen up?" He dangled his car keys in the air. "This is my spare set. I left the other set in the ignition."

"Why would you do that?" Mandy asked.

"'Cause the legend goes, you leave your keys in the ignition, lock the car, and take off for a bit—"

"How long?" Mandy asked.

"I don't know. Ten minutes."

"And go where?"

"Down the bank to the river, I guess. Fuck, Mandy, who gives a shit? We just have to be out of sight of the car. Then we wait ten minutes. When we come back, the car should be running."

"You're serious?" Steve said.

"As a snake." Jeff stuffed the spare keys in his pocket and started down the bank to the river.

Steve glanced at Noah, who shrugged.

"As a snake," Noah said and followed.

CHAPTER 2

*"It's Halloween, everyone's
entitled to one good scare."*
Halloween (1978)

Thick colonies of blood-red chokecherries and bracken fern and other shrubbery overran the bank, so Steve couldn't see where he stepped. He lost his footing twice on the uncertain terrain but didn't fall. He called back to the others to be careful. A second later Austin stampeded past him, his arms pin-wheeling. Steve was certain his momentum was going to propel him onto his face. However, he crashed into Jeff's back—on purpose, it seemed—which brought him to an abrupt halt, his beer sloshing everywhere.

"Thanks, mate," Austin said jocularly, slapping Jeff on the shoulder and sucking on the foaming mouth of the bottle. Lately he'd been adopting a British accent when he was drunk because he got off on saying words like "lad" and "mate" and "geezer."

Jeff scowled. "I'm giving you the bill for the dry cleaning."

"Fancy rich chap like you can pony up a couple of bucks."

Steve stumbled down the last few feet and stopped beside Jeff, who had produced a mickey of vodka from the inside pocket of his now beer-stained jacket. Jenny appeared next, emerging from the fog like a wraith. She was moving slowly, cautious of where she stepped. Her leather pants clung to her long legs, the black elastic top to her small breasts, outlining the triangular cups of her bra. She frowned at the vegetation as she passed through it and said, "I hope there wasn't any poison ivy in there. I got it once as a kid. It bubbles between your fingers."

Steve said, "That'll make gross anatomy interesting."

"I know, right? No one will want us on their dissection team if we can't hold a scalpel."

"Yo, nerds," Jeff told them, "check it out." He pointed to the bridge's piers and abutments. "That's the foundation from the original bridge."

"The original one?" Mandy said, pushing through the last of the ferns. Then, higher pitched: "Oh shoot! My tights!" A good three-inch tear had appeared in the yellow Spandex high on her upper right thigh, revealing white flesh beneath. "Stupid branch!"

"Are you wearing underwear?" Jeff asked.

"Jeff!"

"I can't see any."

"Stop it!"

"Anywho," Jeff said, "the original bridge was an old wooden thing that washed away a while back during a flood. This one replaced it."

"Isn't that bad news for your ghost?" Steve said, trying to ignore Mandy, who was fussing over the tear and inadvertently making it bigger.

"What do you mean?" Jeff said.

"Ghosts haunt old places. Once something's gone, they're gone."

"You're an expert on hauntings now?"

"When was the last time you heard of a ghost haunting something new? You don't go out and buy a new Ford and find it comes with a poltergeist in the trunk."

"You're blind wrong there, my dear castaway. Ghosts haunt the places where they died. The baby died here so it haunts here. It doesn't matter if this bridge is rebuilt a dozen times, it's still going to haunt here."

"What's so scary about a baby haunting anyway?" Austin opined. "I'm telling you, I see any baby ghost waving its spectral rattler at me, I'm gonna punt it so far downriver it'll shit its diapers before it touches down again."

Steve ducked beneath the bridge and was surprised to find almost no fog there at all as if the area was somehow off-limits. And was it cooler? Or was that his imagination? He took a box of matches from his pocket and ignited a match off his thumb, illuminating the sandy loam before him.

"One, two, Freddy's coming for you…" Austin sang.

Ignoring him, Steve troll-walked forward. The dried riverbed was littered with dead leaves that had blown beneath the bridge. He heard someone following him and turned to find Jenny there.

"Where are you going, mister?" she said, tucking her blonde hair behind her ears.

"Seeing what's under here," he said.

"I imagine we would have heard the baby by now if there was one."

"I'm expecting a Garbage Pail-ish thing."

"Cindy Lopper."

"Bony Joanie." She paused. "Hey, where's the fog?"

"Strange, I know."

The bridge was less than twenty feet in diameter, and Steve could make out the other side where the inky shadows gave to the mist-shrouded night once more.

He didn't see the baby shoes until he was nearly on top of them.

They were newish, white, and so small they would only fit a newborn.

"What is it?" Jenny asked, moving up beside him. "Hey!" she exclaimed. "Baby shoes!"

"Some kids probably left them there to propagate the legend."

Jenny studied the ground ahead of them, then turned and studied the ground behind them. "There aren't any other footprints except for ours."

She was right, he realized. "Guess they raked them away."

"It doesn't look like the sand's been raked."

"Well, a baby ghost didn't leave its shoes here, Jen."

"Doesn't this bother you, Steve? Seriously—look at them! They're just here, in the middle of perfectly undisturbed sand."

"Ow!" The flame had winnowed its way down the matchstick to Steve's fingertips. He tossed the match away. He lit another and said, "Do you believe in ghosts?"

"I've seen one before," Jenny stated.

"Where?"

"In my bedroom."

"When?"

"A long time ago. I was just a kid. I woke up in the middle of the night, and a face was staring in my window."

"Maybe it was a neighborhood perv?"

"My bedroom was on the second floor."

"Did your bedroom face the street?"

"It did, as a matter of fact."

"Maybe it was the reflection of a streetlamp?"

"I don't think there were streetlamps on my street."

"It could have been anything, Jen. That's the thing with ghosts and UFOs and stuff like that—just because you can't immediately explain them doesn't mean they're real."

"It doesn't mean they're not real either. I'm simply keeping an open mind."

"I've spent the last year cutting open dead people and sorting through their insides. I've yet to find any evidence of a lurking spirit. Have you?"

"We share different metaphysical beliefs. Let's leave it at that."

"Not so fast," Steve said. "I'm having a hard time believing an intelligent person such as yourself, a future doctor no less, believes in the boogie monster."

"I don't believe in the boogie monster, Steve."

"You said you saw something peeking in your window. That's what boogie monsters do, isn't it?"

"I said a ghost. They're two very different things."

He shrugged. "Okay, a ghost, whatever. But can you tell me why a ghost would want to peek in your window? I mean, you'd have to be a borderline megalomaniac to think something made the effort to cross dimensions just to spy on you when you were sleeping."

"There are more things in heaven and earth, Horatio."

"Shakespeare's not going to bail you out of this one, babe."

Jenny cocked an eyebrow. "Babe?"

Steve frowned. "What?"

"I'm not a 'babe,' thank you very much."

"Jeff calls Mandy babe."

"Maybe Mandy likes being a babe, but I haven't spent the last year of my life, studying eighty hours a week, to become someone's possession."

"Possession?"

"Calling a woman a babe diminishes her to a younger and therefore more controllable state—so, yes, a possession."

"So what am I supposed to call you?"

"There are plenty of other terms of affection that don't have the same degrading connotations, but I can't help you there. It's your job as my partner to choose one. You have to think of something that represents the complexities of my personality."

"I'll give it a hard think, princess."

"And it shouldn't be condescending."

Steve and Jenny continued to the far side of the bridge. When Steve emerged from beneath it and was standing erect again, he stretched his back, popping a joint in the process.

Jenny, still crouching next to him, cupped her hands to her mouth, and shouted: "People! There're some rad baby shoes under the bridge if you're interested!"

"We're shaking!" Jeff called back.

"For real!" Jenny replied.

Austin said something, though Steve couldn't hear what he said.

"Nice friend you have," Jenny said.

"What did he say?" Steve asked.

"Not something I'd care to repeat," she said and started up the bank.

Steve followed, grasping shrubs and saplings for purchase, his glasses bumping against his chest on their cord. At the top, parked on the shoulder of the road, Jeff's BMW was exactly how they'd left it: dark, empty, clearly not idling.

"So much for the legend," he said.

The night was cold and getting colder, and Noah wished he'd brought a jacket, considering all he wore on his upper body was the shirt with the hand-drawn P. To make matters worse, an icy wind had begun to blow. It came and went in unpredictable gusts and was strong enough to tousle everyone's hair and to rattle the skeletal branches of the nearby trees.

Shivering, Noah unfolded his arms from across his chest and produced from his pocket a joint he'd rolled earlier. He was not only cold but restless from the eight-hour drive from New York City and wanted to unwind. Moreover, he had a feeling they were going to be in for one long slog of a night. Getting high would be the only way to make it remotely interesting. He wondered again why he had agreed to come. He wasn't superstitious. Ghosts and ghouls and all that jive didn't interest him in the least. He didn't watch horror movies, didn't read Stephen King. Growing up, he hadn't even liked Halloween. He'd appreciated the candy, sure, but the idea of witches on broomsticks and skeletons lurking in closets and Frankenstein monsters eating brains never did anything for him. He guessed he simply didn't have a scary bone, the way some uptight people didn't have a funny bone.

Noah sparked the joint, took a couple of tokes, and passed it to Mandy, who was standing to his right. She took a mini puff and blew the smoke out of her mouth quickly, probably not inhaling. Noah had to make a conscious effort not to stare at her tits, which were practically bursting out of her top. He thought Jeff

19

was crazy for not appreciating her the way he should. She was drop-dead gorgeous, a real sweetheart too, a rare combination. And she put up with Jeff's bullshit. Someone "more on his level"—a phrase he'd been using a lot lately to describe his ideal woman—likely wouldn't. They'd be clashing nonstop like Austin and Cherry, a recipe for disaster, each with one eye constantly on the big red nuke button.

Noah suspected Steve and Jenny had the best chance of sticking it out together. Even so, this was no guarantee either. They both had another two or three years of med school ahead of them, then equally long and brutal residencies. How much quality time could they possibly spend together? Then again, maybe their workloads would be an advantage. Absence makes the heart grow fonder, right?

The joint did the rounds and returned to Noah, almost finished. He took a drag, then ground the roach out under his shoe just as another blast of wind swooped through the trees, whipping everyone's hair and clothes into a frenzy. Noah turned his face out of the worst of it and found himself looking at Mandy's breasts. Her nipples poked against the thin Spandex of her costume.

Abruptly Jenny called to them from the far side of the bridge: "People! There're some rad baby shoes under the bridge, if you're interested!"

Noah could just make out Jenny and Steve's silhouettes.

"We're shaking!" Jeff called back.

"For real!"

"Blow me!" Austin said.

Jeff slapped him on the back of the head. "Don't be so crass."

Austin frowned. "What's your damage?"

"You barely know her. None of us do. Show a bit more class."

"Why do you care?"

"It's called respect, dickweed." Jeff turned to the others. "So, what do you guys think? Wanna take a look under the bridge for these shoes?"

"It's pitch black," Cherry said.

"You'll be fine," Jeff told her. "You won't even have to crouch."

She glared at him.

Austin said, "Respect, huh?"

"Hey," Jeff said to Cherry, "where's your costume?"

Cherry was wearing an everyday fluorescent green blouse, denim miniskirt, and pink leg warmers.

Austin scowled. "She wouldn't do it."

"Do what?" Jeff asked.

"She didn't bring a costume, so on the ride down here—"

"He told me to take off my clothes and wear my underwear around," Cherry finished.

"Right," Austin said. "A lingerie model."

"Hey, that's not a bad idea," Jeff said, looking at Cherry with X-ray eyes.

Mandy harrumphed and Jeff pulled his eyes away and said, "Well, whatever, Mighty Mouse, if you're too scared to come, stay here. No skin off my back. Noah, Mandy, Austin, let's roll." Without waiting for a response, he turned and ducked-walked into the darkness beneath the bridge.

While waiting at the BMW for the others to return from the riverbed, Steve and Jenny were playing a tongue-in-cheek game that involved one-upping the experiences they'd had thus far at med school.

"Pathology is snooze-worthy," Steve said. He was leaning against the hood of the car, his arms folded across his chest to ward off the chill, studying the trees and thinking about those cutthroats Jeff had mentioned. Although he knew Jeff was only trying to scare them, he couldn't help being on edge, his eyes trying to pick out anything moving in the dark that shouldn't be moving.

"You used that last time," Jenny said.

"Fine...don't ask others about their grades."

"I know! I hate gunners," she said. "Okay. Umm...you'll at

some point walk down the street still wearing your stethoscope and people will look at you like you're crazy."

"Or like you're a pompous asshole." He thought for a moment. "You'll learn that for almost any set of symptoms the answer could be diabetes, pregnancy, SLE, or thyroid problems."

Jenny nodded. "Good one. Okay. At least once a week a professor will think fifty minutes is long enough to get through one hundred slides."

"And fail."

"Miserably."

Just then movement in the vegetation caused Steve to start. He pushed himself off the car, wired. A moment later Jeff appeared, tall and lean, clawing through the shrubbery lining the bank.

Steve relaxed.

"Thanks for the wild goose chase, you two!" Jeff called, crossing the road toward them.

Noah and Austin and the girls appeared behind him, one after the other, single file.

"You didn't see the shoes?" Steve said.

"We checked everywhere, mate," Austin said, tossing his empty beer bottle over his shoulder into the trees. Glass shattered. "But I did smell something foul down there."

"Something dead," Mandy said.

"A chipmunk," Cherry said.

Steve looked from Jeff to Austin to the others. "Are you guys having me on?"

"You don't know when to give up, do you?" Jeff said. "But I gotta say, I appreciate the effort."

Steve chuffed to himself, shaking his head. Then he started away from the car.

"What are you doing?" Jenny asked him.

"Getting the shoes to convert the unbelievers."

Steve made his way down the bank, keeping to the path they'd already forged through the chokecherries and bracken fern. At the bottom he stopped in the center of the riverbed and faced the vacuous blackness that had gathered beneath the bridge. It seemed somehow blacker than it had earlier, threatening even.

It's all in your head, Steve. Now get on with it.

He lit a match off his thumb, picked out his and Jenny's original footprints among all the others, and followed them beneath the bridge to the baby shoes—or where the baby shoes had been.

Because now they were gone.

Frowning, he turned in a circle, searching the sand—and heard a noise behind him. He jerked around and squinted into the darkness. Nothing there. He wondered if it had been the wind. Only right then there was no wind. The night was tomb-still. Besides, since when did wind sound like chattering teeth?

Chattering teeth...or a baby's rattle?

This thought raised the hackles on the back of his neck.

"Hello?" he said, though he didn't wait for a reply. He scurried out from beneath the bridge and up the bank, irrationally convinced a rotting baby corpse was going to latch onto his legs and drag him back down to the riverbed, where the sand and the silt and the clay would swallow him whole just as it had swallowed the baby shoes.

This didn't happen, of course, and when he was on the road again, the night sky above him, he chided himself for spooking so easily.

Everybody was back inside the two vehicles. Headlights pierced the omnipresent fog, turning it iridescent so that it seemed to glow with a radiance of its own. Jeff honked the BMW's horn impatiently.

"Yeah, yeah," Steve mumbled, swallowing the lump in his throat. "I'm coming."

CHAPTER 3

*"You know that part in scary movies
when somebody does something
really stupid and everyone
hates them for it? This is it."*

Jeepers Creepers (2001)

A s soon as Steve climbed into the front passenger seat, the cool leather crackling beneath his weight, Jeff said, "Well?"

Steve looked at him. "Well, what?"

"Show me the shoes."

"Did you take them?"

"Take them?" Jeff said. He was chewing a shoot of beard grass, which dangled from his mouth like a long, limp cigarette.

"Are you going to play dumb?"

"I have no idea what you're talking about."

"The baby shoes," Steve said patiently. "You took them."

"They weren't there?" Jenny said.

Steve shook his head. "They took them."

"Whatever you say, li'l buddy." Jeff tossed the beard grass in the foot well, swallowed a belt of vodka from the bottle in his hand, then tucked the bottle neatly into his jacket's inner pocket.

He turned the key in the ignition slot. The engine vroomed to life. Hot air roared from the vents. "Need You Tonight" by INXS blasted from the speakers.

"I like these guys!" Mandy said. "They're from the UK or Scotland, I think."

Jeff snorted laughter.

"Australia," Steve told her, deciding not to point out that the UK included Scotland. He turned down the volume. "Anyway, I'm serious. Let me see them."

Jeff seemed pleasantly exasperated. "There were no fucking baby shoes, bro," he said. "Mandy—tell him."

"We didn't see them," she said.

Steve shook his head; he didn't care. He knew they were having him on. Now that he thought about it, he wouldn't be surprised if one of them had leaned over the side of the bridge and made that noise he'd heard.

He was about to mention this when a black car thundered past them so fast it left a wake of air that rattled the BMW.

"Fucking hell!" Jeff said, the curse drowned out by Mandy and Jenny's exclamations of surprise.

"Asshole!" Mandy said.

"That was a hearse," Steve said, noting the vehicle's distinctive quarter panels.

"Bloody kids!" Jeff said.

"It was a hearse!" Steve repeated.

In the distance the red taillights flashed, angry red eyes in the eddying fog.

"Look, it's stopping," Mandy said.

The brake lights disappeared, replaced by the sweep of the headlights as the vehicle turned to face them. Two small, bright orbs glowed malevolently.

"Are they coming back?" Jenny said, a tremble in her voice.

"Maybe we should turn around?" Mandy said.

The hearse high beamed them.

"Oh, the little pricks!" Jeff said, grinning. "They've got balls!" He flashed his high beams back.

"What are you doing?" Mandy demanded. "Jeff? Answer me!"

Jeff buzzed down his window, stuck his fist out, and effed them off with his middle finger. It was a pointless gesture, considering there was no way they could see his finger through the mist.

The hearse's engine revved, building into a chainsaw-like screech. Then the vehicle shot toward them.

Jeff released the parking brake, shoved the transmission into first, popped the clutch, and goosed the gas. The tires squealed as the car lurched forward.

"Jeff!" Mandy wailed. "Don't you dare!"

"Stop!" Jenny cried. "Please! I want to get out!"

Jeff smashed through the gears, reaching third and sixty miles an hour in a few seconds.

The g-forces flattened Steve to his seat. He fumbled for his seatbelt, tugged it across his chest, buckled it. He wanted to tell Jeff to stop, but the girls were already shouting at him to do exactly that, and he wasn't listening.

As soon as they shot past the end of the bridge the canopy knitted together and blotted out the sky once more, creating the sensation that they were bulleting down the bore of a pistol.

Jeff stared intensely ahead at the road, his mouth twisted into a bitter grimace, his hands gripping the steering wheel in the ten and two positions tight enough to squeeze the blood from his knuckles.

He was a man who'd just gone all in on the pot of a lifetime, and right then Steve knew that he wasn't going to yield the road.

Steve was suddenly furious. He couldn't believe Jeff was risking a potentially fatal head-on collision, risking all of their futures, to prove he wasn't a chicken.

Mandy and Jenny gave up yelling and buckled their belts. A fear-soaked silence followed, magnifying the purr of the engine and the hum of the tires.

Only a handful of seconds had passed since Jeff gunned the gas, but it felt much longer. Steve's fear had warped his perception of time, slowing it down, and for a crazy moment some mordant part of his brain contemplated jumping out of the speeding vehicle. But it was traveling too fast. He would break his back or neck—and likely get run over by the oncoming hearse. Besides, he was frozen stiff. All he could move were his eyeballs, which he strained to the left so he could read the speedometer. The needle wavered just below seventy miles per hour.

He looked back at the road. The hearse was sixty yards away, the headlights bleeding together to form a blinding wall of shimmering white.

Fifty yards.

We're going to die, Steve thought.

Forty.

He braced his hands against the dash.

Thirty.

"Jeff!" Mandy shrieked.

Twenty.

"*Jeff!*"

Jeff swerved to the left. The hearse screamed past. Jeff yanked the wheel to the right but overcompensated. The car knifed across the dotted line toward the opposite shoulder. He yanked the wheel left again. Right, left, right, left, trying to regain control of the now fishtailing vehicle.

They careened off the road and plowed through a small tree, shattering bark and branches. They hit something that launched the BMW into an airborne somersault. For a moment Steve floated in zero gravity, and he was thinking this was it, this was how he was going to die, and there was nothing he could do to prevent it—

The car struck the ground nose first. The impact accordioned the engine block and slammed Steve with the force of a sledgehammer to the chest. The seatbelt strap bit into his flesh and held him suspended above the dash, which was no longer in front of him but below him. The handstanding vehicle crunched forward onto the roof, where it rocked back and forth before coming to rest in the still, silent forest.

◆ ◆ ◆

Noah had been seconds away from getting out of the Jeep and going to talk to Jeff about the assholes in the hearse when the BMW's rear tires squealed and burned rubber. Through wafts of smoke, he watched the car shoot away down the road.

"He's playing chicken!" Austin exclaimed from beside him.

Noah didn't know what to do, but he couldn't sit there without doing anything. He shoved the Jeep into gear and accelerated.

"He's not going to give!" Austin said. "Jeff's not going to give. The motherfucker's going to get them all killed."

"The hearse will give," Noah said automatically.

"Don't get too close," Cherry said from the backseat in a terrified voice. "Stay to the shoulder. Do you hear me? *Stay to the shoulder.*"

"I'm straddling the goddamn shoulder!" Noah said. He could hear loose gravel spraying the Jeep's undercarriage.

Then, ahead, Jeff arced sharply to the left. For a moment it appeared as though the hearse had plowed straight *through* the BMW, but Noah knew that had to be a trick of the fog and the glare of the headlights. He eased fully onto the shoulder and slowed.

Two seconds later the hearse thundered past, hogging the center of the road, bovine horn moaning. Noah tried to glimpse the driver, but the hearse's headlights blinded him. No one turned to watch the morbid vehicle depart. No one said anything. They were all staring in horror at the slewing BMW ahead of them. In the next instant it bucketed off the left side of the road into the mix of evergreen and deciduous trees.

Cherry sobbed and screamed in the same breath.

Austin shouted: "Go!"

Noah was already accelerating again.

When Steve realized he wasn't dead, and when his shock subsided, he heard moaning from behind him. "Jen?" he said. "Mandy?" He tried to crane his neck around to check on them, and that's when he saw Jeff in the darkened cabin, crawling through a hole in the windshield. Then he realized Jeff wasn't crawling; his lower body was ragdoll limp.

Steve couldn't see the upper half of his friend, the half that had been launched through the windshield, because the glass had gone gummy and opaque with cracks.

"Fuck Jeff," Steve mumbled. "You stupid fucking fuck…"

"Steve?" Mandy said shrilly. "What's wrong? What happened to Jeff? Is he dead? *Is he dead?*"

Steve unclasped his seatbelt and collapsed onto the car's ceiling. He twisted himself around so he could see Mandy and Jenny. They were both layered in shadows, hanging upside down like bats. Mandy was sobbing into her hands. Jenny was either unconscious or dead.

In the distance came the unmistakable drone of an approaching vehicle. The hearse coming back for them?

Steve maneuvered his body in the awkward space so he could grasp the door handle. He tugged it. The door was stuck.

Tires screeched to a halt.

Steve drove his heels into the window. The glass spider webbed. He kicked it again, harder, and again, harder still, until his feet stamped through it. He rolled onto his hands and knees and scrambled through the shattered window. He heard branches snapping, vegetation crackling, and he was suddenly filled with an exquisite terror, sure the driver of the hearse was going to be something with a hole for a face and leathery wings and—

Austin shouted Jeff's name; Noah, Steve's.

"Here!" Steve managed, standing and swooning into the upturned car. Austin and Noah and Cherry burst through the thicket. They came to an abrupt standstill.

"Oh no," Austin said, those two words barely audible but

powerful enough to halt a marching band. "No, no, no…"

Steve pushed himself away from the car on splintered pegs for legs and faced the wreckage. In the frosty light he could see it clearly enough. Jeff's head and shoulders protruded from the windshield like a half-eaten meal. He lay on his back. Given that the vehicle rested upside down on top of him, his nose kissed the hood.

Noah brushed past Steve, dropped to his knees, and pried open the back door. He climbed in and spoke calmly to Mandy while attempting to extract her.

Steve wobbled around the front of the car—the BMW's distinctive headlights and kidney-shaped grille were an unrecognizable mash of metal—and all but collapsed next to Jenny's door. Blood smeared the window. He gripped the handle and pulled, expecting the door to be stuck. It swung open with ease. He felt one of Jenny's dangling wrists for a pulse, but his hands were shaking too badly to perform this action correctly. He unbuckled her seatbelt, lowered her body into his arms, then dragged her out onto the leaf litter. The fog billowed around her, caressed her. He noticed her chest moving up and down and said a silent prayer of thanks.

Meanwhile, Austin had crawled into the gap beneath the hood and now he shouted, "Jeff's alive! He's breathing!"

While Noah and Austin discussed what to do next in urgent tones, Steve patted Jenny on the cheek, urging her to wake up. All the while his heart was filled with guilt. He had invited her on this trip. She had wanted to spend the weekend studying, but he'd insisted they needed a break from school, he'd wanted her to finally meet his friends, and now here she was, lying on the damp earth, bloody and broken.

Her eyes fluttered open.

"Jenny!" he said. "Thank God! Are you okay?"

"Okay…"

"You hit your head."

"Hurts…"

"It's just a little—"

The rest of the sentence died on his lips.

He could smell gasoline.

◆ ◆ ◆

Gas? Jenny thought slowly. What was Steve talking about? Were people camping nearby?

"We have to move away from the car," Steve was telling her now, though it remained difficult to hear him through the ringing in her ears. "I'm going to carry you."

"I can...okay..."

Steve helped her to her feet. Pain flared in the left side of her head. She almost toppled over, but Steve caught her in his arms.

"Let me carry you," he insisted.

"No, I..." She couldn't find the right word. "Just...dizzy."

Jenny allowed him to lead her away from the wreckage. Without warning her trembling legs gave out beneath her. She dropped to her knees. Steve was saying something to her, though the words seemed suddenly far away. Her vision blurred, darkened—and then she was floating above her body, which was lying on the operation table in the cadaver lab, nude and lifeless. Nine fellow students were gathered around the table, everyone wearing brown lab coats and dishwashing gloves to protect against formaldehyde. Nobody seemed shocked or saddened that Jenny was the cadaver today. Professor Booth was giving some sort of eulogy in Latin that she couldn't understand. She wanted to tell them she wasn't dead, but she couldn't speak, only hover, insubstantial, like a ghost.

Belinda Collins stepped to the table. She was one of the gunners in the class, ambitious to a fault. Ever since Jenny scored higher than her on their first assignment, Belinda had done her best to make life miserable for Jenny, and Jenny knew she would be thrilled to be performing the dissection.

Belinda raised her scalpel to make the first incision. Jenny squeezed her eyes shut against the anticipated pain. She felt nothing. Surprised, she opened her eyes again. The cadaver lab had disappeared, replaced by a cold night filled with nacreous fog and towering trees.

"Jen? Jen!" Steve said. "Can you hear me?" He was cradling her head in his lap.

"Where...?" she said, disorientated. Then she remembered with a punch of dread: the hearse, the accident. "Jeff? Mandy?"

"Mandy's fine. Jeff's...okay. I have to go help get him out of the car. Are you going to be all right for a couple of minutes?"

She tried to sit up. It took all her strength, but she managed. She saw the upside-down BMW for the first time. Mandy and Cherry stood on one side of it, Noah and Austin on the other. Everyone was speaking and gesturing wildly.

"Where's Jeff?" she asked.

"He's still inside the car," Steve said. "I'll be right back—" He frowned.

"What?" she said.

"How do you feel?"

"Pummeled."

"How many fingers am I holding up?"

"Two. Steve, what's wrong?"

"Nothing. You hit your head though. I just want to make sure you're okay."

Yet the concern that had appeared on his face a few moments ago was still there. She suddenly wondered whether she'd been disfigured somehow. She touched her lips, her nose. "What's wrong with me, Steve?"

"Nothing."

"Steve!"

"Nothing—it's just your eyes. One's dilated a bit more than the other. Probably nothing more than a mild TBI. It's not a big deal."

Jenny went cold. A traumatic brain injury. If it was indeed mild, she had nothing to worry about. But Steve had no way of knowing whether it was mild or not. It could very easily be moderate or severe. She could have intracranial hemorrhage or brain herniation, both of which could lead to disability or even

CHAPTER 4

*"Goddamn foreign TV. I told ya
we should've got a Zenith."*
Gremlins (1984)

Cleavon sat in his recliner with one eye squeezed shut, the other open, because this seemed to help keep the headache thumping against the inside of his skull at bay. The Sony color television glowed softly in the dark room, though it didn't produce any sound because the volume knob was busted. On the fourteen-inch screen, a customized '86 Toyota Xtra Cab sporting a lifted suspension and oversized tires idled at the track's starting line some five hundred miles away in Mississippi. Then the flag dropped. The truck leaped forward. A dozen cameras flashed.

The truck shot toward the bog, windshield wipers waving back and forth. When it hit the water it sprayed curtains of mud down both flanks, turning the bright red and blue paint job— BAD TO THE BONE airbrushed across the hood—a shitty brown. A few seconds later it got caught up and stopped, shimmying back and forth, dipping and rising, smoke billowing from the raised wheel wells. It made Cleavon think of an antelope or zebra losing their battle to cross a muddy river on one of those nature shows.

"It's them big fat tires," Earl said from his recliner a few feet away. "They just slow you down, am I right?" He reached for a fresh beer from the six-pack in the cooler resting between the two of them. The recliner squealed in protest at the sudden shift in his six-foot-seven, four-hundred-pound body. It was no wonder the fucking thing hadn't collapsed under his weight yet. It wasn't made for someone so big. Clothes weren't either. Earl always had trouble finding clothes that fit him, not that he bought clothes much, a pair of jeans, a few wife beaters every few years, if that. The white, stained tank top he had on now stopped halfway over his gut, above his belly button. The jeans stopped a few inches shy of his ankles. He looked like a fucking retard, Cleavon always told him, but Earl didn't care. Cleavon didn't either. He just liked telling him he looked like a fucking retard.

"The skinnier the better, ain't that right Cleave?" Earl went on. "That's what you always say. Leave them fat meats to the pretty boys who can pay someone to change the bearings and seals every year. That's what you always say, Cleave." He burped, a loud, maggoty one smelling of food left in the sun for a few days. "And he don't got no sense using a stick shift. Not for a big old slop hole like that. Am I right, Cleave? Am I right?"

Cleavon grunted but said nothing to his brother. On the screen a young fella began wading into the waist-deep muck to attach a tow strap to the truck's front hook. Suddenly the picture hiccupped, then went haywire, flickering all over the place.

"For fuck's sake!" Cleavon said.

"It's all right, Cleave," Earl said. "You just gotta leave it for a bit, is what you gotta do."

Cleavon eased himself to his feet and crossed the room, delicately, like he was walking on eggshells, one hand pressed to his forehead. He smacked the top of the TV, the headache making him hit it harder than he'd intended.

"Hey!" Earl said. "That ain't helping—"

"Shut it," Cleavon growled. He began fiddling with the rabbit-ear antennae. "Get the light, Earl, I can't see shit in the dark."

Earl set his beer on the floor, which his gorilla arms reached easily. Then he heaved his monstrous bulk out of the recliner. He lumbered across the room, burping once again, and hit the light switch. The sixty-watt bulb dangling from the socket where their parents' chandelier used to hang blinked on.

Cleavon fiddled with the antennae for a full minute, but all he managed to do was wake his fucking headache. Grimacing, he tore the rabbit ears loose and tossed them across the room.

"Hey, Cleave, why'd you do that?" Earl said, going to pick them up. "That's not helping, throwing them like that. How's that helping? You gonna break them. And you break them, and that's it, they just won't work."

"Shut the fuck up, Earl," Cleavon snapped. "I'm in no mind for your bullshitting right now. I been in the garage all day, I'm beat to shit, and also, I got a headache like a motherfucker. So shut the fuck up with your bullshitting." He went to the cooler, rubbing his forehead. There were no beers left. Four empties sat in a line next to Earl's recliner. "You drank all the beer, Earl?"

"I did not, Cleave," Earl said. "We shared them. They were sitting there, we were sharing them."

"I had two, you had four. That don't sound like sharing to me. That sounds like you having twice as much as me, you fat shit."

"I wasn't counting." Earl shrugged his big shoulders. "Besides, I got them, didn't I? I went to the shed, I told you, I said, the TV got a signal, some monster truck racing, you wanna watch it, have some beers. Then I filled up the cooler with ice and a six-pack. You didn't do nothing but come in here and sit down—"

"Aw, shut up, Earl," Cleavon said. He left the den and went down the hallway to the kitchen. The headache felt like a drill behind his eyes. While he'd been sitting in the recliner, it had almost faded to nothing. But all that fussing around with the TV had pissed it off, and it was drilling like a sonofabitch now.

He stepped into the kitchen and stopped at the sight of the Corn Flakes scattered on the floor, the soured milk puddled on the countertop. "Floyd!" he shouted, then cringed as the headache drilled deeper. "Floyd!"

There was no answer. Cleavon didn't expect one either. Floyd was deaf as a fencepost and had been that way for a good ten years now. You wouldn't believe what happened to the stupid fuck. Cleavon didn't at first. He could still see Floyd as clearly as if it were yesterday, come stumbling back to the farm, clothes torn, blood pouring down his face, looking like he'd gone insane. But he and Earl had never changed their story, not once, so Cleavon believed it happened the way they'd said it happened.

Floyd and Earl had been hunting rabbits. What they'd do, they'd catch one of the rabbits in a trap, tie a stick of dynamite around it, light the wick, and let it go. Nine times out of ten it'd head straight underground. When the dynamite blew, Thumper might turn a couple of his pals inside out, but the rest would leave the warren and hop around in loopy circles. You could stroll right over and pluck them up by their ears, just as easy as picking daisies. Floyd and Earl caught as many as two dozen a day this way. They sold them to Pete Scoble in town, who in turn butchered them and sold them as meat in Akron. It didn't make anybody rich, but it paid the bills and put food on the table.

On the day Floyd lost his hearing he'd been sitting in the pickup while Earl strapped a stick of dynamite to the rabbit they'd caught in the trap. When he let it go, however, it didn't go underground; it made like the devil to the pickup, TNT strapped to its back, fuse burning. Earl had his rifle and tried to shoot it, but he didn't have the best aim, and a moving rabbit was a tough target. The critter took cover under the truck. Earl yelled at Floyd to haul ass, but Floyd had never been quick upstairs, not even back then.

According to Earl, the truck did a big cartwheel, flipping ass over tits before landing on its wheels again. Floyd received a dozen deep gashes to his face and complained of ringing in his ears for a good week. None of the cuts healed properly because he kept picking away the scars, and his ears didn't heal either, because he kept digging his fingers into them to the knuckles.

Nevertheless, Cleavon thought now, being ugly and deaf didn't give him the right to be a pissing slob. Who couldn't make a bowl of cereal without spilling shit all over the place? Cleavon scowled. He would get the lazy oaf to clean up the mess later; he didn't want to deal with any more idiocy right then. He just wanted a beer and a cigarette and some peace.

Stepping on the cereal, crunching it beneath his boots, he opened a counter drawer and rifled through Scotch tape and screwdrivers and a bunch of other junk until he found a bottle of Aspirin. He popped the cap and upended the container to his mouth. He chewed the five or six pills that flopped onto his tongue, thinking they'd get to work faster ground up. Then he opened the old Kelvinator refrigerator and snagged a cold Bud. As an afterthought he bent back down and scanned the near-empty shelves. There were another six beers, a bag of carrots, a carton of milk, a couple of loaves of bread, a bowl of eggs, a jar with two pickles floating in it, and not much else.

He closed the door, twisted off the beer cap, and was about to head outside to have his smoke in the cool night air when the telephone jangled.

He picked up the handset. "Yeah?"

"That was fast you quick sumbitch," Jesse Gordon said.

"I was standing next to the phone," Cleavon said.

"What you doing standing next to the phone? You some mind reader now, know I was gonna call?"

"I was getting a beer from the fridge. On account of the fridge being in the kitchen, and on account of the phone also being in the kitchen, I was standing next to the phone." He paused. "Listen, Jess, what'd'you say about coming over tomorrow for a coupla beers, throw some steaks on the grill?"

"And I'm guessing you want me to bring the steaks?"

"Now there's an idea."

"As much as I'd like to sit around and listen to you bitch about your dumb ass brothers, Cleave, I got other plans."

"Other plans, huh?"

"Plans with the missus."

"Connie? Since when you start having plans with Connie, that fat cow?"

"Since she told me she's making her famous roast pork tomorrow night. She stuffs it, you know? Only cooks it on special occasions. You wanna guess what this special occasion is? I'll tell you—she's starting a diet."

"She gonna cook roast pork to kick off a diet? Shit, Jess, that's why she's so fat all the time, all she does is cook and eat what she cooks. No way this diet's gonna work. She ain't gonna last two days on no diet."

"I don't care she lasts until her midnight snack. I'm still getting her roast pork tomorrow night."

"Maybe I'll come by and try some of that famous roast pork?"

"Don't think so, Cleave. It don't work like that. You can't, you don't just invite yourself over 'cause you don't got no good food of your own. You got a coupla pigs. Go stick one on a spit and you got your own roast pork, bacon, ham, whatever, as much as you want."

"So why you calling me? To tell me your fat cow of a wife is cooking a roast pork dinner that I can't have none of? I tell you, Jess, Connie can't cook for shit, so go on and have your fuckin' roast pork—" He cut himself off. "Shhht—you hear that?"

"Hear what?" Jesse said.

"Someone just picked up." Cleavon and his brothers shared a party line with Jesse and Connie Gordon, and four other households who'd refused to sell their properties to the National Park Service when it started buying up land fourteen years ago. "Who's there?" Cleavon said. "Speak up."

"Cleavon?" a voice said.

"Higgins?" Cleavon said.

"Yeah, it's me Weasel. Who you talking to?"

"Me," Jesse said.

"Jess? Good, that's easy—I was just about to call y'both." He was speaking fast, excitedly. "Boys, we caught us some new does!"

"Lick my leg!" Cleavon exclaimed, unconsciously using a saying his pa had often favored before he blew his brains out with a double-barrel shotgun. "Doe" was code for the out-of-town women they used in the black masses. "How many?"

"Three."

"Three!" Jesse crowed happily. "Good work, Weasel, you sumbitch! They not too, they not like the last one, too cut up, are they?"

"I don't know, Jess."

"The hell don't you know?" Cleavon said, frowning. "You didn't just leave them there, for Christ's sake, did you?"

"You don't understand, Cleave," Weasel said. "They were with four bucks. I couldn't, there were too many, for me to go back. That's why I'm calling. I need help rounding them up."

Cleavon blinked. "Seven in all? The fuck they driving, Weasel —a goddamn limousine?"

"Driving?" Weasel said, playing dumb.

"Hell, Weasel," Cleavon said. "It's just us, nobody else is on the line listening in, now start talking some sense."

"It's just that, Mr. Pratt told us, he said—"

"Fuck Spencer! Now spill it. What were they driving?"

"Cars, Cleave. Normal cars. One was, one was a Jeep, green, if I remember right. Everything happened so fast, you know? The other, blue, I think. That's the one I ran off, that crashed. Ballsy driver. Came right at me straight as a bullet. Never seen anything like it. He kept coming, he held it together a second longer, I might've been the one in the woods."

A silence followed.

Cleavon said finally: "You pulling our legs, Weasel?"

"No, Cleave. Why?"

"Why? *Why?* You better be messing with us, Weasel."

"I'm not messing, Cleave. What's wrong?"

Cleavon's headache, which he'd temporarily forgotten about, was back and worse than ever. He kneaded his eye sockets and tried to keep from throwing the phone across the room like he'd done to the rabbit ears. He had to deal with two retards in Earl and Floyd all day long, every day of the year, he didn't need it from Weasel too. But he got it, didn't he? He sure did. "I'll tell you what's wrong, Weasel," he said. "Those people you ran down—"

43

"Does, Cleave, does and bucks—"

"Those fuckin' *people*," he snapped, "you think, what, they're just gonna sit there where they crashed and have a barbecue? Shit no, Weasel, they gonna get in the second car and go for help. They gonna go to town. They gonna raise hell, that's what they gonna do! Now where the fuck are they?"

"Damn, Cleave, I didn't think, I thought, you know, I thought they'd... Damn, Cleave—they're right near your place, not a hundred yards north of the bridge."

"Listen up, Jess, and listen good," Cleavon said. "Me and the boys're gonna cut through the woods, get this under control. You and dipshit here, you two drive up and meet us quick as you can. I'm gonna call Lonnie now."

"Get him to stop anyone coming his way?" Jesse said.

Cleavon nodded, then realized nobody could see him. "They'll probably stop at his place looking for help. Probably. But who knows for sure. They might drive right on past, so, yeah, get him to stop them whether they want to stop or not."

"Hey, Cleave," Weasel said. "I wasn't thinking, I'm sorry—"

Cleavon slammed the handset down. He waited a few seconds, picked it up again, and began dialing Lonnie's number.

"Cleave?" It was Weasel.

"Get off the fuckin' phone Weasel!"

"Sure, Cleave, okay, see you soon."

Cleavon depressed the switch hook, counted to five before releasing it, then dialed Lonnie's number. After two rings Lonnie's boy picked up. "Hello?"

"That you, Scottie? It's Cleavon McGrady. Your pa there?"

"Naw, he's gone to Randy's for the meat draw."

Cleavon swore to himself, then said, "Scottie, listen up, okay? I have something important you gotta do. You listening?"

"Yeah?"

"Some people might be coming by, on the way to town. They might stop by your place, looking to use the phone. You can't let them do that. You tell them you don't have no phone. You got that?"

"Why they wanna use my phone? Who they calling?"

"It don't matter. You just tell them you don't got no phone. Can you do that?"

"I guess."

"I'm gonna call your daddy now. You remember what I told you."

"I ain't got no phone."

"Good boy. Your daddy will be home soon."

Cleavon hung up and dialed Randy's Bar-B-Q. He knew the number by memory; Randy's was one of only two bars in Boston Mills, the main watering hole so to speak, and he often called there when looking for Jesse or Lonnie or whoever else he wanted to find for whatever reason.

"Randy's," a man drawled in a Southern accent. Randy had lived in Louisiana his entire life, a small claims court lawyer. Then he got in some kind of financial trouble and moved out here—fleeing the law you might say—and opened up the bar. The running joke between Cleavon and the guys was that he was going to need a damn good *criminal* lawyer whenever the IRS or FBI or whoever tracked him down and came knocking on his door.

"Listen, Randy, it's Cleavon, I need to speak to Lonnie. He there?"

"Does shit stink? Hold on a sec."

Cleavon waited. He could hear a cacophony in the background: laughter, talking, someone speaking on a mike, reading out numbers. A long thirty seconds later: "Cleave?"

"Lonnie," he said harshly. "You gotta get back to your place, now."

"My place?" It came out "My plash?"

"Listen to me, you drunk shit," Cleavon said, "and listen good. Weasel got us some new does. But he fucked up, he fucked up good, 'cause there were two cars and one still works just fine. Me and the boys are gonna go round them up now. But if some took off in that second car, they're gonna be heading to town. That means past your place. They might even knock on your door, looking for help. I've already spoken with your boy. He's gonna tell them you don't got no phone. If they're still there when you return, you keep them there until me and Jess arrive. If you see them on the road, you don't let them pass—"

"How many does we got, Cleave? Are they lookers—?"

"Pay attention, Lonnie, for Christ's sake! This is important. You do whatever it takes to make sure they don't get to town. Now get going. We've wasted enough time talking."

"Hold up, Cleave, hold up," Lonnie said, sounding more alert, no longer slurring his words. "How'm I supposed to stop them if they're on the road?"

"You got your rifle in your truck, don't you?"

"'Course."

"So you see them coming, you block the road with your truck. When they stop, shoot their tires. Fuck, shoot the driver, you have to. Just make sure they don't go nowhere 'till me and Jess arrive."

"Yeah, right, okay, don't you worry, Cleave, you can count on me. But you didn't tell me, Cleave, these does, they lookers or not —?"

Cleavon hung up the phone, then returned to the den. The TV picture was still on the fritz. Earl was snoozing in his recliner, snoring and drooling a river. Cleavon clapped his hands loudly, startling Earl awake, and said, "Get up, shithead. And go find your deaf-ass brother. We got business to take care of."

CHAPTER 5

"Ding dong. You're dead."
House (1986)

T he road angled upward. Noah slowed the Jeep to forty miles an hour. Anything faster would be reckless in the fog, which seemed to have become denser and more opaque during the last half hour. As soon as he breasted the summit he started down the other side, which dipped sharply. The slope was so great the bottom dropped out of his stomach. He leaned back against the seat, his arms at right angles to the steering wheel, the way you hold the safety rail while zipping down the big hill of a roller coaster.

The road finally flattened out and came to an abrupt end —at least, to a crude wooden barricade with a grime-covered, reflective "Road Closed" sign.

"A dead end!" Noah said, braking.

"No, it's okay," Steve said. "You can go around it. The road still leads out of the park."

Noah peered into the gloom. Visibility was nearly zero. "How do you know that?"

"Jeff told me. He did the research for this trip, so I assume he knows what he's talking about."

Noah contemplated that. "And if we get lost?"

"We can't if we stay on the same road. And if worse comes to worst, we'll backtrack. We passed a few houses before the bridge. We'll knock on a door, tell whoever answers there's been an accident, get them to call an ambulance. But going straight ahead is by far the fastest option right now."

Accepting that logic, Noah circumnavigated the barricade. The road immediately deteriorated, a victim of the elements and neglect. Weeds overran the shoulders and sprouted up here and there through the blacktop. Low branches bounced off the Jeep's windshield and slapped the roof as if to shoo the intruders away. Noah thought briefly of the vehicle's paint job, then told himself this was a trivial, selfish concern, given Jeff and Jenny's conditions.

And exactly what were their conditions? he wondered with a hollow feeling in the pit of his gut. Was Jeff going to lose his ability to walk? Was Jenny going to live out the rest of her life in a vegetable state until her family decided to pull the plug? Or was his overactive imagination blowing things out of proportion? "They'll be fine," he mumbled to himself.

"What?" Steve said. He had been examining his shattered reading glasses.

"Nothing," Noah said, embarrassed he'd spoken his thoughts out loud. "Have you ever had a bad accident before?" he added, to say something.

"I broke my collarbone skiing in Aspen if you can call that a bad accident."

"Aspen, huh?"

"My parents were both into skiing. As a kid I probably saw every major ski resort west of the Rockies."

"You still ski?"

"Not for years."

Steve tossed the useless eyeglasses onto the Jeep's dashboard, and a silence fell between them. The trivial talk was awkward given the circumstances.

Finally Noah said, "How long does it take to recover from a broken back?"

Steve shrugged. "It depends on the type of fracture."

"How bad do you think Jeff's fracture is?"

"We don't know he has a fracture. There's no way to tell the extent of his injury without an X-ray."

"But if it is fractured?"

"A single fracture, and no associated neurological injury..." He shrugged. "Most tend to heal within a few months."

Noah frowned. "Neurological injury? You mean, spinal cord injury?"

"Yeah."

"Back at the crash, you mentioned he could be paralyzed from the waist down."

"I shouldn't have said anything. I was caught up in the moment. Again, it depends on the extent of the injury."

"But there's a possibility he could be paralyzed?"

"I'm not a spinal surgeon, Noah. I haven't examined him. I don't know."

"Be straight with me, Steve. I'm not his mother."

Steve hesitated. "Yeah, there's a possibility. Even so, there's always rehab, physio..."

"Which could last years."

"Better than never walking again."

"Yeah," Noah said sourly. "Better than that."

Noah saw the gravel driveway and white mailbox at the last moment. He slammed on the brakes. The Jeep squealed to a stop.

"What the hell?" Steve said, alarmed.

"A house!" Noah said, already swinging the Jeep onto the driveway.

The house was set a hundred feet back from the road, barely visible in the spectral haze. It had projecting eaves, tall windows, and a wrap-around porch. Yellow light glowed from behind a window in a square belvedere, which protruded vertically from the eastern corner of the low-pitched roof.

"Thank God," Steve said. He twisted in his seat and checked Jenny's breathing and circulation.

"How is she?" Noah asked.

"Her pulse is weak."

"That's not good, is it?"

"Could be due to shock, or internal hemorrhage."

Noah banged over a pothole.

"Hey!" Steve cried out. "Careful!"

"Sorry, dude," Noah said. "I'm trying. This driveway's in shit condition."

Steve sat forward again.

Noah avoided a few more potholes and stopped next to a waterless stone birdbath. He killed the engine but left the high beams on.

Steve hopped out. "Wait with Jenny. This shouldn't take long."

Noah nodded and watched Steve hurry up the veranda steps. Several spindles in the veranda railing, he noted, were snapped in half or missing altogether. Broken slate shingles littered the scorched-grass lawn, while the paint on the weatherboards and ornate pediments above the windows was blistered and peeling.

Steve knocked on the front door, waited, knocked again, waited longer.

He turned and shrugged.

Swearing, Noah joined him on the veranda. The knocker Steve had used was big and brass and couldn't have gone unheard.

"Someone's gotta be home," Steve said.

Noah rapped the knocker three times, hard, angry.

Silence.

Steve cupped his hands against the small window in the door's upper carved panel and peered inside. Then he reached for the door handle.

"Whoa," Noah said. "What are you doing?"

"Seeing if it's unlocked."

The handle twisted in his grip. The door swung inward.

became angry at everybody and everything and began hanging out with other angry kids. She dropped out of high school in grade eleven, became a compulsive shoplifter, and was in and out of juvie until she was eighteen. That's when her parole officer sat her down and painted a grim picture of her future if she didn't clean up her act. At the same time her father told her she was an adult now and kicked her out of the house. She got a job at Burger King and worked forty-hour weeks just to pay her rent and bills and feed herself. The job sucked, but on the plus side it kept her busy and out of trouble. It was also a wake-up call. Realizing she was going to be working behind a cash register for the rest of her life if she didn't learn an employable skill, she saved enough money to enroll in a three-month fashion makeup artistry program. Once degreed, she found work with a bridal company where she remained until moving on to the Broadway theater scene. By twenty-two she had become the go-to stylist for several top stage performers and had a healthy list of private clients.

One evening in the late summer of 1984 she and her roommate Lisa Archer were in the small upstairs area of a Midtown bar when the waitress—a tall brunette with a Russian or Polish accent—brought a bottle of Dom Pérignon to their table and told them it was from the two gentlemen at the bar. Jeff and another young trader, both wearing Miami Vice suits, waved and smiled at them.

"Invite them over," Lisa whispered.

"Seriously?" Mandy said.

"They're hot!"

"They're sleazy!"

"You know how much that champagne costs?"

Mandy pushed out a spare chair with her foot. Jeff and his pal came over. She took an immediate disliking to Jeff. He was too smooth, too confident, too good-looking. But the longer they spoke, the more he grew on her, and she realized he wasn't putting on airs; he was the complete package. She ended up going back to his place that night, and soon they were spending all their free time together. Although he'd just been starting at the investment management firm then, he was already a big deal, attracting the notice of important people. Consequently, he was constantly invited to fashionable dinners and events. Mandy felt like Cinderella, living the rags-to-riches dream.

At the same time, however, she was uneasily aware that the clock was going to strike midnight at some point. She was just some messed up kid from Queens, the daughter of an accountant, pretty, successful in her own right, but nobody special. She had no business mingling with the Establishment. She knew Jeff was disappointed she had not become the socialite he wanted, knew he was losing interest in her, but what could she do about that? He had successful, intelligent women of high breeding fawning over him whenever he went out. How could she compete with them? The knowledge that she would inevitably lose him gutted her, but she was too proud to let it show. Instead she became snarky, poking fun at him when she could, as she had done in the car earlier. This wasn't winning her any points, but she couldn't help it. She wanted to hurt him as much as she could before he hurt her.

Mandy forced herself to look at Jeff now, and she was flooded with guilt at her petty behavior. His face, yellow in the light from the fire and slick with blood, looked like someone had taken a box cutter to it. He would be left disfigured with a half-dozen scars.

Poor Jeff, my baby, she thought. *My arrogant, narcissistic, beautiful baby...*

She gritted her teeth. If only she had stood her ground, they wouldn't be in this hellish predicament. Two weeks ago a makeup artist named Cindy had invited Mandy and Jeff to her white-trash-themed Halloween party. Mandy had initially accepted, but when she mentioned it to Jeff, he scoffed, telling her he wouldn't be seen dead at such a party. A couple of days later he sprung the idea for the current trip.

"It's called Helltown, babe," he told her while they were getting dressed to go out for dinner with friends. "It's supposedly one the most haunted spots in all of the country."

"It's in Ohio!"

"It'll be a road trip."

"A boy's trip."

"Austin will bring Cherry."

"Whoopee." Mandy had never shared much in common with the Filipina.

"And Steve said he'll ask that chick he's seeing."

"The med student?"

"Whoever. So what do you say? There's a spooky bridge to check out and a couple of haunted cemeteries and other neat stuff."

"If you're twelve years old."

"Sure as hell beats a party mocking the white working class. Don't you realize how crass that is? Would you go to a party mocking underprivileged blacks or Asians?"

"White trash isn't an ethnic group, Jeff," she said, thinking of the teenage deadbeats who'd almost ruined her life. "It's a description of lazy people who make poor life choices."

"I think it'd be a poor life choice to attend such a party."

"It'll be fun."

"Helltown will be fun, babe. I've found us a great little hotel to stay in."

"You've already booked it, haven't you?"

"You'll love it."

"Forget it."

"So that's a yes?"

"It's a no, Jeff!"

But of course it was a yes. It was always a yes. She would have a better chance of giving birth to identical quadruplets than persuading Jeff to do something he didn't want to do.

Austin was pacing back and forth and chain-smoking Marlboros when Mandy said something. He turned to face her.

She was bent close to Jeff as if examining him.

He tossed away his cigarette and hurried over. "What is it?"

"He moved," she said.

"He moved?" Austin repeated, filled with sudden hope. "His legs?"

"No, his cheek. It twitched. At least I thought it did. Jeff?"

He didn't reply.

"Jeff?"

Nothing.

Austin said, "You must have imagined it."

"I don't think I did."

Austin patted Jeff's cheek. "Hey, buddy? You hear me? You wanna open your eyes for us?"

"Stop that!" Mandy said. "You're going to wake him up."

Austin frowned. "So?"

"What if he starts screaming again?"

"So he screams. He'll stop eventually, and we can find out…"

"Find out what?"

"If he can move his fucking legs!" He patted Jeff's cheek again, harder. "Jeff? Wake up, buddy. Jeff!"

"Stop it!" Mandy cried.

Austin ignored her and continued hitting Jeff's cheek. "Wake up, Jeff. Wake up—"

Mandy grabbed his wrist. "Stop it!"

He shoved her backward. She fell on her butt. Tears welled in her eyes. "Fine!" she blurted. "Wake him up! Listen to him scream!"

Austin hadn't meant to push her so hard. "Mandy, I'm sorry."

"Jesus, Austin," Cherry said. She'd been sitting off by herself but joined them now. "Apologize to her."

"I just did!" he said as Mandy covered her face with her hands. He looked at Cherry helplessly. "Can you talk to her or something?"

Cherry crouched next to Mandy and offered words of comfort.

"I'm not hurt!" Mandy said. "I just want to leave this place!"

Austin returned his attention to Jeff. He ran his hands through his Mohawk in frustration. God, he couldn't take this. He really couldn't. He had to know. He slapped Jeff's cheek, hard.

"Don't touch him!" Mandy screamed.

"Just scrape the bottom of his stupid foot!" Cherry said.

Austin frowned. "Huh?"

"If he has feeling below the waist, his toes will curl down. It's instinctual, like when the doctor checks your reflexes by hitting your knee with a hammer."

"Bloody right!" Austin exclaimed. "Why didn't you mention that before?" He tugged off one of Jeff's reddish-brown dress shoes, then a diamond-patterned sock. He dug his key ring from his pocket, chose the largest of the three attached keys, and scraped the tip along Jeff's sole.

His toes didn't curl. They didn't even flinch.

Austin scraped Jeff's sole a second time.

Nothing.

"Try again," Mandy said, staring at him with pleading eyes.

"He can't feel it," he said numbly.

"Do it harder."

"It won't make a difference."

"Do it harder!"

"I did it twice!" he shouted. "He can't feel a fucking thing!"

Austin stumbled away from Jeff's inert body, his collar damp with sweat despite the cold, the air suddenly greasy, unpleasant to breathe. Through a part in the fog he spotted the road and wished he'd taken the case of beer from Noah's Jeep before he and Steve had left for the hospital because if he'd ever needed to get shitfaced, it was right then.

Jeff, he thought. A paraplegic.

Austin blamed himself and the others for this sad fact. Steve had said they had to move Jeff or he would have been barbequed alive. Fine. Austin agreed with that. However, it was *how* they

moved him, half dragging him like he was a heavy side of beef—
that he couldn't get out of his mind. They should have kept their
cool, made a litter, carried him properly.

Austin lit a cigarette and inhaled greedily.

Jeff. A paraplegic.

The words were like oil and water, chalk and cheese. They
had no business being linked. Maybe if Jeff had been some poor
slob the idea of him wheeling around in a chair for the rest of
his life wouldn't have been so hard to accept. But Jeff was the
poster boy for success and vitality. Austin had met him on the
first day of grade nine at Monsignor Farrell High School. Austin
had been sitting in the back row of third-period math when Jeff
had strolled through the door seconds before the bell rang. He
had been tall even then and could easily have been mistaken as a
senior. His blond hair had been brushed back from his forehead,
his maroon school golf shirt perfectly fitted, his gray slacks
pressed and creased, a preppy sweater draped over one shoulder.
He swept his eyes across the room, then started down the aisle to
the empty desk next to Austin, poking students with his pencil
along the way, eliciting nervous chuckles from the victims. Ten
minutes into the lesson he made a *pssst* noise and passed Austin
a note. Austin opened it and read the three words: "Suck my
dick!" He was so surprised he laughed out loud. Mr. Smith, the
bespeckled teacher with a bushy brown mustache and yellow
sweat stains under his arms, paused in his explanation of the
course outline and asked him what was so funny.

"Nothing, sir," Austin replied.

"Stand up, Mr...." He checked the roll call. "Mr. Stanley."

Austin stood up.

"Now tell the class what is so amusing."

"Nothing, sir."

Mr. Smith crossed the classroom and collected the note from
Austin's desk. He read it, his face impassive. "Who gave this to
you?" he said.

"No one, sir."

"You wrote yourself a note?"

"Yes, sir."

"And you laughed at your own note?"

"Yes, sir."

"I'd like to see you back here during the lunch break. Do you understand, Mr. Stanley?"

"Yes, sir."

After class, in the hallway bustling with students, Jeff found Austin and hooked his arm around his shoulder. "Thanks for not ratting me out to Armpits," he said.

"No problem."

"What's your name?"

"Austin."

"I'm Jeff. I'll see ya round."

After that day Austin and Jeff started hanging out more and more. Their personalities complimented each other so much as they were both smart-mouths and troublemakers. Yet this was as far as their similarities went, because while Austin despised sports and could barely keep his grades above water, Jeff made the varsity golf and baseball teams, graduated with a 4.0 GPA, and was one of three students named valedictorian. And while Austin dropped out of community college and ended up buying a crummy bar with his grandmother's inheritance and battling alcohol addiction, Jeff went the Ivy School route and was now trading securities at a top-tier investment management firm, living the dream.

Was living the dream, Austin amended.

A paraplegic.

Fuck.

◆ ◆ ◆

Cherry had moved away from the burning BMW and sat beneath a large tree with a thick trunk, wanting to be alone. The fragile calm that had existed since Steve and Noah left with Jenny had deteriorated quickly. Mandy was a total mess, while Austin seemed ready to explode. She didn't blame either of them. Mandy had dated Jeff for four years; Austin had known him since high school. This was the reason she hadn't mentioned the plantar reflex stimulation earlier. She knew there was a chance Jeff could be paralyzed from the waist down, and she didn't want to verify this was the case, for it would only demoralize the others further. But Austin had totally wigged out. He had been slapping Jeff, inadvertently moving Jeff's neck, which could compound his spinal cord injury. So she told him to scrape Jeff's foot, and the diagnosis turned out to be as bad as she'd feared.

Cherry remained clinically detached from Jeff's predicament. She wasn't close to him like Austin and Mandy were; she didn't even particularly like him. Not only had he been making fun of her height from the moment they'd met, but he was also an asshole in general. Moreover, as a registered nurse, she had become used to seeing sickness, disease, and injury.

Just last week there had been a mentally disabled man in the ER with an infected stasis ulcer in the back of his calf. The necrotic tissue around the black eschar had been gnawed away by maggots that were still in residence in large numbers. During debridement surgery the man decided he had to urinate and could only do this standing up, so he got off the operating table, bleeding and dropping maggots everywhere, and peed in the middle of the floor.

And then there was old Ray Zanetti who had cancer to the mandible. Cherry had been his primary caregiver, and pretty much every time she checked in on him he would be looking in the mirror and peeling away pieces of his flaking skin. By the time of his death his face had all but fallen off.

Situations like these were grotesque and sad certainly, but they didn't faze her anymore. They were simply part of her job, what she experienced daily. All in a day's work, so they say.

Nevertheless, Cherry had never questioned her career choice; it had provided her with a new life, literally. She had been born in Davao, in the Philippines. Her family had been dirt poor. Her father didn't work, while her mother was a housecleaner, mostly for Western expatriates. She earned two hundred pesos, or approximately four dollars, a day. This went to support her husband, Cherry, and Cherry's two siblings. They lived in a cinderblock house with a corrugated iron roof and no running water. They battled lice and rats constantly, and they wasted nothing. Her mother often told her how disappointed she was with her Western employers, whose refrigerators were always full of expired food and spoiled vegetables.

Most of Cherry's friends dropped out of high school to work at McDonald's or one of the big malls. These positions didn't pay any more than her mother made cleaning houses and apartment units, but you got to hang out with your friends and spend the day in an air-conditioned environment out of the stifling tropical heat. Cherry, however, had greater ambitions. She wanted to get a university degree and work in a call center. She would have to work night shifts to compensate for the different time zones in the UK or US or Canada, but the money was decent and, in the eyes of other Pinoys, it was a highly respected profession.

However, when Cherry heard about a friend of a friend who had become unimaginably wealthy as a registered nurse in the US, she promptly changed her degree to nursing. Her mother, starry-eyed at the prospect of having a daughter who could lift her family out of poverty, offered to sell the *carabao*—water buffalo—to help pay for Cherry's schooling, but Cherry refused. She began working at a massage parlor servicing Western expats because the hours were flexible and could accommodate her classes. The company exploited her shamefully, paying her twenty-five cents for each massage she gave, regardless of whether it was one hour long or two. Even so, they turned a blind eye to "extra" service. Cherry was raised Roman Catholic, went to church every Sunday, and was conservative by nature, but money was money. For her, a hand job was a service, nothing more, and depending on how cheap (not poor—Westerners were never poor) or generous her client was, she could make anywhere from ten to fifty dollars for a few minutes of work. She could have made even more by offering sex, for which she was often propositioned, but she would not cross that line. She was not a prostitute.

Once she completed her BS in Nursing four years later, she passed the US licensure exam, applied successfully for a green card, and was offered an entry position with New York Methodist Hospital in Brooklyn. She'd been there for three years now, had a mortgage, a car, and enough money in the bank to send hefty sums to her family in Davao regularly, making them the envy of all their friends.

Cherry pulled her eyes from the ground and glanced at the others, relieved to see they had settled down somewhat. Austin was pacing again, but he no longer seemed like a ticking time bomb. Mandy had stopped crying and was staring inward.

Cherry checked her Coca-Cola Swatch and saw that only ten minutes had passed since Steve and Noah had left with Jenny. How long would it take them to find a hospital, explain what was going on, and bring back help? Half an hour? Longer?

A nippy breeze ruffled the nearby reeds and saplings and stirred the mist into searching, serpentine tendrils. Cherry folded her knees to her chest for warmth, wrapped her arms around them—and spotted three flashlight beams bobbing between the trees some fifty yards away.

CHAPTER 7

"They're here!"
Poltergeist (1982)

Mandy hurried over to Austin and Cherry to watch the crisscrossing flashlight beams approach. She frowned as an uneasy feeling built in her gut. She told herself there was no reason to be concerned, whoever was out here had come to help. But there was something about random people in a dark, unfamiliar forest that scared her silly.

"Do you think they're campers?" Mandy said anxiously.

"Out here?" Austin said.

"Maybe they live nearby?" she said. "They heard the crash and are coming to help?"

"Maybe," Austin said, though he didn't sound convinced.

"Why else would they be out here?"

"I don't like this," Cherry said. "I don't like this at all."

Mandy frowned, momentarily despising the Filipina. She wanted to hear that they were safe, that they were fine; she didn't want to hear fear and paranoia.

Soon the strangers were close enough Mandy could make out the snapping of branches, the crunch of footsteps on dead leaves, the general rustle of disturbed foliage.

"'Lo there?" one of them called.

"Hello," Austin said.

A few seconds later three men dressed in checkered lumberjack jackets emerged from the gloom of the night into the firelight produced by the burning BMW. Mandy gasped silently in surprise and horror. The slim one in the middle sported stringy black hair, bushy muttonchops, and a handlebar mustache. Despite skin the color and texture of old vellum, and a hooked beak for a nose, he appeared normal enough. The other two, however, might have just escaped from a carny sideshow. The freak on the left had a round moon face, piggish eyes, stood close to seven feet tall, and must have weighed somewhere in the neighborhood of four hundred pounds. The freak on the right had misshapen features covered by a jigsaw of wormy white scars and a vacant expression, as though his brains were nothing but mush.

Mandy forced herself not to stare and focused on the middle one, who was shielding his eyes with his hand while he studied the flaming vehicle.

"Good Lord almighty, will ya look at that," he crowed.

"We had an accident," Austin said.

"No fooling," he said. "Anyone hurt?" His eyes fell on Jeff. "Aw, shit. He ain't dead, is he?"

"No!" Mandy said, shocked by the man's blunt manner.

He looked at her. His eyes were dark, unreadable. They appraised her from head to toe and lingered on her breasts. "Well, now," he drawled, "that's quite an outfit you got on, ma'am."

"It's a Halloween costume."

"I reckoned as much. And a good choice at that." He turned his attention to Austin. "How about you, Cueball? No costume?"

Austin twitched at the insult. "I took it off."

"And you, little lady?"

"I didn't bring one," Cherry said quietly.

"All Hallows' Eve, my favorite night of the year, when all the ghoulies come out to play, ain't that right?" He grinned, revealing a missing front tooth. "Anywho, the name's Cleavon.

What can I do to help y'all?"

"Our friends have already left to get help," Mandy said. "They'll be back any minute," she added purposefully.

"Any minute you say?" Cleavon said to her. "When did they leave?"

"Forty minutes ago," Mandy lied.

"Forty minutes, huh?"

She nodded.

"And they ain't back already? Shit, maybe they got lost?"

"Do you live out here?" Austin asked him.

"Over yonder." He hooked his thumb over his shoulder.

"And you wander the woods at night?"

Ignoring the question, Clevon took a few steps toward the BMW and said, "Well knock me down and steal my teeth. It's a genuine Bimmer, boys! Or *was*, I should say. So you some uppity rich kids, that right? Where you from?"

"New York," Austin said.

"The Big Apple! Never been there myself. Always wanted to go, but don't reckon I'd fit in too good. I'm 'bout as country as a baked bean sandwich. Ain't that right, boys?"

The four-hundred-pound freak nodded. "Right-o, Cleave."

"My apologies," Cleavon said. "That there's me brother Earl. And that's me other brother, Floyd. Floyd don't say much. He only got two speeds: slow and stop. And he don't hear too good neither unless you shout." He raised his voice. "Ain't that right, Floyd?"

Floyd nodded.

"Well?" Cleavon said, smiling expectantly at them.

"Well, what?" Austin said.

"Ain't you gonna introduce yourselves?"

Mandy glanced at Austin and Cherry. She saw her fear reflected in their eyes. Cleavon and his brothers were not just assholes; they were dangerous. But there didn't seem to be any choice other than to keep Cleavon talking until Steve and Noah returned with help.

"I'm Mandy," she said.

"Mandy," Cleavon repeated. "That's short for Amanda, ain't it?"

She nodded.

"I like it. Mandy. Suits you." His eyes floated to her breasts.

"I'm Austin," Austin said. "And this is Cherry."

"Austin and Cherry—now those are a coupla fine names as well. Had an uncle named Austin. Sat on the porch all day drinking hooch, his own concoction, from a big ol' jug. By suppertime he would be drunker than Cooter Brown on the fourth of July." He smiled his gap-tooth smile at Cherry. "Never knew a Cherry though. The pleasure's mine, darlin'."

Cherry looked away from him. Her lips were pressed together in a thin line.

"Well," Cleavon went on, "now that we're all fine friends, why don't y'all tell me what happened? What caused this unfortunate accident?"

"Our friend lost control of the car," Austin said simply.

Cleavon eyed Jeff. "That the friend, huh? And just lost control, you say?"

"Another car ran him off the road. It was a hearse."

"A hearse? You sure you don't need to get your eyes checked, boy?"

"We all saw it," Mandy said sharply.

Cleavon held up his hands. "Hey, no need to get worked up, darlin'. You say ya'll saw a meat wagon, ya'll saw a meat wagon. Now, enough talk. How 'bout we give you a hand bringing your friend there back to the house? We got medicine and enough food to feed the lot of you to your heart's content."

"Like I mentioned," Mandy said, "our friends went for help. They'll be back here any minute. But thank you for the offer."

"And if they got lost? Could be hours 'till they get back. We got a telephone. We'll call the sheriff. He knows exactly where the ol' McGrady house is. He'll be there with an am'blance in fifteen minutes."

"We're going to wait here," Austin said tersely.

"Hey! I ain't liking your tone, *boy*," Cleavon growled. "Didn't your mama teach you no manners? When someone offers you help, you be gracious."

"Listen, mister...Cleavon," Cherry said pleasantly. "We appreciate your offer. We really do. But we can't move our friend. He has a broken back. Moving him will make his injury worse."

"Don't worry, darlin'. We'll be careful with him."

"We're not going anywhere," Austin said, stepping forward.

"I'm 'fraid I have to insist," Cleavon said. "Boys, get the cripple."

Floyd and Earl started toward Jeff.

"Don't you touch him!" Mandy shouted. "His back is broken!"

Austin made to intercept them.

"Hold it right there, Cueball," Cleavon said, and to Mandy's horror he produced a monstrous machete that had been hidden beneath his jacket. "I wouldn't do nothing stupid if I was you."

CHAPTER 8

*"They will say that I have shed
innocent blood. What's blood
for, if not for shedding?"*
Candyman (1992)

Austin acted without thinking. He charged Cleavon and jump-kicked him in the gut. Caught by surprise, Cleavon didn't have time to swing the machete. However, the jump kick was uncoordinated and did little more than knock Cleavon backward a few steps while Austin crashed awkwardly to the ground. Before Austin could regain his feet, Cleavon was on him, raising the machete. Austin kicked the psycho in the shins, dropping him to his knees. Austin lunged, driving his shoulder into Cleavon's chest, knocking him onto his back. He grappled for the machete, but the man wouldn't let go. Then Cherry appeared beside him, also grappling for the weapon.

Austin landed a fist in Cleavon's face, then another. Still, Cleavon wouldn't relinquish his grip on the blade.

Abruptly Cherry disappeared, lifted free from the skirmish. A moment later the left side of Austin's head went numb. Cleavon had walloped him with his free hand. The world canted, his vision blackened, but he didn't release Cleavon's other hand, which was still holding the machete. Cleavon struck him again, this time catching his chin. Austin tried to head-butt Cleavon, but his forehead deflected off the asshole's temple. White-hot pain tore through his face. Cleavon was biting him! He shoved himself free, his hand going to his bloody cheek.

The chaotic scene around him registered in a heartbeat. Earl holding Cherry off the ground, arms around her chest, her feet kicking wildly. Mandy on her butt, as if she'd been pushed over, her hands held protectively in front of her face. Cleavon shoving himself onto his knees, glaring at him. He didn't see Floyd anywhere, and knew the man must be behind—

Something heavy slammed into the back of his head.

Mandy was still dazed from Floyd's open-handed slap across her face. Her eyes watered, her cheek smarted, and when she blinked away the stars she saw Floyd looming up behind Austin, swinging a tree branch. It struck the back of Austin's head with a snappish crack. His eyes rolled up in their sockets and he fell limply onto his chest.

This happened so quickly Mandy had no time to react. Now she leaped to her feet and ran at Floyd, screaming at him to leave Austin alone. Floyd kicked Austin in the side of the head twice before she reached him. She grabbed his arm, trying to pry him away. He shoved her aside and kicked Austin again. The impact of his foot striking the side of Austin's skull made a heavy, dead thunk. Mandy felt ill, and all she could think was: *This can't be happening! This isn't happening! He's going to kill him!*

Shouting hysterically—she hadn't quit shouting the entire time—she flung her weight into Floyd, knocking him off balance and away from Austin. While she drummed her fists against his chest, he clutched her around the throat with his hand. She gripped his wrist but could do little else except make rusty, rasping noises. He squeezed tighter, crushing her windpipe. His eyes were shining like a rabid animal—intense yet emotionless.

"…stop…" she gasped.

Her body was going weak. Blackness seeped into her vision.

She tried to rake the freak's face with her fingers, but his arm was outstretched at full length, and his arm was longer than hers. She swiped at air.

He's killing me. He's going to kill me right here.

The realization was like a shot of adrenaline to her heart. She kicked with all her strength and connected with his groin. He bellowed, sagged, and released her.

She ran.

Encouraged by Mandy's escape, Cherry raised both her legs and drove her four-inch heels into Earl's shins as hard as she could. He grunted and dropped her to the ground. She fled in the opposite direction Mandy had gone. The forest was a blur of darkness and fog, shadows layered upon more shadows. Still, she didn't slow. She knew her life had boiled down to two scenarios: escape and live or get captured and die.

Mandy thrashed through the scrub, out of control, like a drowning swimmer. Her throat, already raw from being strangled, was now on fire. Her breathing came in gasping sobs. The scent of rot and evergreen seared her nostrils. She dodged vegetation left and right, leaping and ducking obstacles she saw at the last second, praying she didn't poke out an eye. She raised her arms for protection against the brittle branches clawing at her face, but she could do little to prevent them from piercing the thin Spandex of her costume, scouring her stomach and legs, drawing warm blood from a half-dozen different cuts.

Cherry thought she had lost Earl when a hand suddenly seized her shoulder. She felt resistance, felt herself slowing. Then a loud tear. Her top. She was free, picking up speed. But she only made it a few more steps before Earl seized her shoulder again, this time dragging her to the ground.

She scrambled forward on all fours, the giant clawing her back, her rear, searching for purchase. He snagged her leg, his fingers pinching her flesh. She kicked her foot, once, twice, and connected with his face or shoulder. Yet he wouldn't let go. She rolled onto her back, gasping for breath, struggling to free herself. He raised a fist. She brought up her arms in front of her face to block the blow. His swing came from the side, plowing into her left ear. He raised his fist again. She yelled and squirmed. He smashed her jaw.

Holding onto consciousness by a thread, Cherry shoved her hands into his face, pushing him away. One of her thumbs found an eye socket and she dug deep.

Earl reared up with a startled cry. She wormed out from beneath him, flipped onto her front, and crawled away. She didn't get far. A moment later he appeared next to her and mumbled something that might have been, "Nice try, little girl." He kicked her in the stomach, lifting her clear off the ground, turning her turtle onto her back. He kicked her in her side again and again, relentless. She heard her ribs snapping with twiggy, gristly sounds, and the certain realization that she was going to die filled her with an incomprehensible terror the likes of which she had never experienced.

Mandy blundered blindly into a glade of waist-high grass and cattails. She tripped on a root, pin-wheeled forward, and fell, slamming her chin against the ground so hard her upper teeth punctured her lower lip. Blood gushed into her mouth. She attempted to push herself to her knees but didn't have the strength. Instead, she was reduced to pulling herself forward, like something primordial that had just slithered out of the ocean for the first time.

When a shrill cry shattered the night, Mandy knew it belonged to Cherry. Still, she didn't contemplate turning back. What could she do? She'd tried to fight them, and she'd failed. She was too small, too weak, outnumbered. Cleavon and his freak brothers were animals, crazy, sick. They would surely do to her...whatever they were doing to Cherry.

Cherry wailed again in abject pain and misery.

Somehow Mandy regained her feet.

She ran.

CHAPTER 9

*"I'm the guy that's gonna
save your ass."*
Feast (2005)

"**H**ere we are, I guess," the driver of the white Pontiac Firebird Trans-Am said. "Boston Mills." He had only spoken a few words since he'd picked up Beetle fifty miles back on Interstate 77, mostly to tell him he could take him as far as the Ohio Turnpike. "Sorry it's not someplace bigger," he added. "But I'll be heading east now to Warren. You'll be fine here for the night?"

Beetle nodded. His real name was Frederick Walker, but in the army you got nicknames, and they stuck—enough at least Freddy still thought of himself as Beetle, which he'd received because of his thick eyebrows and square face. "I'll be fine," Beetle said, "and thanks for the ride." He got out and watched the Firebird drive off, vanishing into the fog, there one moment, gone the next, like a ghost ship glimpsed momentarily at sea.

The street was deserted. The only light came from a nearby sodium arc streetlamp that cleaved an inverted copper cone through the mist.

Beetle glanced at his wristwatch. 8:40 p.m. Not so late that there shouldn't be a coffee shop open, or a couple out for a walk.

Then again, it being Halloween night, he supposed everyone had closed up to take their kids out trick-or-treating in the residential neighborhoods.

He started walking in the direction the Firebird had gone and passed the typical businesses you found along the main drag in most small towns: a barbershop, a bookstore, a diner, a druggist, a real estate office, a shoe store. The exteriors were weatherworn, most in need of a coat of paint, the display windows as frost-blank as cataracted eyes. Graffiti covered the boarded-up entrance of an out-of-business tavern.

At the end of the block the street signs told him he was at the intersection of Main Street and Stanford Road.

While deciding which way to go he made out voices and laughter from somewhere ahead of him. Some ten seconds later two silhouettes materialized in the gray gloom before resolving into teenage boys. They were sixteen or seventeen, both dressed in torn jeans and wool football jackets with leather sleeves. The one on left had a buzz cut, the one on the right a mushroom cut with bangs that went to his chin. They were each gripping open wine bottles by the necks. They stopped when they saw Beetle. Their bantering ceased. Then, realizing he was too young to be a parent, they continued toward him with the awkwardness of kids who knew they were doing something wrong and were hoping you didn't say anything about it.

"Excuse me," Beetle said when they were a few feet away.

They slowed but kept walking. Buzzcut eyed him warily. "Yeah?"

"Can you tell me where the nearest motel is?"

Buzzcut stopped. Angry red splotches of acne marred his face. His mouth hung open slightly, and he could have done with a pair of braces, maybe one of those full headset deals. Mushroomcut slouched against a newspaper box and cleared the bangs from his face with a quick, neat jerk of his neck.

"You a soldier or something?" Buzzcut said, eyeing Beetle's woodland camouflage shirt.

"The motel?" Beetle said.

The kid shrugged. "Only two in town. The Pines has an indoor pool, but it's way over on the south side. The Hilltop's closer, down that ways a bit, but no pool." He pointed north along the cross street. "Keep going for a couple of blocks to the edge of town. Then keep going maybe five more minutes. You'll see it right up on a hill like the name says. Can't miss it. Oh, and so you know, the church with the upside-down crosses is another five minutes farther on, right on the edge of the national park."

"Upside down crosses?" Beetle said.

Buzzcut nodded. "That's why you're here, isn't it?"

"To see the church?" Beetle asked.

"The church, the graveyard, the slaughterhouse." His face lit up with an idea. "Hey, you want a guide tomorrow? I can meet you at Hilltop. Five bucks and I'll show you everything."

"I don't have any idea what you're talking about."

"You don't know about the legends?"

"What legends?"

"You know you're in Helltown, right?"

Beetle shook his head.

"So what you doing out here?" Mushroomcut said. "Passing through or something?"

"Or something."

"Huh," Buzzcut said. "Don't get many passer-throughers. Most visitors come to check out the legends." He frowned. "So you don't want a guide?"

"No, but thanks for the directions." Beetle started away, then hesitated. He took his wallet from his pocket, turned back around, and handed Buzzcut a fifty-dollar note. "Split it," he said.

"Holy Christ! A fifty! Thanks, mister!"

Buzzcut took off down the street, hollering like an ape, dollops of wine jumping from the mouth of his bottle. Mushroomcut followed on his heels, grasping for the bill, telling Buzzcut they had to share it.

Beetle continued down Stanford Road, in the direction of the motel.

◆ ◆ ◆

The houses he passed reminded him of those you might find at a military base that had long since shuttered its doors and had been frozen in time, forgotten by the world. Most were dilapidated things with weed-infested front yards littered with rusted bicycles and neglected toys and garden equipment. From inside a bungalow bunkered behind a corrugated iron fence, a woman cried out in a bitter, hysterical voice, something about the dog and dinner and "getting off your ass and helping out!" The husband shouted back, punctuating every few words with expletives.

The arguing made Beetle think of Sarah—or, more precisely, his relationship with Sarah, how it had been at the end. It was funny, he thought, how something so good between two people could go so bad. But that's how it worked, wasn't it? If he and Sarah hadn't loved each other the way they had, they wouldn't have bothered hating each other the way they had.

Beetle had met Sarah shortly after he'd finished Ranger School. He'd already completed Basic Training, Advanced Individual Training, Airborne School, and the Ranger Indoctrination Program. And he'd already been assigned to the 1st Ranger Battalion for the previous eleven months. Ranger School was more of an old tradition than anything else, but it was a requirement for leadership positions within the 75th Regiment.

To celebrate graduating from the two-month course, during which he'd managed on less than three hours of sleep a night and one and a half meals a day, Beetle and a few other soldiers secured thirty-six-hour passes for the weekend. They rented rooms in a Sheraton in downtown Savannah, Georgia, went for dinner at a steakhouse recommended to them by their commanding officer, then moved on to the bevy of Irish pubs the city was famous for. By midnight only Beetle and a guy named Tony Gebhardt remained from the original group of six; the others had either gone off with girls they'd met, or hookers. Beetle and Tony were contemplating calling it a night when Beetle spotted Sarah at the bar. With her dark hair tied into pigtails, and a splattering of freckles across her nose, she was cute rather than sexy, though still quite attractive.

Tony wiggled his eyebrows at Beetle, and Beetle decided what the hell. He went to the bar, waved to get the bartender's attention, and said to Sarah, "Hi, I'm Beetle."

"Hi," she said, giving him a quick up and down. Drinking and smoking were prohibited while on the pass, so he was dressed in civilian clothes to avoid drawing attention to himself.

"I know how this sounds," he said, "but you remind me of someone."

"Punky Brewster, right? I get it all the time."

Beetle laughed. Because she was right. She did look like Punky Brewster, albeit a grown-up version. "Maybe that's it," he said.

"So—did you come over to buy me my drink?"

"Sure," he said as the bartender arrived. "Coors for me, and put, uh—"

"Sarah."

"—Sarah's drink on my tab."

Sarah smiled at him, raised her blue cocktail, then started walking away.

"Hey," he called after her. "Where're you going?"

"My table—join if you'd like."

And so he did. Tony did too, given Sarah was with a girlfriend. The four of them drank and smoked, played billiards and darts, and danced to the occasional song. At last call Tony and Beetle invited them back to the Sheraton. The friend was game, but Sarah wouldn't budge on her "I don't go home on the first night" policy, and Beetle settled for a telephone number and a brief kiss.

In the weeks that followed garrison life at Hunter Army Airfield went on as usual. Physical training, paperwork, squad and platoon evaluations, parachute jumps. Beetle never called

Sarah. The army was his life. He could be deployed anytime. A relationship would be messy. Nevertheless, the next time he was in Savannah on a pass he found himself thinking about her, the fun they'd had, and he discovered he still had her number in his wallet. He called her from a payphone. He expected a snub, but she said she was getting ready to go out with friends and, whatever, if he wanted to come to Congress Street, maybe they could meet up. He got the name of the place she would be at and convinced the guys he was with to change venues. They were all keen except for Tony Gebhardt, who didn't want to see the friend again. But Tony was outnumbered, and they went.

While searching the Congress Street club, Beetle realized he couldn't remember exactly what Sarah looked like, and when he found her on the patio out back, he was surprised by how beautiful she was. They were both soberer than they had been at the Irish pub, and they spent the rest of the night at a secluded table, talking, touching, making out. This time it was her suggestion to return to the hotel.

After that they saw each other as often as possible, and they fell madly in love the way only the young and naïve could. Beetle proposed on the anniversary of the day they'd met. They married a short time later on a beach on Tybee Island. He moved out of the barracks, and they rented a house off post together on a cul de sac in a quiet Savannah suburb. Sarah chose it because of the mature vegetable garden in the backyard. The idea of being able to step outside and pick basil or tomatoes or chili peppers delighted her to no end. Also, they had been talking about having children, and the house had a spare bedroom, which they could convert into a nursery.

Sarah found employment as a receptionist at a small law office, while Beetle was promoted to Specialist, then Sergeant, given a team leader position, and eventually his own squad.

Their lives had been near perfect.

Then, in October of 1983, President Regan issued orders to overturn a Marxist coup. Beetle kissed Sarah goodbye in the middle of the night, and within hours he was on an Air

Force C-130 Hercules four-engine transport, configured to carry paratroopers, heading for the tiny Caribbean island of Grenada.

Beetle arrived at the motel before he'd realized it. Directly to his left a stand of pines had been cleared to make room for a parking lot, which was currently empty. A sign perched atop a twenty-foot metal pole announced in red and yellow neon: "Hilltop Lodge - Vacancy." A tacky, flashing arrow pointed to a cement staircase that carved a path through the trees to the top of the hill.

An icy wind blew in from the west, sneaking down the throat of Beetle's shirt and causing his skin to break out in gooseflesh. Rubbing his arms to generate warmth, he climbed the steps, seventy or eighty in total.

The motel rose two stories behind a grove of twenty-foot fir, which, given their calculated spacing, had been planted some years back. The shiplap siding was rotting in places, though someone had attempted to give it a facelift recently with a rich brown coat of stain. A thick hedge of privet lined the perimeter of the plateau and substituted for a fence to prevent visitors from plunging down the steep slopes. On a clear day those same visitors would have been afforded a sprawling panorama of Boston Mills and the national forest those kids had mentioned, though tonight little was visible behind the drab gray curtains of mist.

Beetle followed a stone path between two towering firs to the reception. A placard in the window read: "Great Rates, Free Movie Channel, Imaginary Friends Stay Free." He opened the glass door, stepped inside, and wrinkled his nose against a spoiled cheese smell. He crossed the thick-pile, hunter-green carpet to the front desk. It was currently unmanned. He rang the small brass bell on the counter. A moment later a wizened old man emerged from the back room. He wore pastel slacks and a heavy wool cardigan buttoned to the neck. Gray hair curled out from beneath a beat-up Baltimore Orioles baseball cap. A rosy blush colored his cheeks, nose, and ears. He fixed Beetle with bright blue rheumy eyes and said, "Help ya?"

"A room for the night, please," he said.

"Ranger, huh?" the man said, reading the bars on Beetle's right sleeve. "Was in 'Nam myself. Spent most my time in a resettlement village, twenty miles southwest of Da Nang, three miles from the 5th Marines Combat Base. Supposed to be hell on earth, target practice for the commies, but I didn't see no combat my entire tour. Never met no Rangers neither. They weren't officially incorporated until a few years ago, that right?"

"A room, please," Beetle said.

The man studied him for a moment, then nodded. "You're in luck." He produced a key attached to a piece of red plastic from beneath the counter and dangled it between his thumb and index finger. "Got one room left."

Beetle thought of the empty parking lot but didn't say anything.

"It's a superior suite so a little pricier than the others," the man went on. "But it got a private balcony and views of the Chaguago National Park you won't soon forget. Guests say they like to sit out there with their coffee in the morning. If you're lucky, you might spot a whitetail or elk. Had a few moose about too. You haven't seen nothing until you've seen a buck with a full set of antlers. They shed them each season, you know. The lot simply drops off. Found a set myself a few years back. Was going to put them on the wall over there, but couldn't find nobody to mount them without charging an arm and leg. How many nights you say?"

"One," Beetle said, taking out his wallet.

"Suit yourself." The man glanced at the wad of bills in the wallet sleeve. It was a discrete glance, no more than a flick of the eyes, easy to miss. But Beetle didn't miss much. "That'll be forty-nine ninety-nine," the man said reasonably. "Say, I'll make it an even forty-nine, give you change for the soda machine."

"Forty-nine bucks for one night, huh?" Beetle said just as reasonably.

The man nodded. "That's right."

"That the going rate or the sucker rate?"

The man blinked. "Huh?"

"I asked you if that was the going rate, or the sucker rate?"

"The sucker rate?"

"Do I look like a sucker?"

"No, sir."

"Then why are you treating me like one?"

"No, sir, I'm not—"

Beetle grabbed the old man around the throat, moving fluidly and quickly. He pulled the shylock's face close to his own. "Let's do this again," he said quietly. "I'd like a room for the night."

"Nineteen...ninety-five..."

"You didn't ask me what type of room I'd like."

"They're all...same..."

Beetle stared into the shylock's terrified eyes. They had popped wide, blood vessels webbing the whites. Why he wanted to live so much, Beetle didn't know, didn't care. He didn't care about anything anymore—not even, he realized, getting ripped off in some shitty backwater motel.

Beetle released the old cheat, who stumbled away, wheezing, cowering. Then he slapped a twenty-dollar bill on the counter and scooped up the key.

Without looking back, Beetle crossed the reception to the staircase that led to the second floor. At the top of the stairs a bronze placard on the wall indicated that rooms 200-206 were to the left, 207-210 to the right. The key was labeled 209, so he went right. Pink carpet and floral wallpaper had replaced the hunter-green carpet and paneled wood of the reception. The spoiled cheese smell remained.

Standing in front of his room, Beetle inserted the key into the lock, opened the door, and flicked on the light. The interior was larger than he'd expected and included a kitchenette with wood-trimmed white cabinets. The lavender bedspread matched the upholstery on the armchair in the corner. A TV was bolted to a Formica table, next to a fake flower arrangement. White satin curtains that looked like they came from the inside of a coffin were drawn across the pair of doors that gave to the balcony.

Beetle upended his rucksack on the bed and messed through his clothes until he found the one-liter bottle of Stolichnaya vodka he'd bought at a Piggly Wiggly in Columbia that morning. He twisted off the cap, took a drink, and set the bottle next to the television set. Next he unzipped a toiletry bag and withdrew a matte black M9 Beretta and a fifteen-round magazine, which he set next to the booze.

Tonight, he decided in a vague, almost blasé way, not wanting to acknowledge what he was thinking. If he did, if he contemplated, reflected, felt, he would become too emotional, and he wouldn't do it. And it had to be done. Sooner or later, it had to be done.

Tonight.

Shrugging out of his fatigue shirt—WALKER embroidered above the right breast pocket, US ARMY above the left—Beetle went to the bathroom and drew water for a hot shower.

CHAPTER 10

*"We don't need a stretcher in
there. We need a mop!"*
A Nightmare on Elm Street (1984)

"**I** just let go," Noah said monotonously, almost to himself. "I didn't push him. He was trying to take the hockey stick from me. I just let it go."

He and Steve were standing a few feet from the dead boy. Both had turned their backs to the body.

"That radiator shouldn't have been leaning there against the wall like that," Steve told him. "It was a hazard."

"Fuck!" Noah ran his hands up and down his face. *"Fuck!* I'm in deep shit, aren't I?"

"It was an accident."

"Yeah, an accident…an accident." He shook his head. "What the hell was he doing, Steve? Attacking us like that? We knocked on the door, didn't we? We called out, said we needed to use the phone. Robbers don't do that, do they? So what the fuck was his problem?" He shook his head again. "This is fucked. This is so totally fucked."

"Listen," Steve said, "I'm going to go give one last look upstairs for that phone. There were a couple of rooms I didn't get to. If I can't find it, though, we need to get moving. We can explain what happened here to the cops after we get help for Jeff and Jenny."

Noah stiffened, his disposition instantly flipping from tempestuous to calculated. "Whoa, hold up a sec, Steve. Slow down. We haven't discussed this yet. I mean, what are we going to tell them?"

"The cops?" Steve said. "What do you mean? We're going to tell them the truth—the kid attacked you. He fell and knocked the radiator on his head."

Noah snorted. "You think they'll believe that?"

"That's what happened, man. What do you want to tell them?"

"I don't know. Maybe, I don't know...but why do we even need to mention the kid?"

Steve stared at him. "Because he's dead, Noah."

"I know that! But, look, nobody knows we've been here, right? Nobody knows we stopped. We can hide the body in the woods or something."

"Hide the body?" Steve said.

"He's already dead."

"Are you kidding me? Jesus Christ, Noah! We're not hiding his body in the woods. *This wasn't your fault.*"

"No one's going to believe—"

"It was an accident—"

"His teeth marks are in my fucking hand! Look!" Noah thrust his hand out so Steve could see the bloody wound. Several deep teeth punctures had formed a half moon in his flesh. "How's that going to look, huh?"

"He attacked you. You were restraining him. It was self-defense."

"We broke into his house!"

"We were getting help for Jeff and Jenny. It was an emergency. The cops will understand that—"

"Dude!" Noah exclaimed. "We're a bunch of boozed-up out-of-towners. Jeff smashes his car while he's half-soused and jumping from coke. Yeah, he was, did a couple of lines when you and Jenny were under the bridge. You think the cops are going to have much sympathy for him? Much sympathy for *us* getting *him* help? Then another boozed-up out-of-towner—this one testing positive for pot—breaks into a house and kills a kid who's trying to protect his home from what he believes are burglars. Shit, Steve, the cops aren't going to be on our side in this. They're going to be gunning for us. What I did might not be premeditated murder, but it sure as hell is manslaughter. I'll go to prison."

Steve frowned. He hadn't thought about the full ramifications of their collective actions. But Noah was right, wasn't he? They'd been drinking. Not only that but Jeff was high on coke and Noah thoroughly stoned. "Fuck, Noah..." He cleared his throat. "Okay, let's say you're right. Okay? Maybe you're right. But hiding his body... It won't work. They'll find it. They'll have dogs."

Noah's eyes brightened, became intense. "Then we drive it somewhere, somewhere far away."

"There's blood all over the floor."

"We can clean it up," he said urgently, almost manically. "I'll clean it up right now." He jerked his head about as if searching for a mop.

"No," Steve said, aware his dithering was encouraging his friend. "No," he added more firmly. "Forget it, Noah. Forget it."

"Dude!" Noah grabbed his arm. "We can do this!"

Steve tugged free. "We have to report this."

"We can't—"

"We're reporting this!"

"Jesus! Don't you—"

"Yeah, I do! I understand!" Steve said, stepping away, putting space between them. "And I'm sorry, Noah, but we're doing this right. We start lying, it's only going to get worse—a lot worse."

Noah shook his head disgustedly.

"It'll be okay," Steve told him. "It will." He softened his voice. "Don't worry, man. We'll sort this all out."

Then he was gone around the corner, back upstairs.

Noah remained where he was, thinking.

Lonnie Carlsbaugh shoved through the front doors of Randy's Bar-B-Q and tottered out into the cold, starless night to his car, trying his best to keep in a straight line. He had driven home from Randy's beer-eyed too many times to count, and he had no reservations about doing so this evening, even after polishing off what must have been seven or eight pints of Coors Extra Gold. Given that it was that time of the month again—that time being the end of the month—he had no cash on hand and put the beers on his tab. Randy knew he was good for it. One thing Lonnie did, and did well, was pay his debts. Every two weeks, after receiving his workers' compensation check from the government, he would stop by Randy's for a beer and clear his tab. Keith and Buck and Daryl and his other pals would show up throughout the evening to get away from their wives, and he'd square up with them whatever he owed them from their Tuesday night Texas Hold Em games. This would usually leave him with just enough money to pay any outstanding utility bills and pick up a few groceries. He didn't eat much himself, but his son Scottie could eat a man out of house and home. Last week Scottie's cunt of a schoolteacher had the nerve to call up Lonnie in the middle of the day like he had nothing better to do than waste his time talking to her, and ask if Scottie was eating breakfast because he had been caught stealing his classmates' snacks at recess time. She also blamed what she called "hunger pains" for his rowdy behavior and poor attention span. Lonnie told the stupid cunt Scottie was eating just fine, had eggs every morning. And that was mostly true. He ate whatever the hen laid. That was usually one egg, but sometimes it might be two. And on the days the hen laid a zero—well, how was that Lonnie's fault? He couldn't control the biology of a chicken. He wasn't fucking God, was he?

It really pissed Lonnie off, Scottie's teachers calling him up like they did. Didn't they understand he was a single father doing the best he could for the boy? Georgina, his wife and the boy's ma, had died in childbirth from something the doctors had a big fancy word for. That had been shitty luck. Georgina might not have been a looker, but her family had money coming out of their collective gazoo. Her parents bought him and Georgie the house for their wedding gift and furnished it with stock from one of their furniture stores. Lonnie had been in the crosshairs to manage one of those stores. But when Georgie died the family didn't want anything to do with him or Scottie. So he was stuck raising the boy by himself. And it hadn't been easy either. No sir. But he'd done it, hadn't he? He'd raised Scottie fine and well. So what if the boy had a few behavioral problems? Hell, all kids did. What was a parent to do about that? Let them live and learn and fend for themselves, was Lonnie's mantra. That's how you built character. That's how Lonnie's father raised Lonnie, and he'd turned out all right.

Lonnie made it to his rusted puke-green Buick Skylark without falling on his ass and spent a good ten seconds finding the right key to unlock the door. He dropped in behind the steering wheel with a great sigh of satisfaction. His eyes drifted closed, and when he realized this, they snapped back open. He slapped himself across the face to wake himself up, got the car going, and reversed, bumping off a particularly high part of the curb. The Skylark's back bumper kissed the road loudly.

Lonnie mumbled something incomprehensible, shoved the column shifter into drive, and accelerated. He didn't drive too fast because clouds of fog hung low over the streets, turning the largely residential neighborhood into something out of a monster movie. At the corner he turned left onto Westside Lane. Some of the houses he passed had jack-o-lanterns sitting in their front windows or out on their front stoops, though only two were lit from within with candles.

Halfway down the block Lonnie spotted his first trick-or-treaters: a little girl dressed as a princess with fairy wings sprouting from her back and a little boy dressed in a full-body tiger suit with a limp tail that dragged on the sidewalk.

The mother walked a few feet behind them. She was on the chubby side, but not a bad looker. Lonnie had seen her around town before. You saw everyone around town now and then in a township of nine hundred souls. He thought she might work at the art gallery on Edgeview Street, but he couldn't be sure because he'd never gone in, only glanced through the window when walking past on random occasions.

Seeing the woman and her kids made Lonnie think about Scottie again. He'd promised to take the boy trick-or-treating tonight. Scottie had even made a mask to wear. Lonnie frowned. How had he forgotten? Well, he hadn't, had he? Not really. It was more a case of time getting away from him. He went to Randy's for a couple of beers, and those couple of beers turned into eight. What was he supposed to do about that? He couldn't control time, let alone turn back the clock. He wasn't fucking God, was he?

Maybe he'd buy Scottie a chocolate bar tomorrow, surprise him with it at dinner? Sure, that was a good idea. He'd get him one of those Twix bars he liked because there were two cookies in the package, which made him think he was getting more bang for his buck.

Lonnie made a right onto Mayapple Drive, then a left on Colony Drive, passing six more trick-or-treaters. Then he was on Stanford Road, leaving Boston Hills behind him.

Trees closed in around him, their canopy blotting out the silvered light from the full moon. He flicked on the high beams and kept the speedometer needle at sixty miles an hour. The fog was just as bad as it had been in town, and although there might no longer be kids to worry about, there was plenty of deer in these parts, and some of them were plain suicidal. Last summer he'd been driving back from Randy's in the early hours of the morning, nicely licked and minding nobody's business but his own, when a whitetail bounded right in front of him like it got its wires crossed or something. It took out the car's left headlight, crunched the bumper, but at least had the courtesy to die in the process. Lonnie tossed it in the trunk, happy to feast on choice cuts of venison for the next while. The following day he noticed the damage to the car, of course, the blood and fur glued to the broken headlight, but he had no memory of the accident. By the time he discovered the carcass in the trunk a week later it was covered in a squiggling film of maggots, and he had to scoop the goopy remains out with a shovel.

Anyway, a run-in with a suicidal deer wasn't the only reason Lonnie was driving cautiously. He needed time to react, slow down, and block the road if those out-of-towners came his way. Lonnie didn't know why Cleavon couldn't tell him whether they were lookers or not, but Cleavon was like that, a rancorous old crabapple who'd bitch if you hung him with a new rope. Still, if any of the does were half as pretty as the last one—Betty Wilfried, according to her driver's license—he'd be a happy man. It was a shame pretty Betty had gotten so beat up in the crash. Weasel had been too aggressive, scared her a bit too much, because she'd smashed her car bad enough to break half the bones in her body and face. Still, Lonnie hadn't complained. A fuck was a fuck, and broken or not, Betty Wilfried had been a great fuck.

Noah knew Steve was wrong, he couldn't fess up, they had to get rid of the body. Otherwise he was facing prison time— and what was the prison sentence for manslaughter? Five years? Ten? Hell, even one year would be too long. He'd be locked up with murderers and rapists, people who'd been in the slammer before, knew the system, knew how to work the guards. He'd know nothing. He'd be alone, surrounded by sheetrock and iron bars and gang members aligned from the housing projects they came from. They'd each want a piece of a young, straight kid like himself. Some big black or Latino dude trapping him in the shower and telling him how much he was going to love their good time up his sugah ass. And when he wasn't getting raped he would likely be getting the piss beat out of him in the exercise yard, or the cafeteria, maybe even in his goddamn cell. Because he'd be a kid killer, pretty low on the totem pole. It wouldn't matter that the boy's death had been an accident. The lowlifes he was locked up with would believe what they wanted to believe, rumors would swirl, accounts would become embellished. He'd be finished. Hell, he likely wouldn't make it to the end of his sentence alive.

And in the off chance he did...what then?

He could kiss his career in sculpting goodbye. No respectable gallery owner would display his work. He'd be a kid killer in their eyes too, only they wouldn't need to turn him into some depraved pedophile to feel superior. Smashing in the skull of a little boy while drunk and high would be bad enough on its own in their civilized circles.

So what would he do? Get a nine-to-five job? Then again, who would hire him? He'd have to check that little box on all his future employment applications that asked if you had a criminal record.

Why couldn't Steve just cut him a break? All he had to do was turn a blind eye to what had happened, let him hide the body in the forest. Was that so much to ask? The kid was gone. Why ruin a second life?

"What the fuck were you doing?" he said quietly to the dead boy. "Why the fuck were you attacking us, you stupid shit?"

Suddenly, before his eyes, the boy's jeans darkened around his crotch. Noah stared, incredulous, terrified. He bent close and detected the acrid odor of urine.

He was *peeing*?

Feeling suddenly sick, Noah hurried to the front door, threw it open, and stepped onto the veranda. Cool air caressed his face, but this did little to calm him. He stumbled blindly to the banister and leaned over the railing. His stomach slammed his esophagus, acid burned a trail up his throat, and he vomited a jet of watery gunk. This went on for five or ten seconds, one abdomen contraction after the next, a biological pump, until there was nothing left to spew.

Groaning, Noah wiped the heel of his hand across his lips—and made out two headlights approaching along the highway. Instead of continuing past, however, the vehicle slowed, then turned onto the driveway.

"Steve?" Noah shouted in a rubbery voice. "*Steve!* Get down here!"

◆ ◆ ◆

Steve took the steps downstairs two at a time and saw Noah standing outside on the veranda. He stopped next to him and stared in surprise at the car coming toward them through the fog. He recalled the kid's words: *Pa's coming back right now, and you're gonna be in deep shit.*

"What should we do?" Noah said. He had gone white as a ghost.

"I'll tell them," Steve said.

"I killed their kid," Noah said.

"I'll tell them," Steve repeated.

The car shuddered to a stop next to Noah's Jeep. The door flung open and a smallish man appeared. He had warthog hair sprouting from a balding crown, a turned-up nose, and a sallow complexion. He wore sagging jeans and a hounds-tooth jacket over a faded red T-shirt.

He scowled at them. "Who shu'hell you?" he said, slurring his words.

Steve said, "We've had an accident—"

"It's just the two of you? No one else? No girlfriends?"

Steve and Noah exchanged confused glances.

"Well?" the man demanded.

"We've had an accident," Steve continued. "Two of our friends are injured. We saw this house, a light was on, we thought we could use the phone and call the police."

The man's eyes glinted suspiciously. "Well, did ya?"

"Do you live here?"

"What's that to ya?"

"A boy lives here."

"My son, Scottie. And I'll ask you again—what's that to ya?"

"Your son told us you don't have a phone."

The man smiled triumphantly, revealing stained, barnacle teeth. "That's right," he said. "Don't got no phone. Who the hell I need to call?"

"Your son," Steve said, swallowing the tightness in his throat, "started to attack us with a hockey stick. My friend tried to take the stick from him. There was an accident."

The man squinted. "What kind of accident?"

"Sir, I'm sorry. Your son is dead."

"He's *what*?"

"It was an accident. He bumped into a radiator. It fell on him."

The man stood there, staring at Steve like he was speaking Klingon. Then he clicked back to reality and bounded up the steps. "Scottie?" he shouted. "Scottie?"

Steve and Noah stepped aside as the man shoved past them, leaving a trail of cheap cologne in his wake. He went inside the house. "Scottie? *Scottie!*"

Steve stared at his feet as he listened to the man wail and blubber and finally break down in sobs. Then he went quiet. Steve glanced at Noah. He was staring off into the trees. Moonlight glinted off his tear-streaked cheeks.

The man appeared in the doorway. His eyes were bloodshot. Snot hung from his nose, stringing off his chin. "Who did that?" he barked hoarsely.

"I did," Noah said.

"You killed my boy?"

Noah didn't answer.

"*You killed my boy?*"

"It was an accident," Steve said.

The man whirled on him. "An accident? An accident! He don't got no head no more!"

"I'm sorry—"

"Sorry? You're sorry? I'll show you sorry." He hastened down the steps to his car.

Under his breath Steve said, "I think we should get out of here."

Noah rubbed his eyes and nodded.

In the next instance, however, the man withdrew a rifle from his car. He locked it into his shoulder, pressed his cheek to the side of the stock, and took aim at Noah through the open sight. "I'll see you in hell, boy," he said.

Noah's hands shot up. "Wait wait wait—"

The man rocked the bolt to and fro, feeding a round into the rifle's chamber, and fired. The report was like a canon blast. Noah flew backward against the house. His left hand crashed through the living room window, and he crumpled to the ground.

"Noah!" Steve shouted, dropping to his knees. "Noah?" He tilted his friend's head back. A circular hole rimmed with abraded skin and leaking blood marked the center of Noah's forehead like a bulls-eye. His eyes were open and unseeing.

He had died instantly.

Heart pounding, barely able to breathe, Steve bumbled backward like a crab, trying to stand but finding his legs uncooperative. The man tromped up the steps, pointing the rifle at him. He cycled the bolt, ejecting the spent casing. It struck the lumber planking with a plaintive clink.

"Fuck you!" Steve shouted in crazy defiance. "You fucking redneck piece of shit! You killed him! You killed my friend!"

"And you're next, boy," the man snarled as he closed one wild eye, aiming through the rifle's sight once more.

CHAPTER 11

"I warned you not to go out tonight."
Maniac (1980)

P anting, her throat flayed raw, Mandy stumbled to a stop
before a small butte overgrown with vegetation. She
glanced behind her, saw nothing but the dark outlines
of tree trunks in the ethereal fog, and sagged to all fours. She
crawled forward and pressed her back against the rock wall,
wanting to blend into it. She was so deep in shock her brain and
lungs felt encased in ice. She couldn't think or make sense of
anything.

She waited, listened, every nerve-ending tingling, alert. The
night was graveyard silent. She didn't hear any sound of pursuit.
She considered continuing, putting as much distance between
her and the freaks as possible, yet she didn't think she could
coax her body into getting up. She'd only been running for one
minute, two at most, yet she was out of breath and exhausted.
She might be thin and look fit and healthy on the outside, but
her insides were a different matter altogether. The last time
she'd gone for a run—a real run with warm-up stretches and
Lycra tights and Nike joggers—would have been as a junior in
high school. She'd been nothing but skin and bones then. Her
mother had told her this countless times at the dinner table

when she refused to finish her meals. "You're nothing but skin and bones, Mandy," she would say, looking over the top of her bifocals at her in an uncanny impression of a cross librarian. "No man is going to take a stick-and-bones woman for a wife. Men want femininity, fertility, and that means breasts, hips. Even a nice round tush wouldn't hurt. Now, eat up." Whether it was from eating more, or family genes (her mother had been a buxom, curvaceous woman—until the last stages of the cancer, that was) Mandy had developed the breasts, hips, and tush. But in those younger days, as a twelve-year-old girl, it wouldn't have been hard to imagine a strong gust of wind picking her up and blowing her halfway down the block.

Healthy on the outside...rotten on the inside.

Nevertheless, Mandy had gotten away from Cleavon and his brothers. She was safe. As long as she remained still and didn't make any noise, they wouldn't find her—

She made out a distant yellow light arcing back and forth in the fog. Her lungs shucked up in her chest.

For a few moments the light seemed to be angling away from her. Then, to her horror, it bee-lined back in her direction. It came closer, growing larger and brighter.

Mandy watched it, hypnotized. Her muscles stiffened as she prepared to flee. She eased herself onto her knees but froze when the leaf litter crackled beneath her weight. It sounded as loud as a gunshot in the still forest.

She couldn't run, she realized. The person with the flashlight was too close. He would hear her, then see her. He would catch her.

The light came closer.

She pressed her back flat against the rock wall. The person —Floyd? Earl? Cleavon?—was now so close she could hear him. He was stepping heavily, batting branches, making no effort at stealth.

Abruptly he stopped. An unbearable silence ensued. Mandy was sure he had spotted her. But then he aimed the flashlight into the canopy. Maybe he'd heard an animal, a raccoon or possum, or maybe he thought she'd climbed a tree.

He lost interest in the leafless boughs a moment later and started forward once more, sweeping the flashlight beam to his left and right, methodically searching the mist-shrouded night. He couldn't be any more than twenty feet away. If he kept his path he would spot her. She was certain of that. A few more steps and he would cry out in triumph and charge her. She should have run when she had the chance. She should have ignored her exhaustion. What were a few minutes of discomfort when your life hung in the balance? Surely she could have pushed on—

"Cleave?" the man who was now only fifteen feet away shouted. It sounded like Earl. Mandy's stomach dropped as she waited for him to say, "Found her!" Instead he added, "She's gone!"

There was no reply for a long moment. Then Cleavon's voice, gruff and distant, told him to come back.

Mandy said a silent prayer of thanks even as Earl bounced the flashlight beam back and forth a final time. It stopped directly on her, blinding her. She felt as lit up as a fly on a television screen.

If she could have worked her lungs, she would have screamed. If she could have moved her limbs, she would have fled. But she could do neither. She was paralyzed with fear—and it was this instinct that ultimately saved her. Because Earl hadn't seen her after all. The beam moved off her, the footsteps started away.

Mandy expelled the breath she'd been holding and shook uncontrollably.

Mandy remained where she was for another five minutes, making sure Earl's departure wasn't a trick to lure her out of hiding. When she didn't hear or see anything more of him, she decided she was safe.

She sagged with relief. She had never contemplated dying before. But while frozen there, pinned in the flashlight beam, she'd been convinced it was the end. She was going to die.

Mandy—no more.

She couldn't get her mind around this possibility. She couldn't grasp the concept of not being. Maybe older people could. Maybe the longer you lived, the more familiar and understanding you became of whatever awaited you. You came to accept it, the way you came to accept aging.

Nevertheless, Mandy was too young for all this. It was as alien to her as the starving African children on those TV infomercials. She'd watched the LiveAid concert with Bob Geldolf and Michael Jackson a couple of years before. She knew about the famine and disease over there. But she hadn't been able to relate to the images she saw. Babies were supposed to be chubby and gay, not emaciated and buzzing with flies. It had been too far removed from her world. She'd acknowledged that it happened, but tuned out immediately, just as she had always tuned out thoughts on death when they became too philosophical. Even when her mother died, she had not allowed herself to dwell on what became of her soul. Of course she had been overwhelmed with sadness, but at eleven years of age, it was the sadness of loss, of loneliness, nothing deeper.

Slowly, carefully, Mandy stood. She felt strangely energized like she could run a marathon. *She was alive.* Suddenly the concept of living was as invigorating as the concept of death was frightening.

She took a deep breath and tried to figure out what to do next. She couldn't remain where she was. Cleavon and his brothers might resume their search for her in the morning when, without the cover of nightfall, she would be much more exposed and vulnerable.

She contemplated finding her way to the highway. She could flag down a passing car, get a ride into town. Then again, wasn't that what Cleavon would expect her to do? What if he collected his car from the "ol' McGrady house" and prowled the roads for her? She could unwittingly flag him down, just as the distressed damsel always flagged down her tormentor in the movies.

Could she walk all the way to town then? She had no idea how far Boston Mills was, but right then she was determined to walk all night if she had to. She could keep to the verge. If a vehicle came along, she could duck into the woods and hide until it passed—

She nearly slapped her hand against her forehead when she realized what she'd overlooked.

Steve and Noah!

They were likely already on their way back with help. Paramedics, police officers, firefighters. She had to get to the road, wave them down, warn them about Cleavon and his brothers. She wouldn't be fooled. She'd recognize a police cruiser or an ambulance. Their lights would be flashing, their klaxons blaring.

With fresh determination, Mandy went searching for the road.

CHAPTER 12

"That cold ain't the weather.
That's death approaching."
30 Days of Night (2007)

Cleavon was pacing back and forth in the middle of the road when he spotted a pair of headlights beyond the veil of fog. He moved to the gravel shoulder so Jesse didn't run him over and waved his arms above his head. The two orbs of white grew brighter until Jesse's Chevy El Camino appeared and hunkered to a stop before him. Jesse left the engine running as he hopped out one door, Weasel the other.

Jesse was an owlish-looking man who always had his head stuck forward and always looked like he had a question on his mind. His big-framed, thick-lensed eyeglasses made his eyes look bigger than they were, while his perpetually puckered kisser made the rest of his face look smaller. He was freshly shaven and wore a beige jacket zippered to his chin against the chill. He liked to tell people he was the CEO of his own company, and he was, technically. What he didn't tell people was that the company was a one-man operation called JG Outhouse Kleanin Kompany. He also didn't tell people, if they asked, how he got the third-degree burns on his arms. He probably wouldn't have told anybody, ever, had Randy not read about it in the *Akron Beacon*

Journal. According to the story, which was now framed behind glass and hanging on the wall of Randy's pub, Jesse had been working on an emergency toilet hole cleanup job in the middle of the night and had decided he'd needed light and lit a match while down in the hole. He was only lucky he'd been wearing a half-face respirator and goggles, or his face would have gone the way of his arms.

Weasel was still a kid, twenty-one next month, ferret-faced and thin as a rail. God knew why he grew that long-ass goatee because it made him look all the more feral. He was bushy-eyed and eager to please and more times than not dumber than a bucket of coal. He wasn't a retard like Earl or Floyd, but he was prone to doing stupid shit—like what he did earlier this evening. Cleavon didn't think Spencer should have given him so much responsibility in the first place. But nobody else wanted the job of skulking Stanford Road for does. High-speed chases were dangerous, even if you were the chaser.

Weasel's folks ran a café and restaurant over in Peninsula. It was successful enough that they opened another larger restaurant in Akron, where they moved to a few years back. Weasel remained behind in the family house, receiving a comfortable allowance every month for doing nothing but sitting on his ass all day. Why someone so stupid got such a lucky break in life, Cleavon didn't know. Cleavon himself had worked like a son of a bitch for most of his miserable life, and he'd never once been given a break.

"That them?" Jesse said, looking at the bodies lying on the ground some twenty yards away and illuminated by the fire from the blazing wreckage: Cueball, the mocha-skinned girl, Cherry, and the handsome cripple. The way they were lined up side by side, they resembled corpses waiting for their coffins.

"'Course that's them," Cleavon said. "Who the fuck else they gonna be?"

"What I meant is, where's the rest of them?"

"Already gone when me and the boys arrived." Cleavon scowled at Weasel. "You see how you fucked up, Weasel? You see what you did now?"

Weasel stared at his boots. "I know I fucked up, Cleave, and I said I'm sorry."

"Sorry, huh? They get to town, if Lonnie don't stop them and they get to town..." He shook his head. He wasn't going to entertain that thought right now. "Jess, you bring the fire extinguisher?"

"Ayuh. On the back seat."

"Weasel, go put out the fire. You can do that, can't you?"

"Yeah, Cleave." He started toward the burning car.

"You gonna put it out with your fuckin' hands? Get the extinguisher!"

Weasel blushed. "Right, Cleave." He opened the back door, grabbed the red fire extinguisher, and trotted toward the burning car.

"That boy got about as much sense as God gave a goose," Cleavon muttered.

"Ayuh," Jesse said, though he was still looking at the three bodies. Given the hungry glint in his eyes, Cleavon suspected he was looking more at Cherry than the other two. Sprawled how she was, her denim skirt pushed up her thighs, she was showing more than leg.

Just then Earl and Floyd emerged from the forest, their flashlights pointed at the ground ahead of them, their heads lowered. They knew they were in trouble and trying to play ostrich. Fucking retards.

"Earl!" Cleavon shouted, cupping his hands around his mouth. "Get your ass over here."

"The hell they doing in the woods?" Jesse said.

"Looking for the one that got away."

Jesse raised his eyebrows. "The one that got away?"

"I had the bitch by the throat, I *had* her, then she goes and kicks me right where it hurts and got away."

"Shit, Cleave, how we gonna find her?"

"We're not, not now," he said. "Where she gonna go? It's the others we need to think about right now. We gotta deal with them first. Then we can worry about finding the bitch."

Earl approached in his lumbering size sixteen-boot gait, red-faced and out of breath. Floyd was behind him, also huffing and puffing. Unless you gave Floyd a direct order—one he could understand, mind you—he'd simply follow Earl everywhere.

"We couldn't find her, Cleave," Earl said shyly, staring at his boots. "She took off like a rabbit, and we couldn't find her. If you didn't let her go, if you didn't do that, we woulda had her, we woulda had everyone. Why'd you let her go, Cleave? She's nothing but a girl."

Cleavon wanted to kick Earl in the nuts and see how quickly he reacted afterward, but he didn't dare. Earl had a temper like you'd never seen. You get him worked up, you better be faster than a striped-ass ape. It wasn't that Earl got it in his head to kill you; he simply might do it unintentionally. He didn't realize his strength, or if he did, he forgot about it when he got worked up and emotional.

Back when Cleavon was twenty or thereabouts he'd been feuding with Earl over some fucking thing and had gone into Earl's room and took his pet mouse from the aquarium and cut off the thing's head with a straight razor. Earl, only fifteen but already huge, caught Cleavon red-handed and went crazy, tossing the bed out of the way to get at him. He slammed Cleavon against the wall hard enough to knock all the pictures to the floor. Then he heaved Cleavon up like he weighed nothing and launched him straight out the second-floor window. Luckily it had been winter then, and a couple of feet of snowfall had cushioned Cleavon's fall. Still, he'd broken his left arm and split open his chin against his knee. When Cleavon came back from the doctor's with a cast on his arm and stitches in his chin, Earl had been profusely apologetic, said he hadn't meant to hurt him, wouldn't do it again. Since then he had lost his temper only a few other times. This wasn't due to discipline on his part as much as everybody else having the good sense not to provoke him. You could call Earl a shithead all you wanted, but you didn't go kicking him in the nuts, no matter how much he was smarting off, not if you wanted to be walking the next day.

"Shut your yabbering and listen to me, Earl," Cleavon said, feeling as though time was getting away from them all too fast. "You, Floyd, and Weasel are going to take those three there back to the house. Then you come back here with the wrecker and get what's left of the bimmer to the garage. You got that?"

"Sure, Cleave. That's easy. And back at the house, can I, I mean, I've been thinking, and I'm wondering, I know you're gonna say no—"

"Spit it out, man!"

"Can I give the bucks to Toad and Trapper?"

Cleavon stared at him. "To your *snakes*?"

"Can I, Cleave, please? They just shed, they're real hungry—"

"Judas Priest! You must be dumber than you look! There ain't no way those snakes can eat a full-grown man."

"Sure they can, Cleave, they can easy. Trapper's twenty-six feet now. Toad's only a bit shorter, I just measured them last month. They can eat the bucks easy."

Cleavon frowned, thinking about that. They were damn big snakes. Monsters. If they could eat fully grown humans, well, that would be two fewer graves to dig.

"Also," Earl went on, "it'd mean they don't need to eat no rabbits for a couple of months, and more rabbits equal more money for us, that's what you always say—"

"All right, all right, enough yabbering, for fuck's sake! You wanna feed baldy and the cripple to your snakes, feed them to your snakes. Just don't lay a hand on the girl. That means no 'playing' with her either. I swear to God, Earl, I find one mark on her when I get back, I don't know, but I'll tell Spence it was you this time, no more covering, and he'll kick you out of the club forever. You got that, Earl?"

Earl nodded solemnly. "I won't touch her, Cleave. I promise."

"Your promise ain't worth shit," Cleavon said. "You just remember, you touch her, no more does, never." He turned to Jesse. "C'mon."

They climbed in the cab of the El Camino just as a light rain began to fall, and within moments they were speeding north along Stanford Road, on their way to Lonnie's place.

CHAPTER 13

"Be afraid... Be very afraid."
The Fly (1986)

When Jenny came around on the back seat of Noah's Jeep, she couldn't make out whether what she was hearing was animal or human. It took her a good three or four seconds to realize it was the latter—the warbling, forlorn cries of a man suffering great anguish. Thinking of Jeff, his broken back, she sat up quickly and cried out herself as a bomb seemed to go off inside her head. She moaned and sank back in the seat, afraid to move for fear of setting off another bomb. She remained like this until the pain receded and her vision cleared.

The horrible wails, she noticed, had ceased. She leaned forward gingerly and peered through the rain-specked windshield. Steve stood next to Noah on the veranda of some house. A grimy little man pushed between them and stomped down the porch steps. Jenny barely had time to wonder who he was before he reached into the car parked next to the Jeep, retrieved a rifle, and aimed it at Noah.

Jenny didn't scream a warning, didn't jump out of the Jeep and tackle the man from behind. She didn't do any of this because everything inside her had ceased to work. Fear and confusion and disbelief had shut her down, made her a spectator in what was about to play out.

The man fired the rifle. The report was a toneless bang, like a firecracker. Noah collapsed. Steve shouted his name. The man started toward them.

Jenny broke her paralysis and fumbled with the door handle. She thrust the door open and fell out of the vehicle, landing on her hands and knees on the damp gravel driveway. The air reeked of cordite smoke. Light raindrops plinked off the nape of her neck. For a split second she considered turning toward the road and fleeing, running as fast and far as she could because she didn't know what was going on here, only that it was bad, really bad, and Noah might be dead and she might be too if she stuck around. Yet even as she contemplated this she was scrambling forward. She hit the porch steps on all fours and used the banister to pull herself to her feet.

The man had stopped a few feet ahead of her, oblivious to her presence, rifle pointed at Steve. He was saying something, but Jenny didn't know what, couldn't make sense of the words right then, and it didn't matter, because he was about to shoot Steve in cold blood.

"No!" she cried, throwing herself at the back of the man. She grabbed him by the shoulders and used her weight to drag him backward off balance. The rifle swung skyward as he fired. The bullet split a chunk of wood from the porch roof.

Jenny crashed to her side. The man came down on top of her. He elbowed her in the gut, knocking her down the steps. She brought her arms up to protect her head, but still smacked her cheek against one tread hard enough to see stars and taste blood in her mouth. At the bottom she rose to her knees, expecting to hear another gunshot and to feel a round tear through her.

Instead she found Steve grappling with the grimy little man for the rifle. Bellowing like a caveman, Steve tore the gun free, shoved the barrel into the man's stomach, and squeezed the trigger. The bullet passed straight through the man, exiting his back in a jet of blood. The man clutched his gut and fell facefirst to the deck.

Jenny scrambled up the steps toward Steve. He jerked the rifle at her. His eyes were glassy and sightless, like a doll's, empty of whatever made him *him*.

"Steve! It's me! Jenny!"

Steve returned his attention to the now dead man, who lay on his stomach, blood pooling around him. He tossed the rifle away as if it had burned him.

"He killed Noah," he said softly.

Jenny glanced at Noah, crumpled against the wall, his head bowed against his chest as if he were snoozing. But he'd never be snoozing again, would he? He'd never be doing anything again. She hadn't known any of Steve's friends well, had met them for the first time this evening, but Noah had seemed most normal of the bunch. Jeff was a shmuck who thought he was God's gift to women. Austin was immature, and from what Steve had told her, a borderline alcoholic. Mandy was funny but an airhead. And Cherry, well, she was named "Cherry" and dressed like a prostitute to boot. It was only Noah—soft- spoken, dark, brooding, Noah—whom she had thought she would be happy getting to know better in the future, especially if he found a nice girlfriend and the four of them could double date.

"Are you sure he's dead?" she asked, the words coming out wooden.

"The fucker shot him right in the forehead." He drove a foot into the man's side.

The man groaned.

"He's alive!" Jenny said and felt his neck for a pulse. "Steve, he's alive!" She slipped her hands beneath the arm closest to her and flipped the man onto his back. His red T-shirt was saturated with blood. "Give me your pullover."

"Why?"

"To stop the bleeding!"

Steve came back from wherever he'd been. "Stop the bleeding?" His brow knit. "Let him bleed! Fuck, Jen! He killed Noah! He tried to kill us!"

"You're a medical student, Steve. You have a duty to—"

"Don't give me that bullshit."

"You want to have his death on your hands? Is that what you want?"

"It was self-defense."

"That's not what I meant. Christ, Steve!" She tugged her black elastic top over her head. She had nothing on beneath but her bra. The cool air bit her bare skin.

"Okay, Jesus, okay, Jen, here..." Steve removed his pullover and held it out for her.

She put her top back on, accepted the pullover, and pressed it against the man's abdomen. "This is only going to give him a bit more time. You have to go call an ambulance."

"There's no phone."

She stared at him. "What?"

"Noah and I already checked. That's what started all this..." He shook his head. "Anyway, we checked. And the kid said they didn't have one—"

"The kid? Where—"

"He's dead. It was an accident."

Jenny felt as if she'd been slapped. *A dead child?* But she didn't have time to wonder about this. The medical student inside her had taken over. The man before her was still alive. He could still be saved. He was the priority. It was her duty to help him.

"Get Noah's keys," she said. "We'll drive him to the hospital ourselves. We'll tell them about this child, and Jeff, and— Jesus, just get the keys!"

Nodding, Steve stood and said, "Oh shit."

"What?" But she saw what he did.

A car had turned off the highway and was bumping down the driveway toward them in one heck of a hurry.

Steve picked up the rifle and held it across his chest so it was clearly visible. Jenny was asking him what he was doing. He wasn't listening. Every instinct in his body was telling him that this wasn't right, that he was in danger. He couldn't say why this might be the case, not right then, not keyed up on adrenaline and stressed out of his mind with horror and grief. But now was not the time to question his instincts.

The approaching vehicle sported the roofline of a sedan and the flatbed of a pickup. It skidded to a halt behind the Jeep and Buick. Both front doors opened and two men emerged. The driver was bookish and harmless-looking, and Steve might have let down his guard had it not been for the other man. He was tall, maybe six feet. Beneath shoulder-length greasy black hair he had a hard, no-bullshit face, and beneath a protruding brow he had hard, no-bullshit eyes to match. The mutton chops and handlebar mustache shouted "redneck," and he might have been a comical stereotype had he not been so...hard. That was the word that kept coming back to Steve. Hard.

Steve tightened his grip on the rifle.

"Jesus Mary!" the bookish man exclaimed. "Lonnie? That Lonnie? You shot Lonnie, you sumbitch!"

"Who are you?" Steve demanded.

"Who'm I? Who'm *I*? You shot Lonnie, you motherfucker!"

The hard man held up his hand, signaling the other to calm down. "We're from next door," he said. His manner wasn't pleasant, but it wasn't angry or disapproving either. It was like a cop's: cool but alert, aloof but calculating. "We heard the gunshot, came to see what happened. He dead?"

"He's alive," Jenny said. "He needs to get to the hospital."

"Right-o." He took a step forward.

Steve pointed the rifle at him. "Stop."

The man stopped.

"Steve!" Jenny said. "They can help!"

"Jenny, get inside."

"Steve—"

"Get inside!"

"Whoa there," the hard man said. "That's no way to speak to a lady."

"How many gunshots did you hear?"

The man didn't smile, not quite, but his face twitched as if he were smiling to himself, and Steve knew right then it didn't matter the answer he gave, he was dangerous. The man's eyes flicked from Noah to the man named Lonnie and he said, "Two."

"Jenny, get inside," Steve repeated.

This time she didn't argue. She stood and backed up slowly. Steve backed up also.

"Now, say," the hard man said. "What's the matter?"

"I don't know who you are or why you're here," Steve said, "but you come any closer, I'll shoot you." He pulled the stock tighter against his shoulder.

"Hey, okay, take it easy—"

Stumbling backward across the threshold into the house, Steve slammed the front door shut, flicked the thumb lock, and shot the bolt.

CHAPTER 14

*"Good Ash, bad Ash. I'm the
guy with the gun."*
Army of Darkness (1992)

Beetle turned off the shower taps and dried himself with the towel he'd draped over the curtain rod. He wrapped the towel around his waist and stepped over the lip of the bathtub. Steam had turned the mirror above the sink opaque. He cleared a circle with his hand to view his reflection. He ran his fingers over a few of the shrapnel scars that tattooed his chest and right shoulder. He hated the sight of them, the feel of them. They reminded him that he should have died with the rest of his platoon on the beach in Grenada. He wished he had. Sarah would have remembered him fondly, with love. She would not have grown to hate him. They would have avoided all the pain and suffering of the last two years.

It could have been different, of course—Grenada, his life with Sarah, everything. If the chopper hadn't missed the designated beach drop-off in front of the university campus, if it hadn't set down hundreds of yards away in the middle of enemy territory, the mission to rescue the American students could have gone as planned. But that was the thing with life: there were no second chances, no rewinding time.

Burt Jackson and Big Dave died within seconds of each other. Small arms fire erased their faces, flinging them to the ground and knocking off their helmets. Shortly after this a mortar round blew Oklahoma Eddy into confetti. The detonation was close enough to Beetle that it charged the air around him and splattered him with Eddy's blood and guts.

The rest of the platoon was slaughtered similarly. In the chaos and confusion only Beetle and two other Rangers made it to the shanties beyond the shoreline, where they escaped into the zigzag of back streets and hunkered down in a derelict café. Otter, an anti-tank gunner, had been shot in the back, Pips, a sniper, in the leg. Beetle put pressure on Pip's wound and told him he was going to be okay, lies, he knew, because the bullet had severed a main artery or vein. Pips died listening to those lies a few minutes later. Knowing Otter was next if he didn't receive proper medical attention, Beetle set off on his own to the nearby abandoned Russian Embassy in the hopes of finding a two-way radiotelephone. He killed two Cuban soldiers he came across with his bare hands so as not to raise an alarm and reached the embassy undetected. Inside he discovered the power was out and retrieved a first-aid kit as consolation. While leaving he turned a corner and bumped chest-to-chest into a lone Russian diplomat.

Beetle recognized him immediately. The day before the man had driven alone to Point Salines to deliver an official message from his government to the senior American commander at the recently captured airfield. Beetle and another Ranger had searched him and his car. He had been polite and respectful and thanked them when they finished their search and handed him back his wallet, inside of which he carried a photograph of two daughters, one attractive, the other not so much.

The diplomat didn't recognize Beetle, not bloody and dusty, his face painted in black camouflage, his eyes alight with the craziness of watching several of his brothers die and killing two men with his bare hands, all within the last hour.

The diplomat tried to run. Beetle caught him easily and tied him up with a telephone cord. It took him ten minutes of agonizing before he worked himself up to kill the man. It had to be done, he told himself. He didn't know how long he and Otter were going to have to hide out on the small island, behind enemy lines. It could be weeks or months. The man might be a civilian, and a father of two, but he was still allied with the enemy.

Beetle killed him as he had the Cubans, wrapping his arms around the man's head from behind and twisting sharply to the right. Back at the café Beetle disinfected Otter's wound and bandaged him up. They spoke of their families until they fell asleep, but when Beetle woke in the middle of the night, Otter was dead.

The following day US Forces took control of Grenada, the leader of the rebellion was captured, and just like that the invasion was over—and Beetle was sent home to resume life as normal.

A knock at the door caused Beetle to jump. He realized he'd been staring at his reflection for five minutes or so. Long enough, at any rate, for the mist to clear from the mirror.

Beetle exited the bathroom. The door to the hallway didn't have a peephole.

"Yeah?" he said.

"Open up." The voice was rough, deep.

"Who is it?"

"Open up!"

Beetle went to the bed. He tossed the towel onto the mattress, then pulled on a pair of laundered boxers from his rucksack.

"Hey!" the man shouted. "This is your last warning!"

Beetle dressed in the same pants and woodland camouflage shirt he'd had on earlier. He slipped the Beretta into the waistband of the pants, fitting it snugly against the small of his back.

He returned to the door. On the other side of it he heard at least two people conversing in low tones. A moment later a key turned in the lock. The door swung inward.

Two large men wearing wool sweaters and reeking of BO

stood shoulder to shoulder in the doorway. The one on the left had a shaved head and a bulldog face with flaxen, almost nonexistent eyebrows. The one on the right had dark hair and a matching goatee. The family resemblance, however, was unmistakable. Behind them, scowling, was the shylock from the reception.

"This him, Dad?" Bulldog said.

"That's him," Shylock said.

Bulldog's scowl mimicked his father's. "So, you like beating up old men, do you?"

"He tried to rip me off," Beetle said simply.

"It don't matter what he did. You don't go beating on old men, especially when it's my dad."

"Would you prefer me to beat on you?" Beetle asked.

Bulldog's eyes widened in surprise, then narrowed in anger. "Is that a threat, you piece of shit?"

"You come to my room, you bang on my door, you get in my face. If you don't want a beating, what the fuck do you want?"

"I want you out of my motel!" Shylock crowed, wiping his red nose with the back of his hand. "And don't even think about asking for no money back."

"You're kicking me out?" Beetle said.

"Damn right I am."

"I don't think that's going to happen."

"I don't care *what* you think, asshole," Bulldog said, reaching for him.

Beetle swatted his hand aside and stepped backward, luring him into the narrow entryway.

Bulldog took the bait, lunging forward. He grabbed Beetle's shirt with both meaty fists. Beetle—who was trained not to think in a fight, only act or react—instinctively kicked Bulldog's right kneecap, causing him to cry out and sink to his other knee. Beetle curled his hand into a rock and drove his fore knuckle and middle knuckle into the bridge of Bulldog's nose. There was an audible crunch. Blood gushed.

"My nose!" Bulldog cried. "Owww! My fucking nose! Owww!"

Beetle struck him again in the same spot. He shut up and fell to his side, cupping his nose and rocking in agony.

Goatee was trying to get to Beetle without stepping on his brother. Beetle backed into the room, giving them both space to maneuver.

Goatee came at him, swinging a haymaker. Beetle stepped into the attack, blocking the blow with his left arm while chopping Goatee across the ribs with his right hand. Goatee grunted. Beetle drove a straight right into his gaping jaw, probably dislocating it. Goatee made a noise that sounded like "Oh?" and dropped to the floor.

Beetle moved purposely toward Shylock, who stood statue-still in the hallway as if rooted there by fear. Beetle withdrew the Beretta and shoved the barrel against the man's forehead. He didn't say anything. He didn't trust himself to speak. His breathing came in quick, rough snorts. His trigger finger quivered.

Beetle waited for Shylock to give him a reason to pull the trigger, but the old cheat only made a pathetic, whimpering sound, and just like that Beetle came back to himself. He blinked away the red haze that had crept over his vision, and he heard himself growl: "You're going to go into my room, you're going to collect your sons, and the three of you are going to get out of my sight. You come back, you bother me again, I will kill you. You and whoever you bring. I will end all your miserable, meaningless lives right then and there. Do you understand that? Do you believe me?"

The old cheat bobbed his head.

Beetle lowered the pistol—reluctantly. "Then get to it before I change my fucking mind."

CHAPTER 15

*"Who will survive and what
will be left of them?"*
The Texas Chainsaw Massacre (1974)

"They have guns," Steve said. He had turned off the foyer light and was peering through the front window. The Jeep's and utility coupe's high beams allowed him to see in the black night clearly enough. The bookish man had retrieved a rifle from the car. The hard man had produced a machete—*a goddamn machete*—from where it had been tucked against the small of his back. The rain had begun to fall harder, but neither of them seemed to notice or care.

"Who are they, Steve?" Jenny said in a frightened voice. She stood a couple of feet behind him.

"I don't know," he said.

"Why are they here? If they were lying about hearing the gunshots, how'd they know to come? *What the hell's going on?*"

"I don't know," he said.

"Maybe we should, I don't know, maybe we should—

"Shit."

"*What?*"

"They've backed into the fog. I can't see them anymore."

"Wait—that's good, right?" she said hopefully. "Maybe that means, maybe they're going?"

"Without their car?"

"Well, what then? What are they doing then—"

"I don't know!" Steve snapped.

"Steve, don't yell. I'm scared, okay? I'm freaking terrified. Are we going to die? *Are we going to die?*"

"Jenny, shut up!"

"Don't yell, Steve! Don't!" He could hear her hyperventilating. "I, we, God, we need to call the police—"

"There's no phone."

"There has to be."

She began fussing around the room, yanking open drawers, tossing boxes aside. Steve didn't move from the window. He assumed the two men had retreated out of sight to converse privately. It seemed pointless, considering he couldn't have heard them anyway. Maybe they thought he could read lips.

Jenny crossed the hallway to the dining room.

She screamed.

For a moment Steve was convinced she'd been shot. But when he turned, she was standing in the entranceway to the dining room, both hands covering her mouth. He went to her, put his arm around her shoulder, and led her away from the dead boy.

"What did you *do*, Steve?" she whispered, her eyes glistening with tears. "What did you and Noah *do*? That's why they're coming after us, isn't it? They know you killed that boy, and now they're going to kill us for payback."

"That's impossible, Jen. The boy died, it was an accident, the radiator fell on him, but that only happened ten minutes ago. The old man came home minutes later. He didn't call anybody. Nobody called anybody. Nobody could have known."

"Then why are they here?" She was whispering hoarsely.

"Go upstairs," he told her. "Keep searching for the phone. You're right. There has to be one. I must have overlooked it."

Steve guided her toward the staircase. Jenny hesitated, then tromped up the steps, zombie-like. Steve didn't believe he'd overlooked the phone, but if she didn't do something to occupy her mind she was going to have a nervous breakdown right then and there.

He returned to the window, pulled the floral-patterned curtain aside, and peered outside.

Nothing but fog and rain.

What were they doing? he wondered. What could they be discussing at such lengths? Were they hiding from him? Did they think he was going to pick them off with the rifle? Would he attempt that given the chance, without knowing who they were or what they were doing here? Would he even be able to hit them? A few years ago he'd fired a handgun at a friend's cottage in the Pocono Mountains. They'd set up beer cans as targets and shot at them with the cheap .25 caliber Saturday Night Special his friend's father kept in the cabin. Steve had missed the cans more times than he'd hit them, and he'd only been twenty feet away. So, rifle or not, how would he fare striking a mobile target at fifty yards?

Not good, he suspected.

Abruptly the man with the muttonchops and handlebar mustache emerged from the mist into the headlights. He held his hands over his head, the machete gripped in the right one. "Don't shoot, boy!" he called. "I just wanna talk about this."

"Talk about what?" Steve shouted.

"We don't wanna hurt you, y'hear? We only wanna get our friend some help."

Steve hesitated. Could this be true?

In a show of peace the man turned and set the machete on the hood of the utility coupe. He turned back, smiled, and stepped forward.

"Hold it!" Steve said. "You can get your friend, I'll let you get him, you can take him to the hospital, I won't shoot. But first tell me what you're doing here."

"I told you, we heard—"

"You heard nothing! There were three shots, not two!"

"That's what I said earlier. Three shots."

"Stop bullshitting me!"

"I ain't bullshitting—"

Steve sensed movement to his right and dropped to the floor just as a gunshot boomed and a bullet whizzed past his head, so close he heard it. In the second it took the bookish man to cycle the rifle's bolt and fire again, Steve had moved fast and far enough to avoid the second shot. He charged the man, driving him into the dining room table and chairs. They collapsed in a tangle of limbs, dropping their rifles. They were roughly the same size and their struggle became a grappling match that had them rolling back and forth. Steve gained some leverage and kneed the man in the groin and shoved them apart.

Steve considered scrambling for one of the rifles, but the man got to his feet just as Steve did. His eyeglasses sat askew on his nose. Blood smeared his mouth and chin. He raised his fists like a boxer, taunting Steve, then launched a punch. Steve dodged it and kicked him in the right knee. The man buckled. Steve went for the nearest rifle and grabbed it just as the man wrapped his arms around Steve's midsection. Steve jammed the rifle's stock into the man's gut. They stumbled backward and crashed into the dining room table a second time. The impact knocked the wind from Steve's lungs but also broke them apart. Spinning, Steve swung the rifle with all his might. It cracked against the man's shoulder. He cried out in pain and sank to his knees, holding onto the table to remain upright.

Steve raised the rifle over his head. He was going to bring it down on the fucker's head, he was going to crush him like an insect, he didn't care if he killed him, he was half insane right then and in a fight to the death, and he was going to—

Steve sensed someone behind him. He spun to find the hard man a foot away, machete at the ready. The man didn't say anything. He didn't smile. He showed no emotion at all.

Steve opened his mouth, to plead for his life, but the blade ended it first.

Jenny heard the reports of two successive gunshots. At first she thought it was Steve firing through the window, but then she made out the commotion of a scuffle. *They're inside!* Her first impulse was to rush downstairs and offer Steve whatever assistance she could. Yet reason nixed that idea. The men were both armed. She was five-foot-five, one hundred twenty pounds. She couldn't help. She could only die, and she didn't want to die. More than anything she'd ever wanted in her life, she didn't want to die.

Glancing frantically around the bedroom, Jenny searched for a place to hide. There was nowhere—nowhere but under the bed. She contemplated returning to the hall, fleeing down the staircase, out the front door. But it was closed and locked. She wouldn't be able to escape before the men captured her. She had to hide.

She dropped to her chest and wormed beneath the bed. She lay perfectly still. She was so afraid she felt simultaneously flushed and chilled, headachy and nauseous, almost as if she were in the initial stages of the flu.

Something loud crashed downstairs. Steve cried out, what sounded like a roar.

Of triumph? she wondered. *Was Steve winning the fight? Should she return and help him after all?*

She listened but heard nothing except the blood pounding in her head. No—she heard footsteps. Coming up the staircase, quickly. Only one set of footsteps.

Please be Steve, please let it be Steve, please God please.

The footsteps stopped outside the bedroom. They moved away, into the room across the hall. Jenny's hope was already curdling into doom. If it were Steve, he would have called her name by now. So it wasn't Steve. Steve was dead. Just like Noah was dead and she was going to be dead next. As soon as the man finished searching the room across the hall he was going to come into this room and he was going to—

The footsteps returned to the hall.

"Darlin'?"

The word iced her blood. It wasn't spoken with singsong cockiness but softly and monotonously, almost as if it were a scolding.

The man entered the bedroom where she hid. Jenny's left cheek was pressed flush to the floorboards. She could see his black boots. He took three steps into the middle of the room and stopped.

Jenny became acutely conscious of her breathing. It sounded far too loud. It was going to give her away. She bit her lip and tried not to go insane as she waited for the man's face to appear upside down, peering under the bed at her. He would grab her by the hair and drag her out and kill her.

Abruptly Jenny found herself praying for a quick death. She didn't want to experience it. She didn't want to lie there, bleeding out, in excruciating agony, *waiting*. She didn't want to see her life flash before her eyes. She didn't want to think about never seeing her mother or father again, her two older brothers, her friends. She didn't want to think about everything that could have been. She wanted a painless bullet in the head—

The black boots shuffled in a circle, then left the bedroom.

Jenny knew she couldn't remain beneath the bed. It had been stupid to hide there in the first place. She had trapped herself. She needed to get out of the house, run for the trees.

She wiggled out from the small space and went to the window. The upper sash appeared fixed in place. The lower one, however, slid vertically in grooves in the side jambs. She tried to shove the sash upward. It didn't budge. Had sloppy paint sealed it shut? Had the wood swelled or distorted? Fighting frustration and terror, she felt along the top of the sash and found some kind of metal latch. She worked the keeper free and shoved the panel upward. This time it slid easily.

She climbed through the opening.

Having checked all four bedrooms, and not finding the thin blonde in any of them, Cleavon suspected she would be behind the last door on the right. What he discovered instead was a steep set of stairs leading to the main floor.

He took the steps three at a time and emerged into the kitchen.

A back door led outside.

Cursing, he hurried to the door and found the deadbolt engaged.

Which meant the girl couldn't have left through it.

Jesse appeared in the hallway, eyeglasses busted, face a bloody mess.

"Where is she, man?" he asked. "Where'd she get to?"

"Go wait by the front staircase," Cleavon told him, then returned upstairs.

◆ ◆ ◆

Arms and legs spread wide, back pressed against the house's weatherboards, Jenny inched away from the window along a thin horizontal strip of molding. Blinking rain from her eyes, she glanced to the fog-frosted ground twenty-five feet below and suffered a moment of vertigo. It was too far to jump. She'd break her legs. Fifteen feet to her right, though, a tall maple tree grew close to the house. She thought if she could reach the branches, she could climb safely down.

She continued inching sideways, her fingernails clawing the wet wood for a grip that didn't exist. With each small step she half expected to lose her footing and plummet to the ground. Still, she pressed on. She didn't have a choice.

"Well, fuck me blue!"

Jenny was so startled she pitched forward. For a sickening second she was convinced she was going to fall. But then she flattened her back against the weatherboards once more.

She turned her head to look the way she'd come. The man with the mutton chops and handlebar mustache was leaning out the window, leering at her.

"Come back inside, darlin'. You gonna kill yourself out there."

"Leave me alone!"

"Come on back. I ain't gonna hurt you."

She resumed edging sideways.

"Shit, darlin', I wanted you dead, I'd shoot you right now with this rifle. Now come on inside."

That was true, she realized. He could shoot her easily. So why didn't he?

Because he wants to rape you first.

Swallowing a moan, she continued her progress.

"Jess!" the man shouted.

"You find her?"

"Get outside! To the side of the house. She's gone out the window."

"Okay!"

Jenny glanced at the tree. She wouldn't reach it in time. The other man would be down below her any moment, waiting for her.

She only had one option remaining.

She jumped.

Cleavon stared in disbelief as the stupid cunt jumped off the small ledge. She hit the ground with a hundred-pound thump. For what seemed like a long moment she didn't move, didn't make a sound, and he thought she was either unconscious or dead, and it served her right—

She began to scream, high-pitched and glassy, like a stuck pig.

"What did you expect, darlin'?" he muttered, then went downstairs to see how badly she was hurt.

◆ ◆ ◆

Jesse was bent over her when Cleavon got to them. She was still screaming and crying at the same time. It wasn't doing his headache any good. But he didn't think she'd quiet down no matter how nice he asked, and he didn't have a sock to stuff in her mouth, so he ignored the noise the best he could.

"It ain't pretty," Jesse said, his owlish face frowning.

Cleavon studied the girl. She had large blue eyes and what would have been a pretty face when it wasn't wet with tears and rain and twisted in pain.

"You see what you did?" Cleavon told her. "You went and broke your goddamn legs. I told you I wasn't gonna hurt you."

Jesse said, "What we gonna do, Cleave?"

"Give me a hand getting her to the car."

"I mean, about all this." He swallowed. "Lonnie's dead, for fuck sake, Cleave. Both Lonnie and his boy. How we gonna cover this up?"

"Just give me a fuckin' hand getting her to the car." He crouched next to the girl and set Lonnie's rifle and his machete in the mud. "You take her left arm. I'll—"

"We gotta call Mr. Pratt."

Cleavon paused, one hand on the girl's shoulder. She was moaning now, which was better than screaming. "What the fuck is Spence gonna do?" he snapped. "He some sort of clean-up man, Jess? He gonna come out here and clean up this mess? What's calling him gonna do?"

"He might think of a way to explain all this."

"What needs explaining, Jess?"

"Lonnie's dead, Cleave! Lonnie and his boy. How're we gonna explain that?"

"We're not."

"We're not?"

"We were never here."

"We were never here?"

"Do I have a fuckin' echo? No, we weren't never here. Whatever happened, happened between some out-of-towner and Lonnie and his boy. We weren't here. We don't know nothing."

"But won't the sheriff wonder where that buck inside, where his friends went? Surely they told people where they were going, people're gonna know they were traveling together, they'll wonder what happened to the rest of them."

"Let them wonder, Jess. No one took a picture of us, did they? We weren't never here. That's all that matters. Now give me a fuckin' hand with the girl."

Jess set his rifle aside and took her left arm, Cleavon her right arm, and they hefted her upright. She shrieked but there was little else she could do with no good legs. They carried her between them to the Chevy El Camino and set her in the flatbed.

"Why...?" she said between sobs, propping herself up on her elbow. "Where...what are you...doing to me?"

"Keep your hands and feet inside the vehicle for the duration of the ride, darlin'," Cleavon told her. "And if you try another jumping stunt once we get going, and don't break something fuckin' else, you better believe I'll do it for you."

He slammed the tailgate shut.

CHAPTER 16

"These are godless times, Mrs. Snell."
Carrie (1976)

"Would you like any more potatoes, dear?" Lynette asked Spencer Pratt, her husband of seventeen years—who, she was nearly positive, was cheating on her with another woman.

He dabbed his lips with the cotton napkin. "Thank you, no," he said.

"Are you going to the hospital this evening?"

"Are you so eager to have the house to yourself?"

"Of course not. I was just wondering," she said, collecting her dishes and taking them to the kitchen. "You've been spending a lot of time there this year."

"Yes, well, work's work, isn't it?" he said, following her with his dishes. He set them in the sink and rinsed them with hot water. "I have two new patients who require...extensive work."

Lynette placed the jug of milk in the refrigerator. "Work that can't be done during regular working hours?"

Spencer didn't reply, and Lynette wondered whether she'd said too much, overplayed her hand. Smiling kindly, she turned around, assuming the role of the doting, naïve housewife. Spencer was scribbling something in a notepad he had taken from his pocket, apparently oblivious to her question.

Lynette went to fetch the rest of the dishes from the dining room table. They'd had roast pork, vegetables, and mashed potatoes with gravy. As usual, Spencer finished off most of the pork and potatoes but barely touched the vegetables. When she returned to the kitchen, Spencer was still scribbling notes.

He was the Psychiatrist-in-Chief of the Boston Mills Psychiatric Hospital, which had once been called the Boston Mills Lunatic Asylum. Lynette still thought of it as the latter. She had grown up in Boston Mills, and her first memory of the asylum had been overhearing her parents talking about a lunatic who'd gone on a rampage and killed a caseworker and two nurses. At six or seven she didn't know what a lunatic was, but she could tell by the way her parents were acting that she should be scared. Her mother would use this fear to keep her in line with ominous sayings such as, "You better be good or the lunatic will get you." She would also threaten to ring up the director of the asylum to have Lynette committed, telling her, "It's a rat trap, very easy to get in, impossible to get out." These threats were made all the more real and frightening because Lynette's father, a gardener at the hospital, brought home any number of stories about what went on there. Patients who would be forced to eat everything on their plates at mealtime even if it made them vomit it all back up. Patients who would be tied to their beds with wet sheets layered in ice in the pit of winter. Orderlies who would beat patients to within inches of their lives with Wiffle ball bats before locking them away in solitary confinement. An old woman who wandered into a closed-down ward and died, her corpse remaining undiscovered for so long it left a permanent body-shaped stain on the floor. And then of course there was the debacle in 1962 when a man escaped the asylum and murdered a local woman and lived in her house for a week, eating her food and dressing in her clothes, before being discovered by the mailman. After this the community came together to form a civic association that convened with hospital administrators on how to keep the community safe, an association that existed to this day.

Given how terrified Lynette had been of the lunatic asylum growing up, it was ironic she would wind up working there. But when you grew up in a small town and had no ambitions of leaving it, you took whatever work came your way. After graduating high school, Lynette was hired as a part-time receptionist at the local doctor's office to cover for a woman away on maternity leave. When the woman returned a short month later, Lynette worked the odd shift at a dairy bar before hearing about a position as a medical transcriptionist at the asylum. Thankfully most of her father's horror stories proved to be false. The lunatic asylum was by no means paradise. There were metal doors that locked behind her everywhere she went, most of the patients wandered in circles, and only a few had teeth due to the psych meds that dried out their mouths. However, there were no sadistic orderlies or rotting bodies or murderous patients—none that she came into contact with, at least.

When Spencer began working there as a psychiatrist, Lynette fell for him right away. He was not a particularly attractive man. He was stout and had a weak chin. But he had a full head of glorious red hair, and he was positively charming. They went steady for six months before he proposed to her. They married soon after and tried for years to conceive a child but were never successful. Eventually, after several consultations with their doctor, it was determined that Lynette was infertile.

Over the next decade they grew apart. Lynette stopped working at the asylum and became something of a lonely spinster, while Spencer did the opposite, immersing himself in the community and his work. Their relationship deteriorated to such an extent she now sensed he privately resented her, as if she were his ball and chain, preventing him from fully enjoying his life. She no longer thought of him as a husband but more of a stranger—a stranger living in her house and sleeping in her bed. This was accentuated by the fact that Spencer, physically, barely resembled the young man who had swept her off her feet. Some years ago he'd gotten into bodybuilding, and he could no longer be described as stout; he was a wrecking ball, with a bull neck, barrel chest, and bulging biceps. Also, he'd grown a beard. It had been her suggestion because she'd known how self-conscious he'd been about his weak chin. But he continued to grow it out until it reached its current length, which stopped just short of his waistline.

Lynette dumped the remaining dishes she'd collected in the sink and filled the basin with hot water and dish soap. Spencer stuffed his notepad back in his pocket just as the telephone on the nearby table rang.

Spencer picked up the receiver and said hello. He listened for a few seconds, turning his back to her. "Stay there," he said finally in a low voice. "I'm coming right now." He hung up.

"Has something happened?" she asked.

"Yes," he told her curtly. "You'll be fine by yourself?"

"I think I'll draw a bath, then retire early. I've been a little tired recently."

"Can't imagine why," he said. "You never leave the house." He cleared his throat. "I didn't mean it that way."

"No, you're right. I should look into a hobby of some sort."

"Why don't you join that book club at the library? They meet every Tuesday, I believe."

"I'll think about it."

He nodded, took the car keys from the pegboard, then left through the back door.

Without his briefcase, she noted.

Lynette watched Spencer through the window over the sink as he hurried through the rain to the garage, pulled up the roller door, and stepped inside. A few moments later headlights flooded the gravel driveway and his silver Volvo sedan appeared momentarily before disappearing from her line of sight.

Lynette dried her hands on a dish towel, then hurried to the front of the house. She pulled aside a blind in the darkened foyer and peered through the small beveled window as the Volvo continued down the driveway and turned left, disappearing behind the forest of trees.

Lynette went immediately to Spencer's study. She'd been contemplating divorcing Spencer for some time now, but she'd been reluctant to file the necessary paperwork. She knew Spencer would be furious at the embarrassment it would cause him, at the hit his sterling reputation would take, and he would paint Lynette as a disillusioned, raving housewife. The small community would turn against her. She wouldn't be able to go to the supermarket without someone talking about her or snickering behind her back. She would be ostracized from the town in which she had grown up, the only home she knew. However, if she could produce proof Spencer was having an extramarital affair, nobody would believe the lies he whipped up. She would be viewed sympathetically. She could live out the rest of her life in relative peace. A fly on the wall, a nobody. And that was fine by her. Better a nobody than the target of scorn and ridicule.

Lynette stopped before the door to Spencer's study. She turned the brass knob and found it locked, as she knew it would be. Last year Spencer began locking it whenever he went out. The reason, he told her, was to protect confidential patient information he kept in his filing cabinet in the rare chance the house was broken into and burglarized. Initially Lynette accepted this explanation. But when he started spending more and more nights at the "hospital," she decided there was another reason altogether why he locked the study: to hide evidence of his affair.

She had been tempted on several occasions to search the study while he was in the shower or outside planting in the garden. However, she could never bring herself to do this, fearful she wouldn't have enough time to conduct a proper search, or Spencer would appear unannounced and catch her in the act. Instead she decided to remove the study key from his keychain and search the study while he was at the asylum. This carried risks as well, as she didn't know whether he would notice the missing key while at work, or whether he would head straight to his study when he returned home before she had a chance to replace the key. Nevertheless, it was the best option she could think of.

So earlier today, when Spencer informed her that he would be going to the asylum later, she slipped the study key from his keychain while he'd been in the garage changing the oil in the Volvo. She kept it in her pocket all evening and was irrationally convinced Spencer knew it was there, could see it through the cotton of her dress. But of course he couldn't, he was none the wiser, and now he was gone, and it was time.

Lynette removed the key from her pocket and stuck it in the keyhole. She half expected it not to work, or for it to break in two. It turned easily. She eased open the door. The study was dark. She reached a hand inside and patted the wall until her fingers brushed the light switch nub. She flicked it on.

The room resembled something you might see in a men's club. Maplewood paneled walls, stodgy button-tufted furniture, a wall-to-wall bookcase. Two stuffed gray wolves stood on either side of the stone fireplace, trophies from one of Spencer's hunting trips. She had always hated them. They reminded her of that three-headed dog in Greek mythology that guarded the gate to the underworld.

Lynette went directly to the oversized desk and opened the top drawer. She sifted through the sundry items, careful not to disturb their positions. She uncovered nothing more interesting than stationery supplies and hospital memos, certainly nothing incriminating. The contents of the three smaller drawers proved equally unremarkable.

She went to the antique wardrobe next and opened the mirrored doors. Several starched white shirts and dress pants hung from the clothes rack. Spencer kept these here instead of the bedroom closet so he could change without waking her if he had to leave for the asylum early. She checked the shirts for lipstick, smelled them for any trace of perfume. They were all freshly laundered. She stuck her hand into each pant pocket. They held nothing.

There was a shelf above the hanging space, but it was too high for her to access. She dragged a wooden chair over, climbed onto the seat, and discovered three shoe boxes. The first contained several envelopes bursting with receipts, though none from jewelry purchases or expensive out-of-town dinners. Most, if not all, were utility bills from AT&T, the Ohio Edison Company, and Aqua America. The second shoebox contained stacks of aging photographs wrapped in rubber bands. Lynette's chest tightened with nostalgia as she shuffled through photos taken when she and Spencer were twenty years younger, smiling, in love. She promptly moved on to the final box. It held nothing but miscellaneous junk Spencer hadn't been able to throw out: broken watches, a torn wallet, a faded issue of *Playboy* magazine, a suede brush, a personal grooming kit, a toy pistol, a silver napkin ring, a bottle of still-corked glycerin.

Lynette stepped off the chair, closed the wardrobe doors, and looked around the study. Where next? she wondered with a growing sense of desperation. Her eyes paused on the bookcase. Could Spencer have hidden a telephone number or a love letter inside one of the books? She gritted her teeth in frustration. This would have been much easier had she known what she was looking for. Still, she wouldn't quit; she would make the most of this opportunity while she had it.

The first three bookshelves contained hardback tomes on psychiatry and psychology and science and medicine. She found nothing inside them any more interesting than a bookmark or an underlined passage that was meaningless to her. She retrieved the chair and climbed on it again so she could reach the uppermost shelf. She frowned at the first book she examined. It was bound in leather and titled: *The Book of Baphomet*. She flipped through the pages and discovered shocking illustrations of grotesque demons and people wearing animal heads and naked women in submissive poses. Her revulsion turned quickly to confusion, then fear as she realized all the books on the shelf were dedicated to the occult, books with titles such as *The Left-Hand Path*, *Arcana*, *The Infernal Text*, *Blood Sorcery*, *The Lost Art*, and so forth.

Why did Spencer have books on devil worship?

Why so many?

Was he—could he be—?

While stretching her arm for a large red book just out of reach she lost her balance and leaped off the chair. She stumbled when she landed and collided with the ottoman, bumping it across the floor. Something inside it rattled.

Kneeling, Lynette discovered the padded, upholstered top lifted away to reveal hollow storage space. She frowned at the contents it held. There was a silver chalice, black candles, incense, what might have been folded black robes, and a stack of photographs bound by an elastic band like those in the shoebox.

Lynette swooned, momentarily lightheaded. What did all this mean? Was her husband a *Satanist*? And if so, what did he do with this stuff? Sacrifice virgins to his dark god? For a moment she experienced a strange mix of relief and disappointment. Was there no affair after all? Was this the reason he went out at nighttime, to play dress-up and *Dungeons & Dragons* with a group of like-minded associates at the asylum? Yet this seemed so unlike Spencer...

The stack of photographs was facedown. She picked it up and turned it over—and gasped.

The top one was a headshot of a young woman. Her eyes were open and unseeing, her skin pale. She appeared to be lying on a slab of stone.

She almost looked dead.

Heart suddenly pounding, Lynette removed the elastic band and cycled through the rest of the photos. There must have been three or four dozen, all females, all headshots, all closed-eyed, all pale-skinned, all—

Dead, she thought as the photos fell from her fingers. *Not almost. Definitely. Definitively. Dead. All of them, dead, dead, dead.*

And then she recognized one of the women: the teased hair,

the heart-shaped face, the beauty mole on her chin. She had gone missing from Boston Mills the year before. What was her name? Debra? Darla? Her fiancé, Mark Evans, owned the auto repair shop in town—or had owned it. After he admitted to police that Darla went missing the same evening she caught him having sex with an employee from the ski resort, rumors swirled that he'd murdered her. Although no evidence could convict him of any crime, none could clear his name either. His clientele stopped patronizing his shop. The townsfolk whispered about him behind his back and avoided him on the street. Children invented stories of how he fed Darla into a woodchopper, buried her dismembered body parts in the national park, or tossed her off the top of Brandywine Falls, where you could see her haunting at midnight on a full moon. Eventually Mark sold his business and moved out of state. No one had heard from him, or Darla, since.

But Spencer has a photograph of her face—her dead face.

Had he killed her?

Had he killed all these people—?

Lynette buried her face in her hands and found herself wishing her husband had been having an affair after all.

CHAPTER 17

"Somebody once wrote, 'Hell is the impossibility of reason.' That's what this place feels like. Hell."
Platoon (1986)

I n the current nightmare, Beetle was back on the beach in Grenada. However, no bullets whizzing past his head, no Marine Corps Sea Cobras decimating the quaint beachfront hotels and cafés with machine gun fire, no fighter-bombers flying gun runs overhead. Instead the beach was ominously deserted. He stood there alone, the sun burning in the sky, the surf foaming at his feet, the palm trees waving in the breeze. He began to walk, pretending not to see the blood staining the bright sand or the drag marks where the tide had ferried bodies to their watery graves. Eventually the beach tapered to an end. Sarah stood where the sand met the jungle, waiting for him. At the sight of her, his heart raced. He wanted to embrace her and tell her he was sorry and promise her he would change. But she wouldn't let him get a word in. She yelled at him for being covered in blood, for killing the Russian diplomat, for drinking so much, for becoming a stranger to her.

He became enraged. Didn't she understand what he'd been

through? Couldn't she understand that and empathize with him? No, no she couldn't. All she could do was yell and accuse, yell and accuse—

Suddenly the USS Caron, a destroyer armed to the teeth, towered beside him, an impossibility in the shallow water, but there nonetheless. His lieutenant, a brown-noser who looked like a dentist and often pulled rank, yelled to him to put down the pistol, to turn himself in. Beetle pressed the barrel beneath his chin and squeezed the trigger—

Beetle jerked awake bathed in sweat, disorientated, gutted, afraid. It took him a moment to realize he was sitting on a rickety wooden chair on the balcony of the room at the Hilltop Lodge. The full moon hung in the black sky, a moldy white disc poking out from behind a smudge of dark clouds. It had started to rain, which had cleared away some of the fog, or at least thinned it, so he could see much of the forest stretching away below him. He swallowed, discovered he was parched and picked up the bottle of vodka on the ground next to him. He took a three-swallow belt.

"Yuck!" a woman's voice said. "That would make me puke."

Beetle fell sideways off the chair, though he somehow managed to keep the bottle from spilling or breaking. He looked to where the voice had originated and found the woman leaning on the wooden banister that separated the two balconies.

She was tall and had lidded, amused brown eyes beneath arched eyebrows. Her features were too long, her face too gaunt, to be considered beautiful, but she had an unusual attractiveness. "I'm so sorry!" she exclaimed. "I didn't mean to startle you so much." She had a strong German accent.

"It's okay," Beetle said, pushing himself to his feet and returning the chair upright. He remained standing, looking at the woman, waiting for her to go away.

"What terrible weather," she said. "It reminds me of the weather in Bavaria. That's where I'm from, in Germany. My name's Greta." She stuck her hand out over the banister.

Beetle hesitated, then shook. "Beetle." His head was spinning

Jeff maneuvered himself onto his elbows. He tried moving his legs. They didn't respond. He tried harder, focusing all of his concentration on them. Nothing. It was like trying to move a third arm.

He swallowed the panic that wanted to explode from his mouth in a needle-sharp scream.

"Steve…?" he said instead, his voice rusty, barely a whisper.

No answer.

He felt rough wooden floorboards beneath his palms. He moved his right hand, exploring blindly for his legs. He found them where they should be, though they didn't register his touch; they felt like someone else's legs. Nevertheless, they were there. They weren't amputated.

Jeff's eyes adjusted to the dark, and he discovered that the blackness was a little less black to his right. He stared in that direction until he understood he must be looking at a door. Dim light was seeping through the crack at the bottom of it.

So he was in some sort of a room. But why were the lights off, and why was he lying on the fucking floor? Shouldn't he be in a hospital? Had Steve and the others gone to get help? Why would they all go? Wouldn't someone stay behind?

"Mandy…?" he said.

Nobody replied.

Jeff squinted. There was something in the far corner of the room, something large and lumpy. A piece of furniture? Or someone else?

"Noah…?"

Jeff sniffed, detecting the putrid odor for the first time, though he suspected it had been there all along. Urine? Yeah, urine. But not his own. His pants were dry.

Urine and…something musky.

Swallowing fresh panic, Jeff eased himself to his side as gently as he could. His back screamed in protest at the movement. It was as if his vertebrae were being held together with razor blades.

"Ignore it," he mumbled to himself, blocking out the pain.

Using only his arms, he began to drag himself forward on his belly. His body felt as though it weighed a ton, and it took all of his upper strength and willpower to move inch after excruciating inch. He didn't stop once, fearing he wouldn't be able to start again, and then he was close enough to make out the shadowy shape in the corner.

"Austin?" he croaked in relief at seeing his friend's face—though it seemed strangely puffy, especially his lips. "Austin—"

Jeff froze in terror.

A gigantic snake was coiled around Austin's body, from his feet to his shoulders. Its jaw, unhinged and opened impossibly wide, was attached to the top of Austin's skull in a toothless smile as it worked on swallowing him headfirst.

Austin was having the nightmare again, only this time it was different and somehow worse than all the others. He was in his bar. It was late, long past closing. He was alone. From the back office came the now familiar sneaky, scuffling sound. He knew what was causing it from past dreams. It was his grandmother. He would go back there like he did every other time, and he would find her rifling through the filing cabinet in which he kept all his receipts and bills. She would tell him she was looking for the inheritance money she'd given him. She would say it had been a mistake leaving it for him, he didn't deserve it, he was going to blow it all on a stupid investment.

Austin reached for the handle of the door to the office, intent on confronting his grandmother, telling her purchasing the bar wasn't a mistake, it was doing all right, but his arm didn't respond. He glanced down, certain he would see a stump where it once existed. His limb was intact. He simply couldn't move it.

"That's my stuff, Nana!" he shouted. "Leave it alone!"

The door swung open.

Across the threshold his grandmother lay on the floor, on her back, swaddled in what looked like spider silk. She was missing her eyes.

"Nana?" he said. "What happened? What's wrong? What happened to your eyes?"

From the darkness Jeff appeared, stopping behind Austin's grandmother's head. He was all blond hair and smiles and dressed in the maroon golf shirt and gray slacks of his Monsignor Farrell school uniform. "Hey, dickweed," he said, buddy-buddy. "How's it hanging?"

"You can walk?" Austin said.

"How 'bout that?"

"You were in an accident, and you couldn't move your legs." He frowned. "What happened to my grandmother?"

"Hell if I know. It's your dream."

"I can't move my arms."

"It's not so bad. You'll get used to it."

"Get used to what?"

"Being a paraplegic or quadriplegic or whatever you are now."

"How did you fix your legs?"

"Don't you know what's going on?" Grinning easily, the way he would grin when chatting up women he wanted to take back to his place, Jeff stuck his fingers in his mouth and whistled. "Dinner time, 'lil buddy."

Slowly, almost ponderously, Steve slithered from the shadows. But it wasn't Steve, not completely. He was green and fat and he just kept coming. His tongue flicked in and out of his lipless mouth.

"Jesus, Steve!" Austin said. "You're a snake!"

Steve headed straight for Austin's grandmother.

"No!" Austin shouted. "Steve, stop! Don't touch her!" He tried to intercept his friend, but he still couldn't move.

Steve reached Austin's grandmother and slinked around her torso, one loop, then two.

Austin screamed, or at least he tried to. He no longer had any air in his lungs, and nothing came out of his mouth.

Then he was awake, his mouth open, still trying to scream, though the sound remained sunken within his chest.

Something tight and solid squeezed his body, pinning his arms against his sides. His first thought: he'd been locked up in a straightjacket. It took all of one second for his waking mind to understand what his sleeping mind had already surmised.

A snake! A fucking snake's wrapped around me! Where's its head? Where's its fucking head?

Then he saw Jeff. He was a few feet away, on his side, staring at Austin with an expression alien to his usual cocky confidence: helplessness.

Austin wanted to beg him to help, but he couldn't get any words out, so he begged with his eyes.

Help me, goddammit! It's suffocating me! It's crushing me!

Suddenly he became aware of something wet on his head. It felt like an ill-fitting cap, though he knew it was no cap.

Overcome with dismay and repulsion, Austin struggled madly but futilely before giving up and exhaling from the wasted effort.

The snake squeezed tighter.

◆ ◆ ◆

Jeff hated snakes. They disgusted and terrified him on a primeval level. He couldn't hold a harmless garter in his hands without shivering. Regardless, this was not the time for phobias.

Austin was dying. Hell, he was being eaten alive.

Steeling his nerves, Jeff dragged himself forward, toward the snake's tail. He'd once read that's where you started if you wanted to uncoil a snake that somehow got wrapped around your arm or leg.

The snake's tail was exposed, not buried beneath its tubular body. It trailed away from Austin's feet in lazy curlicues, terminating in a tip no thicker than a banana. However, the snake was at least a foot in diameter where it was coiled around Austin's ankles.

Jeff gripped the plump length with both hands, grimacing at the dry and satiny feel of the skin. He pulled. He couldn't budge it, not an inch. He punched the thing with his fists, more in frustration than in any hope of causing it harm. It was like punching a sandbag.

Jeff changed tactics and dragged himself toward the snake's head. Austin's eyes, he noticed, were bloodshot and bulging and crazed.

The snake's eyes, on the other hand, were black, beady, emotionless.

Jeff hesitated, thinking he didn't have the balls to do what needed to be done.

"Do it, goddammit!" he told himself.

Grimacing, he wedged his fingers into the corners of the snake's mouth. A moment later he cried out and yanked his hands back. Teeth he hadn't seen had pricked his fingers. He thought about bashing the serpent's head with his fists or elbows, but that would injure Austin as well.

Then, with a pelican-like gulp, the snake's grinning mouth jerked over Austin's eyes and nose, so only his mouth and chin remained visible.

"No!"

Jeff stuck his fingers in the snake's mouth again, one hand gripping the upper jaw, one the lower. He pulled with all his strength but still couldn't pry them apart. As if to prove it was undaunted by his effort to steal its prey, the snake's coiled body undulated and its mouth moved farther down over Austin's face, all the way to his neck.

With a moan, Jeff rolled away from the demonic thing, unwilling to watch it devour the rest of his friend. He closed his eyes, gripped his hair with his hands, and touched his forehead to the floor.

He wasn't aware of the second green anaconda slithering silently through the darkness toward him.

CHAPTER 19

"Something came out of the fog."
The Fog (1980)

Accalled to Mandy's gold wristwatch—a gift from Jeff—she had been wandering through the ghostly forest for a little over an hour, though it seemed much longer than that. She had started away from the small butte in what she'd thought had been toward the highway, but she'd never arrived at it, and now she had to admit she was completely lost. She wasn't surprised. The forest would have been difficult enough to navigate correctly in the daytime. The thick, soupy shadows and coalescing fog made it near impossible. It seemed every five or ten feet she had to circumvent another tree, ducking beneath the low sprouting branches, each time veering more and more off course. To make matters worse, it had started to rain twenty minutes ago. This had cleared some of the mist, improving her visibility, but it had also soaked through her silly Cheetara costume, making the Spandex cling uncomfortably to her cold and clammy skin.

Nevertheless, despite all this, Mandy had to remind herself she was lucky. She had escaped Cleavon and his brothers. God knows what the others were going through right then. She could still hear Cherry's screams in her head. What had Cleavon or his brothers done to her? And why? Moreover, why had they attacked Mandy and the others in the first place? What was their motivation? Were they a bunch of sick, depraved rednecks that ran some sort of torture operation back at the "ol' McGrady place?" Or were they simply psychopaths, who killed for the sake of killing?

She tried to convince herself that Steve and Noah had returned to the scene of the accident with the police and paramedics in time to rescue Cherry and Austin and Jeff. But something told her they would return to find nobody there. They would think Austin and Mandy and Cherry had carried Jeff off in the hopes of finding help. They would organize some sort of search party, but they wouldn't find them. And this was why Mandy felt so frustrated she hadn't reached the road. She wouldn't be able to tell the police about Cleavon and his brothers —and by the time she made her way out of the forest and contacted them, it would likely be too late.

A branch clawed Mandy's face. She cried out at the burning sensation in her right cheek. She touched the cut and felt warm blood.

Suddenly tears welled in her eyes and threatened to spill down her cheeks in great torrents. This wasn't fair. This shouldn't be happening. This was supposed to have been a fun weekend, a chance for her and Jeff to rekindle what had been lost in their relationship. She shouldn't be wandering around wet and lost and...hunted...in some god-awful national park. She should be in the cozy hotel room in town that Jeff had rented for them, warm, the TV on, snuggling with him under the bed covers.

It's all your fault, Jeff, she thought with a hot-blooded surge of anger. If you hadn't felt the need to play chicken with that hearse, we wouldn't have crashed. We wouldn't have run into Cleavon and his brothers. Everything would have been as we'd planned it—

Mandy stopped on the spot. Ahead of her, visible between the crosshatch of branches, illuminated in the cold light of the autumn moon, an old derelict school bus sat in the center of a small glade.

She remained unmoving for several long seconds, trying to comprehend what a bus would be doing out here in the woods, and when no answers came to her, she approached it cautiously, quietly, half convinced it might disappear at any moment, like a mirage.

It didn't disappear, of course. It was as real as the cedars, firs, and pines that had grown up around it. Judging by its beat-up, weathered condition, it had been there for a very long time. It rested on flat tires and canted to one side, perhaps a result of a broken axle. Many of the windows were cracked or missing altogether.

What was it doing here in the middle of the forest? she wondered again. A car, she could understand. This land might have once been someone's property. The owner might have abandoned a broken-down sedan when he moved away, leaving it for nature to claim as its own.

But a school bus?

As Mandy ventured closer she made out graffiti scribbled along the vehicle's shadowed flank. It was similar to the stuff they'd seen beneath the bridge: inverted pentagrams, upside-down crosses, crude drawings of Satan, a goat's head sprouting evil-looking horns. In blue spray paint: "DANNY WAS HERE, 82!" In red: "look behind you..."

Despite herself, Mandy glanced over her shoulder. She found nobody lurking there.

She stopped before the bus's bi-fold door, conflicted. It was cranked open, allowing entrance. It would be dry inside, out of the rain. She could curl up on a seat, wait until the rain stopped, maybe wait until morning arrived.

Then again, was the bus safe? What if the floor had rotted out and she fell through it, her legs shredded by rusty metal? Or what if the ceiling collapsed on her?

She folded her arms across her chest and glanced to her left, to her right, seeing only the thin veil of slanted rain, the dripping

must have because her jaw was swollen. Her probing tongue had found several gummy gaps where her teeth had once been. And her chest, God, that's where she hurt the most. Each breath was torturous as if her lungs were encased in an iron maiden with nowhere to expand but into razor-sharp points.

Cherry couldn't know for certain why Cleavon and his brothers had attacked them, but she had a pretty good guess. She had seen the lustful look in Cleavon's eyes while he'd been talking to them and pretending to be civilized. It had taken her back to her days as a masseuse in Daveo. At the end of each massage she would finish massaging her customer's head, and she would say, "Finished, sir," and he would open his eyes and look at her how Cleavon had looked at her and say, "How much for extra service?" and she would giggle and say, "No, sir, I don't do that," because that's what they wanted to hear, and he would grin and say, "Come on, just a hand job," and she would pretend to think about it and give an exorbitant amount like two thousand pesos, and sometimes the customer would pay no questions asked, or sometimes he would work her down to one hundred pesos, which was as low as she would go, and then she would jerk him off and, afterward, ask to use his bathroom to wash the semen off herself, and then she would collect her money, tell him to request her the next time he called her company, and she would wait out front his building for the driver on the Honda motorbike to arrive, who would take her back to the housing where she and the other massage girls lived, and she would try not to think about what she'd done, she would tell herself it was just to pay for nursing school, and she would do it all over again the next day.

Nevertheless, as much as Cherry had detested that period of her life, at least she had been in control then. She had been the one setting the rules. She had never agreed to intercourse, no matter how much money was offered. To this day she remained a virgin, and she vowed to uphold her chastity until she married. Austin had not been happy with this declaration, but he'd accepted it. Maybe he thought he could change her mind at some point, or maybe he wasn't planning on sticking together with her for long enough for it to matter, but whatever the reason he had accepted it.

Now, however, Cherry was no longer in control. Now there were no rules, and that terrified her like nothing else because if Earl or Cleavon or Floyd wanted to fuck her, they would fuck her, they would fuck her and take her virginity, and they would likely kill her when they were done and bury her body in a shallow hole somewhere.

Earl burped and scratched his groin. He reached into the cooler next to his recliner, retrieved a fresh beer, and twisted off the cap. Judging by the empty bottles on the floor next to him, this was his fifth one. Cherry didn't think that would be enough to get him drunk. It would probably take ten or twelve to get someone his size drunk, maybe more than that. So it wasn't likely he was going to pass out any time soon. It wasn't going to be that easy to escape.

Cherry knew she needed to free her legs. If she could do that, she was confident she could outrun Earl. He was big and would have a large stride. But he was also fat, and she was confident she could escape.

He glanced at her suddenly. She squeezed her eyes shut. Too late. She heard him push out of the recliner, cross the room, the floorboards protesting beneath his girth.

"Hello?" he said, and she could almost feel his shadow looming over her. "Excuse me? Little girl, wake up. I know you're awake, I saw your eyes, and they were open, so open them up again."

She didn't.

"Hey," he said, angrier. "Did you hear me? I said open your eyes." He kicked her in the side. He didn't put much force behind it, but she had three or four broken ribs, and if felt as though he'd stuck her with a hot poker.

She cried out and opened her eyes and stared up at him.

"Hi," he said, smiling.

"Hi," she managed.

He sat down before her and crossed his legs. He smelled rancid like he'd soiled himself two days ago and hadn't gotten around to cleaning himself yet. He reached out a massive hand and patted the top of the head, the way you pat a dog.

He didn't say anything. She didn't either.

Then, abruptly, Cherry began to cry. She couldn't help it.

"Hey," he said, and he sounded alarmed, almost scared. "Don't do that, I didn't hurt you, so don't cry, don't do that."

"I wanna...go home," she said between sobs, throwing herself on his mercy.

"I can't let you go, I'd get in trouble, I'd get in real trouble, my brother would be madder than...he'd be really mad."

He was still patting her head. It was driving her crazy.

"Stop!" she shrieked. "Stop touching me!"

"Hey!" he said, recoiling from her. "I didn't hurt you, I was just petting you, there's nothing wrong with petting, I'm allowed to do that."

Cherry forced herself to calm down. The crying was making her lungs heave inside the iron maiden. She half expected to begin vomiting blood at any moment.

"I didn't do nothing," Earl grumbled, getting to his feet.

"Wait..." she said. "Wait..."

He frowned down at her.

"I need...the bathroom..."

"You gotta hold it in until my brother gets here."

"I can't."

"You gotta."

"Please?"

Earl twisted his mouth indecisively. "A deal?" he said. "Okay? I let you go, I let you use the bathroom, you let me kiss you, that's the deal. Okay?"

Cherry didn't know if he was joking or not.

"Okay?" he said.

"Okay," she said.

Grinning hideously, he bent over, gripped her beneath the arms, and lifted her as if she weighed nothing.

She resisted the urge to cry out; she didn't want to scare him off.

"I can kiss you?" he said.

"After...I go."

"I wanna kiss you now." Without waiting for her to answer he knelt before her, tilted her chin upward with his hand—on his knees he was still taller than she—and pressed his lips against hers. They were wet with beer. The stubble around them prickled her skin. She kept her mouth squeezed shut until he pulled away. He grinned at her proudly.

"Bathroom?" she said.

"Can we do it again? Can I kiss you again? Just one more time, real quick, can I?"

"After I go to the bathroom," she said.

"Okay, after you go, but you promised, you promised I can kiss you again." He heaved himself to his feet and got to his armchair before realizing she wasn't following him. He glared at her. "What's wrong? The bathroom's this way."

"I can't walk," she told him. "You need to untie my feet."

"I can't do that, I'm not allowed, but you can hop, like a rabbit."

"I can't."

"Then I gotta carry you, is what I gotta do, I gotta carry you, that okay?"

"No!" she said and began to penguin-walk. When she waddled past Earl, he placed his hand on her shoulder, gently, the way one might guide a young child or a blind person.

They left the living room this way, the captured leading the dumb, and followed a hallway barren of pictures or any other décor. A 1960s-looking kitchen opened to the right. The bathroom was across from it. The hall ended another ten feet or so farther on at a windowless door she hoped led outside.

Cherry extended her arms in front of her so Earl could untie the rope. He stared at her.

"You need to untie my hands," she told him. It felt as though she were speaking between sausages instead of lips. Even so, she was feeling better, stronger, more clearheaded. She suspected the adrenaline coursing through her veins had something to do with that.

Earl shook his head. "I told you, don't you listen, I said I can't untie you, not your feet, not your hands, I'm not allowed."

"How am I supposed to use the toilet?"

"You can still use your hands, they're just stuck together, that's all. You can still pull up your skirt. Look." He demonstrated, pressing his wrists together, as if they were handcuffed, and groping for her skirt.

"Stop it!" she told him, alarmed. She shuffled into the bathroom and elbowed the door closed. "Don't look."

Earl stuck his foot between the door and the jamb. The door bounced off his boot. "I have to watch," he said. "My brother, he said tie her up and don't let her outta your sight, so I can't let you outta my sight, I gotta watch."

"I need privacy."

"My brother said—"

"I won't kiss you again. Not if you watch me."

For a brief moment it was as though a black veil had lowered in front of Earl's face, and she feared he was going to strike her. But then the veil lifted and he said, "If I don't look, you'll kiss me?"

"Yes."

"Two times?"

"Once."

"Two times?"

"Fine."

Earl removed his foot. Cherry elbowed the door closed again. To her dismay she discovered there was no lock. She voiced this.

"So?" Earl's voice came back.

"Don't peek! If you peek, I'm not kissing you."

"You promised!" He tried opening the door.

She pressed her body against it. "If you don't look!"

"I told you I wouldn't, didn't I?" He gave up his effort to get in. "Now go on, go pee, go quick, my brother, he'll, he'll be back

161

soon."

The bathroom, Cherry observed, was no more than six feet in length by four feet in width. Hunkered into the small space was a sink marred with toothpaste gunk, a toilet with a partially unhinged seat, a shelf lined with half-used toilet paper rolls and two bars of withered soap in a shallow ceramic dish, and a medicine cabinet.

Cherry caught her reflection in the medicine cabinet's mirrored front. Her hair was disheveled, her naturally tanned skin so pale it was almost white. Mascara streaked her cheeks like black tears. Blood smeared her mouth as if she had just finished a strawberry pie eating competition.

She opened the medicine cabinet door, praying the hinges didn't squeak. They didn't. Inside she found a bottle of Aspirin, two cans of Gillette shaving cream, three toothbrushes all poking out of the same glass caked with green grime, and—
thank you, Lord—a straight razor with a rust-free blade.

She snatched the razor by the wooden handle, eased the medicine cabinet closed, and lowered herself onto the toilet seat.

A moment later Earl shoved open the bathroom door and stuck his head in.

"Don't look!" she cried.

"I'm not, I'm just checking, that's all—"

"Get out!"

He obeyed. Cherry said another silent prayer of thanks, because although she was sitting on the toilet seat, she hadn't lifted her skirt, or pulled down her panties.

Quickly, not trusting that Earl wasn't going to stick his head in the bathroom again, she used the razor to saw through the rope binding her ankles. In her haste she sliced the pad of her left thumb open. Blood squirted to the floor. She bit her lip but kept sawing until the last of the twine snapped apart.

She unwound the length of the rope and tossed it aside. Then she unbuckled her stilettos and left them next to the discarded rope. She stood, barefoot, and flushed the toilet. She went to the door, terrified yet at the same time oddly calm. She cupped the razor with her bleeding hand.

"I'm done," she said, opening the door.

Earl smiled down at her, no doubt in anticipation of his two kisses. The smile turned into a frown when he noticed the blood dripping off her hand.

"Hey," he said, "what happened? And where's the rope for your feet—"

Cherry slashed his throat with the straight razor. His eyes bloomed; he tottered backward, his hands going to the wound. She ran toward the windowless door. For a moment she was positive it wasn't going to lead outside, it was going to open to a cellar, she would be trapped, Earl would recover, catch her, kill her—

The door handle turned easily in her hand and then she was outside. A cry of elation escaped her as she fled down the porch steps into the night, through the rain, through the mud.

Her eyes were searching for the best path to take into the forest when she spotted a wood-paneled pickup truck parked at the end of the gravel driveway.

She risked a glance behind her, didn't see Earl, and made for the vehicle. She didn't think she'd be lucky enough to find the keys inside it, but this wasn't the city. She had to check.

Just as she reached the truck she heard Earl exit the house behind her. She opened the driver's door with her bound hands. The overhead light blinked on.

A key was inserted into the ignition lock.

Cherry's heart sang. She heaved herself up onto the bench seat and she turned the key. The engine vroomed to life. She tugged the column shifter into drive and was about to tromp the gas when Earl appeared next to the open door, one hand pressed against the bleeding tear across his throat.

Shrieking, Cherry swiveled in the seat, brought her knees to her chest, and kicked as hard as she could. Her left foot breezed past him. Her right connected with his gut. He grunted—more of a bloodied gurgle—and stumbled away.

She stepped on the gas. But Earl managed to snag her hair.

The truck lurched forward; her head snapped backward. Her foot came off the pedal.

The truck jolted to a stop.

Earl tugged her head, hard, as if trying to pull her from the vehicle. Her toe, however, found the pedal. The truck shot forward. Earl released her hair but kept pace next to the door. She stamped the gas at the same moment Earl fell and grabbed the steering wheel. His weight yanked it to the left.

The pickup truck arced on a dime, the cornering force tipping it onto two wheels. Cherry's stomach lurched. She thought of bracing herself, grabbing hold of something, but she couldn't with her bound hands.

The truck crashed onto its side. She heard the juxtaposition of crunching metal and shattering glass, followed by a dead silence.

◆ ◆ ◆

Pain. Nowhere. Everywhere.

Cherry had no idea how long she lay in a crumpled heap in the crashed pickup truck, half cognizant, but then the pain sharpened, becoming more localized, coalescing inside her head and chest. She opened her eyes and tried to push herself upright. She cried out as sharp teeth bit into her hands. She glanced down and saw she lay on a bed of gummy safety glass. Where the driver's side window should have been was jagged gravel.

Earl, she thought, and her fear of the man mobilized her into action.

Grimacing—not thinking about how broken her body was right then, though "smushed" seemed an appropriate description—she stood and became perpendicular to the seats. The engine hadn't shut off. The dashboard clock read 12:11 a.m. The steering wheel protruded from the dash at her face level. A pair of sunglasses had somehow remained clipped in place to the sun visor.

Cherry tried to shove open the passenger's door above her

head with her bound hands. She cracked it a foot or so but didn't have the height or leverage to push it all the way. She wound down the window—the simple act of turning the crank took a Herculean effort—but she accomplished it. Then she climbed, using whatever she could for purchase: the driver's seat, the center console, the dashboard, the steering wheel.

With a final groan she pulled herself atop the door. She didn't rest or congratulate herself. Carefully, slowly, she slid to the ground. Her knees buckled on impact and she collapsed.

She wanted to remain there, on the prickly gravel, on her side. She wanted to close her eyes, go to sleep, forget the pain. But she couldn't do that, of course.

Focusing, steeling her determination, she regained her feet and shuffled around the pickup truck's hood. She stopped.

Earl lay on the ground, next to the exposed undercarriage. His ugly, piggy face was turned toward her, his eyes closed, his expression slack. Blood covered his pasty-white neck and singlet.

Was he unconscious or dead?

Cherry glanced about for the straight razor and realized with dread it must be somewhere inside the truck. For a moment she contemplated jumping up and down on Earl's skull with her bare feet. But she didn't. Because what if he was faking, playing possum, waiting for her to come close enough he could spring awake and snatch her?

Earl's body hiccupped. A moment later his eyes opened. Cherry wasn't sure whether he could see her or not—then his sightless eyes fell on her. They thundered over. He pushed himself to his knees, weakly, wobbly, like a calf only minutes out of the womb.

Cherry stumbled back around the pickup truck's hood and limped down the driveway. She glanced over her shoulder. Earl was up and loping after her, weaving back and forth like a drunk, one hand to his throat. They were both moving with the speed and grace of geriatric patients, and the scene likely would have been comical had the consequences of getting captured not been so horrifying.

Cherry forced herself to move faster and concentrated on not falling over. She barely felt the sharp crushed stone beneath her bare feet.

Earl, she noticed when she glanced back yet again, was no longer weaving and was closing the distance between them.

Knowing he would soon catch her, Cherry veered left, into the thicket that lined the driveway. Her feet sank into the wet leaf litter and she lost her balance but didn't fall. She pressed forward blindly, recklessly, batting her way through the spindly branches with her bound hands.

Finally, when she could go no further, she stopped to recuperate. She listened. She could hear Earl behind her, panting, cursing.

Getting closer.

Cherry pressed on. She should have been focused on survival, getting as far away from Earl as possible, and she was, but at the same time her mind was also lecturing her for detouring to the pickup truck. She should have made a straight break for the trees. She might have been alone and wet and lost, but she would have been in a better predicament than she was in right then.

Cherry stumbled into a patch of thigh-high bush. Instead of backing out and feeling her way around, she waded through it. The scratchy shrubbery snagged her skirt and blouse and held her captive. She tugged her clothing, heard the fabric tear, and freed herself.

She only made it another ten feet, however, before she rammed her forehead against a tree trunk and buckled to the ground. She listened for Earl but couldn't hear anything over her ragged breathing and the drone in her ears.

She didn't know how long she lay there, waiting to be discovered, drowsy with pain and despair. Maybe one minute, maybe ten. The cool October air had slipped its icy hands beneath her skin, caressing her bones, whispering for her to relax, to give up the struggle, to slip away—

No!

Consciousness returned with bright urgency. Everything that had occurred over the past ten minutes exploded inside her head in a collage of images—and even as she fought for clarity— *Where was she now? Why was she on the ground? What happened?* —she found Earl towering above her, his face slabs of fat and severe shadows, his eyes dusty white and gleeful.

"Gotcha," he said, and reached for her.

CHAPTER 21

"They strike, wrap around you.
Hold you tighter than your true
love. And you get the privilege
of hearing bones break before
the power of the embrace causes
your veins to explode."
Anaconda (1997)

After Jeff's failed attempt to rescue Austin he dragged himself to the door, gripped the knob, and found it locked. Of course it was locked. What had he expected? Someone to open it and tell him, "Golly, what a mix-up! How did you end up in here?" Nevertheless, this understanding didn't prevent him from shouting as loud as he could, begging for someone to get him out of there, off the fucking slaughter floor. When his throat became raw from this effort, he slumped against the door—and thought his eyes were playing tricks with him. The room was black but not pitch black thanks to the light seeping beneath the door sweep, and in that light he swore he could make out the snake directly ahead of him, perhaps ten feet away. The longer he stared the more convinced he became he was right. But it couldn't be the snake that had eaten Austin;

that nightmare creature wouldn't be moving for the next few months while it digested its man-sized meal.

So a second snake?

Jeff's heart pounded. The snake—yes, there was no mistaking it for shadows now—lay curled upon itself like a giant garden hose, watching him watch it.

Then it began to move.

Its improbable bulk slinked back and forth, propelling it across the floor toward him. Jeff wanted to scream, but he had no voice. He wanted to run, but he had no use in his legs. All he could do was sit there and watch it come for him.

It went for his legs first. Its serpent head nosed beneath his ankles, lifting them with ease. It looped itself over his shins, then beneath his calves, then back over his shins again. It was one big muscle, he could *feel* its power, and it manipulated him as if he were nothing but a stuffed doll.

As the snake wrapped itself around his waist, it corkscrewed him onto his chest. Screaming now, Jeff thrashed his upper body and pounded the snake with his fists, but none of this did any good.

The eyes! he thought desperately. *Where are the eyes? Claw the bloody eyes!*

But by then it was already too late.

Jeff was floating in a perfect void—perfect because in the void there was a rule, and that rule was no thinking or reflecting or regretting or worrying. All you could do was float and be. Then, he didn't know when exactly, only at some point during his floating and being, he realized he was thinking after all. But he wasn't thinking about Austin's purple and puffy face. Nor was he thinking about the second snake that had slipped itself around his own body and was now in the process of working its monstrous mouth down over his skull. All he was thinking about was his childhood, and that, he decided, was okay, that he would allow.

Specifically, he was thinking of all the Saturday mornings when, after the cartoons had finished, he would go to his garage, stuff a basketball into his backpack, hop onto his BMX dirt bike with the yellow padding around the middle bar so you didn't smack your balls on it, and ride to the neighborhood school, where he would meet his three closest friends and play whatever game they were into. Bernie Hughes always preferred boxball because he had a curveball you couldn't help but chase out of the strike zone. Alf Deacon liked Checkers because he was fat and lazy and you didn't have to run playing Checkers. Chris Throssell always picked basketball because he was taller than the rest of them and could get most of the rebounds.

Jeff, on the other hand, never cared which game they chose. He was equally good at all of them. He hit the most home runs in box ball. He was always one move ahead of them in Checkers. And despite being a few inches shorter than Chris, he scored the most baskets in basketball, zipping around the beanpole, layup after layup.

Jeff didn't know why he excelled so naturally at sports. He didn't have the ideal build for them, not then at least. He'd been one of the shortest kids in all his classes up until grade eight when his growth spurt kicked in. It was true he'd always been coordinated. That helped, he supposed. But it wasn't only athletics he'd excelled at. It was everything. Schoolwork, conversation, visual arts—it all came naturally to him. And being coordinated surely didn't help with math problems or vocabulary quizzes. So it was something else.

Ironically enough, he got off to a slow start in life. He didn't start walking until he was well into his first year, and he didn't start speaking until he was nearly three. Originally his mother feared this might be indicative of some intellectual disability. But their pediatrician assured her that Jeff was in perfect health. And he was right. In his fourth year Jeff was not only speaking but reading fluently. When he entered school at five and a half he found the games and activities of his age-peers babyish and showed little interest in their company. His teacher recommended he skip grade two, though his mother didn't allow this, fearing it might cause him emotional difficulties down the road.

Nevertheless, in the following years Jeff continued to impress his teachers with his mature questioning, intense curiosity, desire to learn, and advanced sense of humor. In grade five his physical precocity kicked in, and he was constantly picked first for teams during recess or gym. In grade six he was the runner-up in the state's science fair competition. In grade seven he won first place in the same competition. Whenever his teachers told the class to pair up, everyone wanted to be his partner. Part of this was because he was popular, but it was also because he'd do all the work himself, or at least figure it out, and then explain it to the others.

He never paid much attention when his parents and teachers called him "gifted." He simply took for granted he was smart and talented and athletic. That was his life, it was easy, and it would always be easy.

Yet now, drifting in the void, Jeff understood how foolish and naïve his worldview had been. Because life was never easy, not for anybody. It threw you curveballs much more devious than Bernie's had ever been. Models were disfigured in freak accidents, millionaires lost their millions in bad investments, celebrities had their deepest secrets exposed in the tabloids. People like Jeff, who'd won the genetic lottery, lost the ability of their legs and were fed to grotesque-sized snakes.

If Jeff could have, he would have laughed at the absurdity of it all, and by "all" he meant life. But he couldn't, his lungs were just about crushed to nothing, and as the blackness of unconsciousness and death closed around him, these last thoughts faded from his mind, and he let himself float and be.

CHAPTER 22

*"All work and no play makes
Jack a dull boy."*
The Shining (1980)

Boston Mills Psychiatric Hospital was an imposing Victorian structure composed of staggered wings, pointed roofs, and a bevy of turrets. When Spencer Pratt first began working there, doctors were performing lobotomies and electroshock therapy on a whim and sending the unruliest patients into comas with large doses of insulin and metformin. Today, of course, that no longer occurred. Today, in the great and noble year of 1987, you were held accountable for your actions, and accountable people didn't perform sadism and torture on others—at least not in public anyway.

Spencer parked the Volvo in his reserved parking spot and shut off the engine. He climbed out and darted through the rain across the lot, spotting four other cars. They would belong to the night shift orderlies and nurses. He skipped up the front steps of the main administration building and pressed a four-digit code into a metal box affixed to the brick wall. A beep sounded, the locks unclicked, and he stepped inside.

He shook the water from his blazer and proceeded down the drab hallway, his rubber-soled loafers squawking on the polished laminate flooring. He was greeted by the usual smell of cleaning solutions, antiseptic, and laundry starch.

Spencer enjoyed coming to the hospital at nighttime to work. One, it got him out of the house and away from Lynette. Two, it was serene, peaceful even, the opposite of the controlled chaos that reigned during the day.

At the end of the hall he stopped before the nurse's station. The duty nurse, a twenty-four-year-old local named Amy who had albino skin, horse teeth, and blowfish lips, looked up from the trashy paperback romance novel she was reading.

"Good evening, Dr. Pratt," she said, flashing an ugly smile that made Spencer wonder if she had ever been laid. "Burning the midnight oil again?"

"Work keeps you young. Isn't that what they say?"

"I don't know how you do it, Doctor. All of your late hours, I mean. I think it would make me go crazy." She pressed her hand to her mouth and looked about, as if fearful she had insulted eavesdropping patients. "Oops, I didn't mean it that way."

"Quite all right, Amy. We're all a little crazy, aren't we? If you need me for anything, I'll be in my office."

"Thank you, Doctor. But it's pretty quiet here at night, as you know."

Spencer continued to his office, which was located at the end of the adjacent corridor. He withdrew his keys from his pocket, opened the door, and flicked on the overhead light. Without entering, he locked and closed the door again. A window opened to the hallway. The sheers were drawn, but you could see that a light was turned on inside. He didn't think Amy would need to contact him for any reason, but if she did, she would see the light and assume he was somewhere else in the building.

Spencer exited the hospital through a side door that led to manicured gardens bordered by neatly trimmed hedges. He made his way back to the parking lot and his car.

Satisfied with the alibi, he started the engine, turned up the heat, and continued on his way to Mother of Sorrows church.

◆ ◆ ◆

Spencer Pratt had not always been a Satanist, but he had always been a killer. He'd grown up in Shaker Heights, an affluent suburb of Cleveland. His father had owned a shoe factory, which made him a wealthy man when it became one of the manufacturers and suppliers of boots to American soldiers fighting in World War Two. Spencer, Cleavon, Earl, and Floyd had all attended the same prestigious private school. While Spencer was a stellar student, and Cleavon a mediocre one, Earl and Floyd were both born with chromosomal abnormalities linked to inherited mental retardation and were enrolled in the special education program. They weren't trusted to walk home unsupervised, so at three o'clock each afternoon either Spencer or Cleavon—they rotated the responsibility every other day— would escort them. There were two routes you could take. The first kept to the sidewalks. The second cut through a hundred-acre swath of undeveloped woodland. The latter was quicker and more scenic, but a group of bullies often hung out along the path and would throw rocks and sticks at Spencer if he were by himself. That's why he only cut through the woodland when he had Earl and Floyd tagging along. Everyone in school knew Earl was not only big and strong but also a lunatic. They knew if you teased him he would break your arms or legs if he could catch you. He earned this reputation when he was in grade four and beat up a kid two years his senior so badly the boy didn't return to school for a month. Kids would taunt Earl and pelt erasers at him from a distance because they knew they could get away with that; Earl could never remember faces long enough to hold grudges. But no one risked getting up close and personal with him.

On the day Spencer committed his first murder at thirteen years of age, he was walking through the woodland with Earl and Floyd. It was warm, sunny, June, a few weeks before summer vacation commenced. They didn't run into the bullies but instead came across a girl named Genevieve. She was in special ed with Earl and Floyd. Whenever Spencer stopped by the special ed classroom to pick up his brothers, he would try to tap Genevieve on the head because it set her off yelling and banging around the room like a human tornado.

Spencer spotted Genevieve in the long grasses off to the sides of the path, her shirt held in front of her like a pouch, holding a dozen or so freshly-picked wild berries. He called her name in a singsong way which also drove her nuts. Earl and Floyd joined in, repeating everything he said and chuckling stupidly at their ingenuity. Genevieve shouted at them in the inarticulate gibberish that passed as a language for her. Hands held up, palms facing outward, as if he were an ambassador of peace, Spencer got close enough to tap her on her head. She threw her arms into the air, dropping all her berries at the same time. She spun in circles swatting the air and herself until she tripped on her feet and fell. Spencer stood over her, watching her dissolve into a blubbering mess on the ground. He didn't feel guilt. He didn't feel pity. He didn't feel disgust. He didn't feel anything but curiosity—curiosity at what it would be like to kill her. That's all he remembered thinking at that moment.

He knelt beside her and plugged her snot-dripping nose with his thumb and index finger. She wailed and tried to pull away. He placed his other hand over her mouth, pressing her head to the ground. She flailed her arms and legs and was surprisingly strong. Earl and Floyd shouted at him to stop. He ignored everything except Genevieve's eyes. He stared into them and saw that she understood she was dying. This gave him great satisfaction. Then, eventually, her eyes glazed over and she went still.

That's when Spencer returned to himself, when his nerves kicked in. He wasn't remorseful at what he'd done; he was scared white at getting caught.

He told Earl and Floyd that they would all be in really big trouble if they didn't help get rid of Genevieve's body, and so they obeyed him without question. The three of them carried her to a waterhole where Spencer had gone swimming once, and where his mother had banned him from going ever again, telling him swimming unsupervised was how little boys died. The waterhole was a third the size of a baseball field and filled with sludgy brown water. They loaded Genevieve's pockets and backpack with rocks and sank her in the middle of the pool.

For a few weeks it seemed as though her disappearance was all anybody talked about. Spencer often overheard his parents speculating what might have happened to her, while the kids at school had their own more fantastical theories. Yet after a month or so Genevieve became old news. She was gone, she would never be seen alive again, she was best left forgotten.

Spencer didn't kill again for six years. He thought about doing so on most days. He might see a girl in the supermarket or riding a bicycle on the sidewalk, and he would imagine getting her alone somewhere and suffocating her to death as he had done to Genevieve. He never followed through with these fantasies, however, because he was too afraid of getting caught. Killing Genevieve had been a spur-of-the-moment action. He knew he had been very lucky. Someone could have seen him and Earl and Floyd cut through the woodland that June afternoon, or seen them while they were disposing of her body. The waterhole could have dried up and revealed her skeleton and perhaps some link to Spencer. Earl or Floyd could have talked.

In the end it was the move from home to his dorm at Case Western Reserve University that kicked him into action. The freedom he found living on his own at college intoxicated him and gave him the confidence he had until then been lacking. He had a private room. He had no curfew. He could come and go as he pleased, no questions asked. He could do anything and everything he wanted.

Spencer found the person he would kill in the classified section of *The Plain Dealer*. Her adult-services advertisement read: "Sensual massage to forget your stress and worry. Black, busty, 24 y/o Monique will make all your desires come true." He chose Monique over the other illicit masseuses after consulting the Rand McNally Cleveland Street Guide and confirming her address was a residential property far away on the other side of the city.

Spencer's parents had bought him a brand new Mercury Comet as a high school graduation gift—this was still several years before his father would lose all his savings in a series of bad investments and declare bankruptcy—but he left the car in the college parking lot and instead opted for public transit. He had grown into a cautious man—perhaps because of so many years of waiting for the police to knock on his door and haul him off for the murder of Genevieve—and he was determined not to leave any evidence that could point back to him.

After getting off the bus at Detroit Avenue and West Fifty-eighth Street, he started along a quiet tree-lined street, his head down, his face hidden by his hoodie. The masseuse's home-cum-workplace was a bungalow with a knee-high stone property fence. A white sign on the front lawn read, "Oasis Massage Clinic," and below that in handwritten letters, "Please use side door."

Spencer turned down the driveway. A placard on the side door invited him inside. The reception was dimly lit and smelled of lavender incense. A cash register and a telephone and some pamphlets sat on a six-foot-long counter. Given that it was unmanned, Spencer figured the masseuse was with another customer. He was about to leave when Monique pushed through a beaded doorway. She was indeed black, but she was only busty because she was twenty-five pounds overweight. She wore a short skirt and tight top that did little to cover or support her braless breasts. She was definitely older than twenty-four, maybe early to mid-thirties. Spencer, however, didn't care. This wasn't about what she looked like. It was more intimate than that.

"Hi," she said pleasantly though with little enthusiasm. "I'm

Monique. You can come this way."

She led him to a dark room and told him to take off all his clothes and lie facedown on the table. Spencer never had a massage before, but he didn't think Monique was adequately skilled at what she professed to do. She mostly trailed her fingernails across his back and along his legs like a bored student doodling in her notebook. The massage was advertised as an hour, but fifteen minutes into it she tickled her fingers up and down the inside of his thighs and said, "Time's up, hon. Do you want something extra?"

He didn't and told her so. She seemed surprised by this but then shrugged, replied curtly that it was his loss, and left the room. He got dressed again and pulled on a pair of leather gloves he'd kept in his pocket until then. Monique was behind the reception counter waiting for him. He walked up to her, ignoring her protests that he was on the wrong side of the counter, and seized her around her plump neck. He was still skinny then, having not yet discovered weight training, and it took all of his strength to wrestle Monique to the ground. He pinned her shoulders with his knees and continued to squeeze her throat, preventing her from breathing or screaming for help.

Throughout this he stared into her eyes and saw in them the same understanding she was dying as he'd seen in Genevieve's eyes, and once again this brought him great satisfaction. Afterward he took a Polaroid of her lifeless face, so he wouldn't forget it as he had Genevieve's, then left her for someone else to clean up.

After earning his MD, Spencer wanted out of Cleveland and chose to perform his residency at UCLA. While in his first year there a friend invited him to a party in San Francisco. The venue turned out to be a strange little black house in which the owner, a man named Anton LaVey, kept a lion and a leopard as household pets. Spencer had no idea who LaVey was then, but according to the other guests he was a local eccentric: ghost-hunter, sorcerer, organist, psychic. He was also an intellectual who spent much of the evening ranting to those gathered about the stagnation and hypocrisy of Christianity. In place he argued for a system of belief, or black magic as he called it, that emphasized the natural and carnal instincts of man without the nonsensical guilt of manufactured sins.

Spencer left the party that evening a different man, for he had found in Anton LaVey all the answers he had been seeking for much of his adolescent life. He was not an outcast, a deviant, a sexual predator—or if he was, there was nothing wrong with any of that. Life was not about self-denial and the hereafter; it was about pleasure and the here-and-now.

Over the next six months Spencer attended all of LaVey's soirees, mingling with artists, attorneys, doctors, writers, and even a baroness who'd grown up in the Royal Palace of Denmark. LaVey continued his rants against Christianity, though he was not a soapbox preacher. He wanted to start a real revolution, one that would free people from the blind faith and worship that life-denying Christian churches demanded.

To accomplish his goals he knew he could not simply present his ideas to the world as a philosophy, which could be too easily overlooked. He needed to do something shocking, and so he ritualistically shaved his head in the tradition of medieval executioners and black magicians before him, formed a new religion he called the Church of Satan, nominated himself as the high priest, and declared 1966 Year One, *Anno Satanas*—the first year of the reign of Satan.

For a while LaVey's Friday night lectures and rituals continued as cathartic blasphemies against Christianity. But then LaVey, drawing upon Spencer's expertise in psychiatry, began to focus more on self-transformational techniques such as psychodrama, encouraging his followers to enforce their own meaning on life. This proved hugely popular with the masses, and within two years LaVey was getting coverage in major magazines such as *Cosmopolitan*, *Time*, and *Newsweek*. By the time he published *The Satanic Bible* in 1968, the Church of Satan had ten thousand members and he had become an internationally-recognized Satanist labeled the Black Pope by the media.

Over the next couple years, however, LaVey allowed himself to become charmed by his own hype and grandiosity, causing Spencer to lash out at him one evening in September of 1971, accusing him of turning the church into a cult of personality. The following day Spencer discovered just how much he had overestimated his position and influence within the Magic Circle —or underestimated how crypto-fascist LaVey had become— because LaVey kicked him out of the church, what had become his family.

Disillusioned and lost, Spencer returned to Cleveland and did his best to get on with his life. He often consoled himself with the knowledge that LaVey was a lie and a phony. The man wrote and preached that Satanism was about becoming one's own god and living as one's carnal nature dictated, but he never had the balls to move beyond the conformities of the masses and follow this teaching fully. He never raped or killed or indulged in any other of the most basic of human desires—desires repressed inside everyone—which made him as hypocritical as the hypocrites he professed to hate.

Spencer, on the other hand, indulged more than anybody ever knew. During his time in LA he killed seven women, while over the next sixteen years he killed dozens more, experimenting with everything from necrophilia to cannibalism to human sacrifice. What kept him from getting caught, he believed, were two simple rules: he never killed anyone he knew, and he never killed anyone in or around Summit County.

He broke both those rules in the winter of 1985.

Her name was Mary Atwater. She was committed to Boston Mills Psychiatric Hospital during a blizzard three days before

Christmas day. As Psychiatrist-in-Chief it was one of Spencer's responsibilities to interview each incoming patient. Based on the photo in her files he knew Mary was attractive, but he wasn't prepared for her extravagant beauty. Armenian-American, she had glossy jet-black hair and piercing chestnut-brown eyes and a wide, handsome mouth. She wore a blue silk kaftan with a silver-and-turquoise necklace and an armload of silver bracelets. She had been born in Chicago where she enjoyed a normal, stable childhood. She became a cello prodigy in her teenage years and married her former college professor. They relocated to Cleveland when she was twenty-five, where, quite out of the blue, a combination of heritability and her daughter's birth precipitated a catastrophic mental breakdown from which she never recovered. It's what landed her in Ward 16 of Boston Mills Psychiatric Hospital, an "acute admissions" ward meant for patients in highly disturbed states who needed around-the-clock care and medication. They were all sectioned, a euphemism for legally detained (hence the hospital's barred windows and locked doors), and most were never discharged, instead withering away in the long-stay wards until they died and were no longer burdens on the system.

Mary was deeply and irremediably psychotic with the most extreme form of what used to be called manic depression and is now known as bipolar disorder. On the day Spencer first met and interviewed her, she was in a relatively good spirit and mind. She spoke with an educated accent and, had you not known better, you would have thought she was a perfectly healthy young woman.

But Spencer had treated enough patients with bipolar disorder to know this was a deceptive calm in what would be a stormy, unforgiving life. Indeed, the very next day Mary sank into her depressed state and refused to get out of bed. She simply lay there unmoving, unspeaking, barely eating or drinking. She would be torturing herself inside her head, Spencer knew, rehearsing ever bad thing she had every done, every bad thought she'd ever had, telling herself she was trash, filth, perhaps contemplating killing herself. This terrible low continued for several days until her manic state took over and she became wild, uncontrollable, ripping off her clothes, screaming obscenities at the orderlies and other patients, and once attacking the charge nurse, taking a bite out of her arm.

Seven weeks after she was committed she escaped from the hospital while under the influence of one of her manic phases. The Ward 16 nursing station sat between both the male and female dormitories, with a twenty-four-hour lookout spot. After ten o'clock only one nurse remained on duty. That night it was Ron (the night nurses were always male), who admitted to falling asleep for what he called in his statement to the police a "brief spell." Spencer, who had been working late at the hospital as usual, alerted Alan Humperdinck, the Summit County sheriff, to Mary's disappearance, and an impromptu, sleepy search of the hospital grounds commenced. When Mary wasn't found, the search was called off until the first light. Spencer left the hospital at 3 a.m. that morning—and discovered Mary when he pulled out of his parking spot. She had been hiding beneath his Volvo, presumably to get out of the wind and snow, and had fallen asleep.

Instead of installing her back in her room, Spencer set her in the backseat of his car. The situation was too serendipitous to pass up. The police knew she was missing; Ron had already copped blame. Everyone would assume she'd died from exposure to the elements and was buried by the snow.

While Spencer drove her to one of the abandoned houses that littered the national park—now wide awake and buzzing with the adrenaline and excitement that always preceded a kill— Mary woke and went into a psychotic episode, screaming at him, clawing his face with her sharp nails, pulling his beard.

Spencer lost control of the car and plowed into a tree. He struck his forehead on the steering wheel and incurred a three-inch-long gash that gushed blood dangerously. Mary hadn't been wearing a seatbelt and flew into the windshield, her head smashing through the reinforced glass up to her shoulders.

Holding onto consciousness by a thread, Spencer nevertheless understood he was in serious trouble. If he'd been heading in the direction of Boston Mills, he could have explained he'd been returning home when he spotted Mary alongside the road and picked her up before she went ballistic on him. But he hadn't been returning to town; he'd been driving in the opposite direction, into the national park. He couldn't lie about this fact. The police would want him to take them to the scene of the accident. Nor could he dump Mary's body somewhere and pretend nothing happened. Scratches raked his cheeks, Mary's blood coated his windshield, and he was in no condition right then to clean up himself or the car.

With a desperate, half-formed idea in mind, Spencer reversed onto the road and drove to what he thought simply as The House in the Woods.

His father had built the house years ago after the bank took his Cleveland residence. It had been little more than a two-room shack then. His mother and father lived in one room, Earl and Floyd in the other. This arrangement, however, only lasted a few months. That was how long it took their father to work up the nerve to fill his wife with buckshot before turning the shotgun on himself. Cleavon, who'd been living in a trailer park in Akron and working the odd construction job, moved into the shack to look after Earl and Floyd, for it was either that or commit them to Boston Mills Psychiatric Hospital. Over the next several years he collected wood and materials from the nearby abandoned houses and enlarged the shack until it resembled some post-apocalyptic hideout with eight or nine ramshackle additions in total.

Spencer didn't remember the drive to the house or his arrival there. He woke the next morning in a bed with Earl sitting on a stool next to him, patting the top of his head gently. He batted Earl's hand away and explored the gash in his forehead, finding it had been sewn closed with stitches.

"Where's the girl?" he asked hoarsely.

"She hasn't woke up yet," Earl said, and put on a sad face. "We got her out of the car, and fixed up her neck, but she didn't never wake up, and Cleave, he says—"

"Where's Cleavon?"

"He's in the garage, fixing up the Mustang. That's what it's called, ain't it, Spence? It's a Mustang, ain't it?"

"Get him."

Cleavon arrived a short time later grease-covered and cranky as usual, though his eyes were alight with a shit-eating grin.

"Who did this?" Spencer said, touching the gash in his head.

"Hell if I know, Spence. I thought it was from the car accident."

"The stitches."

"That was Lonnie," Cleavon said, wiping his greasy face with a greasy dish towel. "You were bleeding a fuckin' river, and Lonnie said he'd fixed up his boy a couple of times when he'd cut himself. He said he just needed some fishing wire and a hook."

"You called Lonnie Olsen?"

"Nah. Lonnie was already here, Lonnie and Jesse and Weasel. We were playing cards earlier and they got shitfaced and passed out. Well, that was until you came driving your car right into the fuckin' porch. The girl's okay. Breathing at least." Cleavon cocked an eyebrow. "Say, Spence, what was she doing in her pajamas? Rather, what were you doing driving her around in the middle of the night in her pajamas?"

Spencer didn't reply. He was numbed with dismay as he imagined Lonnie Olsen sitting in Randy's Bar-B-Q right then, telling all the other drunks how Spencer had plowed his car into Cleavon's porch with some girl's head poking out of the windshield like a crudely mounted game trophy—

Lonnie Olsen appeared in the bedroom doorway, rubbing his eyes as though he'd recently woken up. Jesse Gordon and Weasel Higgins crowded behind him.

"Hiya, Spencer—Mr. Pratt," Lonnie Olsen said awkwardly, clearing his throat. "Or is it 'Doctor?'"

"Everyone's still here?" Spencer said, surprised.

"Where else would we be?" Lonnie said.

"So what the fuck happened last night, Spence?" Cleavon said. "We won't say nothing."

"Speak what you want to whom you want," Spencer said poker-faced, though his mind was racing, for he thought he might be able to dig himself out of the mess after all. "The woman's name is Mary Atwater. She's a patient at the hospital. She believes she's possessed by a demon."

"A demon?" Earl said in awe.

Spencer said, "I wanted to try a kind of psychodrama therapy —"

"Psycho-what?" Cleavon said.

"A type of role-playing. It employs guided dramatic action to help individuals examine issues they might have. I was taking her to one of those abandoned houses where we were going to perform a black mass to ask Satan to deliver the demon from her body. It's all in her head, of course, but acting her fears out rather than just talking about them can reap substantial results. However, on the way there she had a psychotic episode and attacked me."

Spencer paused, reading their reactions, and decided they bought it. After all, why wouldn't they? He was the psychologist-in-chief of a large hospital and one of the most respected men in all of Summit County.

"Now, I'm still prepared to carry out this black mass," he went on confidently, swinging his legs off the bed and standing upright. "And I don't mind an audience if you gentlemen care for a once-in-a-lifetime spectacle? Come, truly, you'll find it... engrossing."

Spencer gathered the supplies he would need for the black mass—a can of primer paint and a paintbrush, a hammer and nails, a carving knife from the kitchen, a bottle of bourbon, a candle and matches, a wilted carrot, a beer stein—then he led Cleavon and the others on a half hour hike through the forest, with Earl carrying Mary over his shoulder. At the first abandoned house they came to he painted an inverted pentagram on the floorboards of a dirty, moldy room to serve as an altar. Cleavon constructed a six-foot-tall crucifix with two pieces of scavenged timber, which he positioned upside down against the wall behind the altar. Earl placed Mary, who was still unconscious, in the middle of the pentagram. Spencer cut her pajamas from her body with the kitchen knife, to the muted delight of those gathered.

Then, when Spencer had everybody's full attention, he crossed himself in a counterclockwise direction with his left hand and began the black mass. Channeling the intonation and charisma of Anton LaVey, he recited a collection of passages from the Satanic Bible from memory, moving from the Introit to the Offertory to the Canon to the Consecration. Cleavon and the others watched him in an enraptured state, saying nothing, not even when he inserted the withered carrot/host into Mary's labia—but he saw the lust in their eyes. It burned like black fire.

During the fifth and final segment of the mass, the Repudiation, Spencer passed around the beer stein/chalice filled with bourbon. When everyone had drunk from it he said in a commanding voice, "Brothers of the Left-Hand Path, the penitent has proved a worthy neophyte in our high order. It is now time to free her from the bonds of ignorance and superstition. Cleavon, come forth and partake in your desire."

"Huh?" Cleavon said as if coming out of a trance.

"Do you desire this woman?"

"I, well...I guess."

"The Dark Lord Lucifer has granted you all that you desire. Now take her!"

"I don't know—"

"Lonnie? Quick! We must conclude the mass. Take her!"

"Hell ya!" Lonnie Olsen said, coming forward, unbuckling his belt. He was fully aroused as soon as his pants hit his ankles. Then he was on his knees before Mary's prone body, his pasty, pockmarked buttocks clenching in rhythm to the thrusting of his hips.

"*Eva, Ave Satanas!*" Spencer chanted. "*Vade Lilith, vade retro Pan! Deus maledictus est! Gloria tibi! Domine Lucifere, per omnia saecula saeculorum. Amen!"*

Moments after Lonnie removed himself from Mary, Cleavon took his spot, then Jesse, then Weasel, then Earl, and finally Floyd. When they had all been sated, Spencer knelt next to Mary with the kitchen knife. Before anyone could protest, he sank the blade into her chest, into her heart. Her eyes popped open at this, and he watched as her life drained from them.

"And so it is done," he said softly.

Afterward, in the guilty, bewildered silence that followed, Spencer held each man's gaze in turn and said, "Thank you, gentlemen. It is as she wanted. She is at peace." He hesitated before adding, "And you all must know, of course, that in the name of your self-preservation, what happened here this morning can never be spoken of to anyone, ever."

Two months later Spencer read a story in the Boston Mills *Tribune* about a young couple who had disappeared while visiting "Helltown" in the hopes of spotting the mutants said to inhabit the national park (the Satanist rumors wouldn't begin in earnest for another year or so). Nevertheless, Spencer didn't think much about it. When he read a second story two months after the first about another missing couple, he had his suspicions. These were confirmed a week later when Sheriff Humperdinck discovered several makeshift crosses and Satanic graffiti at several different abandoned houses in the national park, which he attributed incorrectly to "troublesome out-of-town folks coming here and giving our town a bad name."

Spencer thought long and hard about what to do before visiting Cleavon at the House in the Woods and telling his brother, "If you and your friends are going to keep this up, you may as well learn to do it right."

Since that encounter Spencer had inducted the six of them—Cleavon, Earl, Floyd, Weasel, Jesse, and Lonnie—into his "club" and had led them in eight other black masses, all of which he had enjoyed tremendously, especially the psychodrama involved, which he'd never incorporated into his private killings but which was proving to be wonderfully erotic. As a bonus he no longer had to leave Boston Mills to find his victims. Weasel took care of this in the ugly black hearse Cleavon had picked up from some junkyard.

Even so, Spencer had always understood this convenient arrangement wouldn't last forever. There were too many people involved, too many chances for something to go wrong.

And that something had gone wrong tonight, very wrong.

Ever the cautious man, however, Spencer had prepared for this eventuality from day one, prepared and planned, and he knew exactly what needed to be done.

Ahead, through the gray drizzle, he spotted Mother of Sorrows Church jutting from atop the small rise on which it had been built, and he went over for the final time the massacre he was about to commit.

CHAPTER 23

"I think people should always try to take the bad things that happen to them in their lives, and turn them into something good. Don't you?"
Orphan (2009)

Mandy crouched next to the bus's window, peering out into the rain-swept forest, searching for the source of the scuffling she'd heard again. Seeing no animal or person, she made her way quietly to the front of the bus and exited through the bi-fold doors. She wanted to run and disappear into the mix of evergreens and deciduous trees, but then she spotted eldritch blue cigarette smoke drifting out from behind the end of the bus. She started along the flank of the rusted yellow relic, suddenly, happily, convinced she would discover Noah back there. He and Steve had returned from the hospital with the police. They had come looking for her. Noah found her sleeping inside the bus, didn't want to disturb her, and so decided to hang around outside it until she woke.

"Noah?" she said.

Noah didn't answer.

Perhaps he was listening to his Walkman through a set of

headphones? Or perhaps it wasn't Noah but Austin. He had escaped from Cleavon and his brothers after all, and he was ignoring her because she told him to stop slapping Jeff's cheek.

"Austin?"

No answer.

Collecting her nerves, Mandy peered around the bus's rear quarter.

A man sat on the jutting metal bumper. He was looking away from her so she could only see the back of his head. He raised the cigarette to his turned-away face.

Mandy noticed blood dripping from his hand—and just like that she had an epiphany. This man had slaughtered the children who'd once occupied the bus. She didn't know how he did this, or why, but he did it, he butchered them, then he killed himself, and now she was seeing his ghost, haunting the spot of his passing, as ghosts tend to do.

The apparition turned to face her. Where its face should have been was a spiraling black void, and that spiraling black void terrified Mandy more than anything had in her life, because it wanted to suck her into it, and this would be worse than death, for she would not merely disappear, cease to exist, she would be *undone*, erased, so she had never been born.

Mandy turned to flee, but her legs had become elephantine. She managed to lift one, to take an impossibly slow step. Her foot sank into the ground to her knee. She glanced over her shoulder, through her stringy bangs and the falling rain, and saw the ghost floating toward her. The black hole that was its face was expanding, cannibalizing its neck, then chest, then arms and legs, consuming its entirety. Then it slipped over her, silently, painlessly, consuming her too, *undoing* her—

Mandy heaved awake, her breath trapped in her throat. She lay on the floor of the bus where she had fallen asleep. Rain drummed on the roof. The wind howled.

A dream, she told herself, exhaling all at once. *Just a dream, a horrible, horrible dream—*

Her relief wilted.

The car accident wasn't a dream. Jeff paralyzed from the waist down wasn't a dream. Nor was Floyd playing baseball with Austin's head, or whatever happened to Cherry to make her scream the way she had.

Despair swelled inside Mandy, despair as cold as the bony finger of death. She fought the tears that once again threatened to burst from her eyes, because if she started crying, she wouldn't stop, not for a long time. Instead she tried to think about something nice, but this proved impossible, like trying to look at the positive side of a funeral. She had no nice thoughts inside her right then.

In her bleakness Mandy sought refuge in her childhood memories. They were neither good nor bad. They occurred too long ago to pass judgment on. They were merely a distraction, a picture of a simpler world when all that mattered were toys and candy and the love of her parents. This was all she'd needed to be happy, day after day, year after year—until when? When had the innocence ended and the real world kicked in? Probably around the time she became interested in boys. That's when "important" things began to matter, like the clothes she wore, or how she did her hair, or who in her grade was developing breasts first, or who was cool and who was uncool.

Nevertheless, the *real* world didn't kick in until her mother's death. Tragedy matures you, ages you, makes you wiser, and thus more cynical. At least it does when it strikes at such an early age.

All of Mandy's priorities went out the window. Her wardrobe became a triviality, boys a nuisance, popularity—she couldn't care less. In fact, she stopped caring about everything. She became petty, self-centered, and bitter. She was miserable, and she wanted everyone else to be miserable too.

But I changed, she told herself defiantly. *I got over all that. I'm a different person now.*

But was she? Was she really?

Because if she had changed, why was she still not speaking to her father? Why was she still angry at him for kicking her out of the house, out of his life—when she had known for some time now that while he had indeed kicked her out of the house, she had deserved it, and he had certainly not kicked her out of his life. It was the other way around. *She* had kicked *him* out of her life. After all, he was the one making the effort to get back in touch. He sent her a letter every month, asking her how she was doing, telling her what he was up to. She kept them all in a folder beneath her bras in her dresser drawer. But she never replied to any...because she was still that selfish little girl who after all these years still wanted someone to blame for her mother's death, something to which no blame could be attributed.

"I'm sorry, Daddy," she mumbled softly to herself, and now the tears came. They flooded her eyes and streaked her cheeks. Yet they were good tears. She had wanted to say those words for a long time, but she always told herself there would be time enough in the future, naively believing there would always *be* a future.

As Mandy wiped the wetness from her cheeks, the despair inside her withered into profound loneliness, and she wanted nothing more than to see her father again, to tell him the words she had just spoken, to ask forgiveness for being a terrible daughter, for rebelling against him when she should have been mourning with him.

Mandy closed her eyes, steepled her hands together, and for the first time in memory, she began to pray.

CHAPTER 24

"You gotta be fucking kidding."
The Thing (1982)

Beetle thought he heard knocking and opened his eyes. He was right. Someone was at the door to his motel room. *Rap, rap, rap.* Pause. *Rap, rap, rap.*

Shylock and his sons? he wondered groggily. Would they be stupid enough to return? Or had they called the police? Shit, the cops were the last thing he needed. They'd run his name, he'd come up AWOL. He'd be shipped back to Hunter Army Airfield where he'd face a court-marshal and likely get tossed in the brig.

Beetle sat up on the bed and swooned with lightheadedness. A dull pulse thumped inside his left temple. The Beretta, he was surprised to find, was gripped in his sweaty hand. The last thing he remembered was thumbing off the safety, pressing the barrel beneath his chin, and counting to ten. Apparently, however, he never reached ten. Or if he did, he wasn't willing to squeeze the trigger. And despite feeling sick and shitty, like he'd just woken up the morning after the bender to end all benders, he was relieved this was the case, otherwise he wouldn't have woken up at all.

But that's what you want, my friend. That's the point. Goodbye, goodnight sweet world. You're a coward, that's all. You don't have

193

the balls to do what you know needs to be done—

"Hey!" a woman's voice called. *Rap rap, rapraprap.* "It's me! Beetle? Are you sleeping?"

Beetle frowned. Me? Who was "me?"

The girl from next door. The tall German with the lidded eyes and the long face who was backpacking through the country to LA.

What the hell did she want?

Beetle stuffed the pistol beneath a pillow and stood, grimacing as the dull pulse in his head became a wicked pounding. For a moment his stomach turned and he thought he might be sick. The queasy sensation passed.

Breathing deeply, he unlocked and opened the door and squinted into the bright light of the hallway. The German —Gertrude? Greta?—stood two feet away from him. Her face appeared flushed, her eyes as wide and round as they'd been, now exaggerated, either in fear or excitement and for a split second Beetle wondered if maybe the motel was on fire.

"You were sleeping," Greta said, more statement than a question. "I woke you."

"No, yeah—sort of." His voice sounded thick and slow in his ears. He cleared his throat.

"I thought so," she said. "You were pretty drunk on the balcony. I would have let you sleep, but I know you would want to see this."

Beetle waited expectantly. He was trying to remember what they'd spoken of out on the balcony and was drawing a blank.

"There are people at the church!" Greta told him in an unnecessary whisper, given they were likely the only two guests in the entire motel.

"Huh?" Beetle said.

"The church! With the upside-down crosses."

"Ah…"

"Three cars just arrived. Right now."

Beetle frowned, struggling to make sense of the meaning and significance of this. Who would attend church at this hour, and why the hell did it matter?

Greta read the confusion on his face and said, "The legends! Remember?"

The legends. Right. What had she told him? Something about mutants…and a graveyard? Or a school bus? He shook his head.

"Satanists!" she blurted. "They're there right now!"

Beetle almost smiled—almost.

"You don't believe me," Greta said. "I can see that in your eyes."

"What time is it?"

"Two in the morning. Who visits a church at two in the morning?"

"You really think there're a bunch of Satanists over there?" His eyes shifted to the door.

"What?" she said.

"Huh?"

"You want me to go?"

"I'm a bit tired, and I have a headache…"

"You want to go to *bed*?" She seemed incredulous.

"I'm sure you'll be safe," he assured her. "Just lock your door —"

"I don't want to hide. I want to *see* them—and you have to come with me."

"To the church?" Beetle was already shaking his head "I'm not going to the church."

"You'd let me go by myself?" She became indignant. "What if they kidnap me? What if they *sacrifice* me?"

"No, I don't think you should go either. It's late. Go to bed. In the morning you can check it out, see if they left anything behind."

"And miss a real Satanic mass? No way! This is why I *came* to Helltown. Now come with me, Beetle. Please? We're wasting time standing here. They might finish soon and leave."

"I'm sorry, Greta. Not tonight. Maybe in the morning."

"I have a car. We can drive there. It won't take long."

Her persistence was trying Beetle's patience. He'd made up

his mind; he wasn't changing it. "I'm not going," he told her firmly. "That's that. Okay?"

Anger flared in Greta's eyes, and for a moment she wasn't uniquely attractive; she was beautiful. Then she clenched her jaw and returned to her room, slamming the door behind her.

Beetle eased his door closed, relieved to be alone again.

He stepped into the bathroom and urinated into the toilet bowl without bothering to lift the seat, fearing the simple act of bending over might ratchet up his headache. Afterward he filled the paper cup on the counter with tap water and drank from it greedily, spilling water down his shirt. He refilled the cup and drank again, albeit more slowly. His parched throat thanked him.

Back in the room he sat on the end of the bed, facing the TV. A news anchor was reporting on a tsunami that had struck Japan's eastern shoreline. Beetle's eyes shifted to the bottle of vodka next to the TV. Roughly a third remained. He was about to fetch it when he realized the idea of drinking more booze right then made him feel more nauseous than he already was.

Then, quite abruptly, a weight settled over Beetle. Not the suicidal depression—that was still there, pressing down on his shoulders like an invisible lead cloak—but something else that made him stare stupidly at the television and fidget with his hands repeatedly.

Boredom. He was bored out of his fucking mind.

He wasn't going to kill himself tonight. He'd already decided that. He wasn't going to continue drinking either. Ideally he would have liked to go to sleep, but right then he felt not only wide awake but wired. If he attempted to sleep he would lie there, thinking thoughts he didn't want to think.

"Fuck it," he grunted, getting up and snagging the motel room key.

Beetle knocked a second time on Greta's door. When she

didn't answer he realized she wasn't ignoring him; she had likely already left for the church. Beetle started along the hallway, noting the zigzagging line of blood that stained the carpet. He passed the clicking ice machine and took the stairs to the first floor. The reception was deserted. The old cheat was likely in bed sleeping, or at the hospital with his sons. Beetle stepped through the front doors, into the rain and wind.

While he was halfway down the steep staircase that led to the parking lot he heard the rev of a car engine. He took the steps two at a time, ignoring the knot of pain bouncing around inside his head.

At the bottom he stepped into blinding headlights. Brakes screeched. Shading his eyes, he went to the car.

Greta rolled down the driver's window and stuck her head out, beaming. "You changed your mind!" she said.

"Yeah, but I think we should walk," he told her. "Because if there are Satanists at the church like you think, we're going to need to be discrete about this."

CHAPTER 25

"Oh yes, there will be blood."
Saw II (2005)

A s Spencer drove through the gate in the split-rail fence and down the gravel driveway toward the House in the Woods, he frowned as he passed Cleavon's pickup truck, which was tipped over on its side like a toy that had been tossed to the broken pile. He parked the Volvo and hurried through the rain to the sagging front porch where everyone was waiting for him: Cleavon, Jesse, Earl, Floyd, and Weasel. There were also two women at Cleavon's feet. They were hogtied and gagged and staring up at him with red, terrified eyes.

"So," Spencer said heartily, "having some car trouble, are we, Cleave?"

"Don't get me started," Cleavon growled.

"I told you, it was an accident," Earl said, holding a bloodied dish towel against his neck. "I didn't mean to, I told you that, she was just too quick."

"What happened to your neck, Earl?" Spencer asked.

"He almost let the tiny bitch get away, that's what," Cleavon said. "She sliced him with my razor, jumped in my truck, and almost got away."

"But she didn't," Spencer said.

"No, she didn't. But look at my fucking truck, Spence! I'm gonna need all new side panels, a new headlight, and a new window. And you think Earl got the money to pay for that? You think his rabbits gonna pay for that?"

"Aw, Cleave," Earl complained. "I told ya, I told ya a hundred times, I didn't mean it."

Spencer held up his hand to command silence. "The truck's not important right now. What I want to know is what exactly went on here tonight. Who would like to explain this to me from the beginning? Weasel? Cleavon tells me this is all your doing?"

Weasel Higgins had his scrawny arms folded across his chest, the beak of his cap pulled low over his forehead as if he were trying to hide. "No it wasn't, Mr. Pratt, I wasn't even here when the truck crashed—"

Cleavon whacked him across the back of the head. "He's talking about Stanford Road and all the shit that's happened 'cause of your stupidity, stupid."

Weasel swallowed. His Adam's apple bobbed up and down like a quickly moving elevator. "I don't know it's fair to say that, Mr. Pratt, to say it's all my doing. Cleave, he's the one who let that redhead get away."

"She wouldn't have gotten away," Cleavon told him, scowling, "if you hadn't gone messing with two cars in the first place." He took an angry drag of the cigarette he was smoking and flicked what remained into the night.

"I'm not blaming anyone," Spencer said calmly. "I merely want an explanation. The account you told me on the phone, Cleave, was brief, to say the least."

"Yeah, well, okay then," Weasel said, lifting his cap and clawing his hand through his oily hair. "Well, I was patrolling Standford Road like we talked about the last meeting. It being Halloween and all, there was gonna be some does, right? So eventually I come to these two cars parked next to Crybaby. Problem was, I drove by so fast I didn't get a good look inside them, didn't know there were so many people. That was the problem." He studied the others warily as if to see if anyone would challenge this claim.

Cleavon jumped on the opportunity. "That's not what you told me on the phone, you lying shit. You told me—and Jess, mind you—you told us there were seven people inside 'em."

"I did not."

"Jess?" Cleavon said.

Jesse Gordon stood off on his own, chewing bubblegum. "Ayuh, Weasel," he said, looking at his feet. "You said seven."

"What the fuck?" Weasel said. "You two ganging up on me?"

"Now, now, Weasel, what's done is done," Spencer said, holding up his hand again. He felt like a school teacher mediating aggressive children. "There's no point arguing about this. Now please continue."

"Yeah, that's right," Weasel said, shooting Cleavon a triumphant look. "What's done is done." He pulled at his goatee, a nervous habit of his. "Anyway, what happened? Well, what happened was, I turned the meat wagon round and high beamed the first car, the Bimmer. It high beamed me back. So it's on, right? So I come straight at it. The driver in the Bimmer was ballsy, but I was ballsier. I kept my cool. Didn't blink. At the last second the Bimmer swerves and shoots off the road faster than a cat can lick its ass."

"Were they screaming?" Earl asked earnestly. "Did you hear them screaming?"

"Naw, Earl, like I said, it happened too fast." He swept his hands together while making a whistling noise. "Now you see 'em, now you don't, just like that. Anyway, I knew they wasn't going nowhere. So I burned rubber all the way home and got on the horn to call Cleave, but he was already talking to Jess, so I told 'em, I told 'em both, what happened. That's when Cleave, that's when he took over. So you see, Mr. Pratt, I didn't have nothing to do with the girl getting away, that was Cleave—"

"There were four of them and only three of us," Cleavon snapped. "Me and the boys took care of them the best we could —"

"Three," Weasel corrected. "One was a cripple. And he was out cold. So there was only three, and two of 'em were girls—"

"I've had about enough of your smarting off, boy," Cleavon said, and shoved Weasel, knocking him into Earl. He shoved him again, this time to his knees.

"Cleavon!" Spencer said. "Leave Weasel be."

"Ehhh," Cleavon spat next to where Weasel cowered. "The little drink of water ain't worth it." He took out his cigarettes and lit up a fresh one while Weasel regained his feet and moved a safe distance away from him.

"So what happened at Lonnie's, Cleave?" Spencer asked, doing his best to appear empathetic. Lonnie Olsen had been one of Cleavon's better friends. "How did he die?"

Cleavon shrugged, showing no emotion—if you didn't know him better. Spencer could tell he was holding back a whole lot of hurt and anger inside. "Happened before me and Jess got there," he said. "But looked like one of the bucks got hold of his rifle and shot him point blank in the chest."

"And his boy?"

"Got it bad, real bad, brains all over the floor. You ask me what happened, I reckon the bucks got into it with the boy before Lonnie arrived for not letting them use the phone. They killed him accidentally, 'cause that's what it looked like with the radiator and all, an accident, and Lonnie came home and went ape shit, killed one of the bucks, then got served himself. But don't take my word for it. Ask the flying princess here. She was there." He kicked the blonde in the side of the ribs.

She moaned and squeezed her eyes shut.

"No, that won't be necessary," Spencer said. "Your account sounds logical to me. Where had Lonnie returned from?"

"Randy's," Cleavon said.

"You called him at Randy's?"

"First thing I done when I hung up with Jess and Dumbass." Cleavon eyed Spencer apprehensively. "What? What's the problem?"

"There's no problem," Spencer said. "You did well."

"Don't bullshit me, Spence," Cleavon said. "You don't think

the sheriff... Motherfuckingshitter! The sheriff, he's gonna find out I called Randy's, ain't he? He's gonna know I was the last person to speak to Lonnie. He's gonna think I had something to do with what went down at Lonnie's. He's gonna put it all together."

"Put what together, Cleave?" Spencer said amiably, carefully. "You just tell Sheriff Humperdinck, if he asks, that you called Randy's to see if Lonnie was going to be around for a while because you wanted to join him for a drink. Lonnie, however, told you he was calling it a night and heading home."

Cleavon screwed up his lips as he thought about this. Then he nodded. "Yeah, that makes sense, don't it? I was just calling to see if Lonnie wanted to stick around for a beer. But what if Randy was standing next to Lonnie? What if he heard something different?"

"Like what?" Spencer asked. "What did Lonnie say to you?"

"Shit, I don't remember his exact words."

"And neither will Randy, even if, by some rare chance, he wanted to snoop in on a call between Lonnie and yourself when he has a bar to run. No offense, Cleave, but you're not the President of the United States." Spencer held his brother's eyes until Cleavon nodded his agreement. "You have nothing to worry about, Cleave," he added. "None of us do. Some out-of-towners crashed their car. On their way to find help they came across Lonnie's place. Something happened, it doesn't matter what, and his son died. Lonnie shot two of them, but not before he got shot himself. The five others fled into the woods. The sheriff will search, of course. But the national park is twenty thousand acres of dense woodland. It will be like looking for needles in a haystack. When no one turns up, the conclusion will be they got lost and died. And that's it. All we have to do is sit tight and wait this out."

"You're forgetting 'bout the girl who got away, Mr. Pratt," Jesse Gordon said, blowing a purple bubble and swallowing it again. "She saw Cleavon and Earl and Floyd. If she gets to town tonight, tells the sheriff about them..."

"Jess's right," Cleavon said. "And we're wasting talk standing round here shooting the shit. Jess, me and you, we'll take the El Camino. The bitch hasn't seen it. She'll think she's flagging down help. By the time she finds out it's us, it'll be too late."

They were correct, Spencer knew. The young woman getting to town would be a disaster—but this was a disaster Spencer wanted. "You're overreacting, Cleave," Spencer told him in a calm, rational, slightly patronizing tone. "It's highly unlikely she could make it to town on foot. That would be a good ten-mile hike—"

"She could—"

"She won't. Not in the middle of the night. Moreover, she'll know you'll be out there looking for her. As soon as she hears a vehicle approach, she'll duck into the woods. You'll drive straight past, never the wiser." He shook his head. "No, she'll bunker down somewhere until morning, when she feels safer. She won't think you'll still be looking for her then. That's when you'll get her."

"I don't know," Cleavon said. "She gets to town—"

"She won't."

"But if she does—"

"She won't," Spencer said with enough decisiveness to signal the discussion was over. "Besides, we have other matters to attend to. We have to get rid of the other out-of-towners in case Sheriff Humperdinck comes by questioning you boys about Lonnie. Speaking of which, where are the other two? There should be—"

"I gave 'em to Toad and Trapper," Earl said in his giddy, booming voice. He shifted his bulk from one foot to the other, almost as if he had to urinate. "Cleave said I could, I asked, and he said I could, 'cause they'd just shed, and they were real hungry, and it would save us giving 'em rabbits."

"You fed them to your *snakes*?" Spencer said skeptically.

"Yeah, Spence," Earl said, obviously tickled blue by the idea. "They're two happy snakes right now, I'll tell you that, you should see them—"

"Show me."

Earl led Spencer through the ramshackle house, down one cracked-plaster hallway, then another, until they stood before a solid oak door.

Earl had purchased the snakes from a pet store in Akron some ten years ago. They were green anacondas, the largest species of snake in the world, though they had only been a few inches long then. They grew fast. After two years they were nine feet in length and devouring a couple of rabbits each fortnight. When they became too big for the timber and wire-mesh melamine cage Cleavon had built for them, Earl demanded they be relocated to the room he and Spencer stood before now. Cleavon put down linoleum tiles to make cleaning the floor easier— they defecated like horses—and he installed a thermostat and humidifier to keep the temperature at eighty-five degrees with ninety degrees humidity. It was a lot of work, and Cleavon wasn't happy about doing it, but when Earl got something in his mind, there was no talking him out of it. There was no ignoring him either, not unless you were prepared to deal with four hundred pounds of single-minded, unreasoning fury.

And then, of course, there was the time one of the snakes tried to make a meal of Cleavon. He especially wasn't happy about *that*. This wasn't long after the snakes moved from the cage outside into the house. Earl would often plunk down in the rocking chair he set up in one corner of the room and sit there watching the snakes even when they weren't doing much of anything, which was their usual state of affairs. On the occasion in question he had been drunk and didn't close the door properly when he left to go to bed. Cleavon woke in the middle of the night shouting. One of the snakes—Toad, Spencer believed—had curled itself around Cleavon's left arm and ankle, swallowing his arm nearly to the elbow. Even Earl, with all his strength, couldn't unwrap the thing. Cleavon wanted him to cut it in half, but Earl wouldn't hear of it. Spencer wouldn't have been surprised if, had it come to it, Earl chose the snake's life over his brother's.

Fortunately the situation didn't devolve into this. Instead

Cleavon had Earl ring Spencer and explain what happened. The telephone call had been chaotic, with Earl blabbering incoherently and Cleavon cursing in the background. Spencer didn't know the first thing about snakes, but he had once read about a boy who had been bitten by a pit bull. The quick-thinking owner of the dog got it to release the boy's arm by dumping half a liter of alcohol down its throat. So that's what he told Earl to do. Amazingly it worked. The snake regurgitated Cleavon's limb and released its death grip from his arm and leg.

Now Earl took the key dangling on a string from around his neck and unlocked the door. He stepped fearlessly into the room, hit the light switch to the left, and said proudly, "See, Spence, I told you, they ate them, they ate them good, didn't they?"

Spencer wrinkled his nose at the sudden stench of feces and urine, and beneath this, the pungent, musky odor the snakes emitted from their anal glands to keep the poisonous organism found in the marshes and swamps of South America at bay.

The two anacondas lay curled in opposite corners. They were both over twenty feet long—nearly twice their length when Toad attacked Cleavon. Their glossy olive bodies dwarfed their heads, which were marked with prominent red stripes. Black oval-shaped markings spotted their backs, tapering down to black spots with yellow centers along their flanks.

Spencer's eyes went immediately to their grotesquely extended middle sections. He stared, fascinated. Despite the massive sizes of the animals, he'd had no idea they could consume fully grown humans. But why not? he thought. Surely if anacondas could swallow caiman and deer in the wild, they could work their mouths around human shoulders.

Spencer wished he had arrived earlier so he could have witnessed the spectacle of the two men's deaths, so he could have looked into their eyes and seen the understanding of their impending doom. Now that would have been something.

"Did I do good, Spence?" Earl asked.

"Wonderfully," he said softly.

"Can I feed 'em more bucks and does in the future? We'll save on rabbits if I do, and all those does and bucks, they just go to waste where we bury 'em out back, so this way we make use of them, and we save on rabbits. I'm right, Spence, am I right?"

Spencer told Earl he could do whatever he wished in the future—an easy proclamation to make considering Earl would not live to see the morning—and they returned to the front porch where they found Cleavon in a heated discussion with Jesse and Weasel. Cleavon was still lobbying to go find the missing woman, while Jesse and Weasel seemed okay with leaving the matter until the first light.

"So what we gonna do till morning then?" Cleavon challenged. "Get pissed and hit the sack like this was any old Friday night? You think any of you gonna sleep knowing that bitch is on the loose out there?"

"Why don't we hold a black mass, gentlemen?" Spencer suggested. "My mistake," he added, casting the bound women a glance. "Why don't we hold *two*?"

All eyes turned toward him.

"Huh?" Cleavon said.

"A black mass," Spencer repeated. "Earl's snakes have taken care of the two bucks nicely. That leaves these two does. It's either bury them out back right now, which would be a shameful waste, or have some fun first. Given we have the time…"

The women moaned and flopped around on the porch like fish out of water. Their struggles only earned the attention of the men present, whose eyes began to burn with primitive hunger and lust.

"I don't wanna waste them," Earl said, squatting next to the small woman and patting her on the head. "I wanna have some fun? Please? Can we, huh? Can we have some fun?"

"Given all the trouble we've gone through to get them…" Jesse said, nodding. "Yeah, I think it would be a mighty shame not to get our due."

"I'm in," Weasel said with alacrity.

"Cleavon?" Spencer said.

"You four go have your fuckin' orgy," Cleavon griped. "I'll

search for the girl myself like I do every goddamn thing else myself round here."

Spencer clenched his jaw. "Weren't you listening to me? She's —"

"Hiding. Right."

"Tell you what, Cleave," Spencer said, playing his final card, "this being our last mass in a while—we're going to have to lay low for several months after this—I was contemplating holding it in Mother of Sorrows church."

"Inside the *church*?"

"That's right. Do a proper mass for once. Also, if that young woman somehow makes it from the forest—and that's a big if—Stanford Road will take her straight past the church. She'll see our cars parked out front and come to *us* for help."

"She'll come right to *us*!" Earl parroted. "Then we'll have her, we'll have her good!"

"Smart thinking, Mr. Pratt!" Weasel exclaimed.

"Hell of an idea, Mr. Pratt," Jesse said, nodding sagely. "Hell of an idea."

Cleavon, however, was ever the pessimist. "Or she might walk right on past the church."

"Would you?" Spencer said. "If you were terrified and alone and you'd just been through what she'd been through, would you pass up the nearest help you came across? Anyway, Cleave, to alleviate your concern, we'll rotate a sentry outside the church while the masses are proceeding, to keep an eye on the road."

Cleavon scratched his stubble. "Well, now we're getting somewhere, boys." He nodded. "I s'pose that might be okay. But the church, it's a bit public to hold a mass, ain't it?"

Spencer shook his head. "There's nothing for miles save that little motel." He made a show of glancing at his wristwatch. "And who's going to be peering out their window with night-vision goggles in the middle of the night? Now, are we all agreed?"

To Spencer's immense relief, they were.

They drove to Mother of Sorrows church in three separate cars. Cleavon, Weasel, and Jesse in the El Camino; Earl, Floyd, and the two women in Earl's old nuts-and-bolts jalopy; Spencer in his Volvo. They parked at the top of the hill on which the church was built and dashed through the rain to the abandoned building.

The sanctuary was pitch black and dusty. The air smelled stale, with the faintest traces of myrrh and spikenard. Spencer turned on his flashlight and led the way down the center aisle to the small nave. The others followed, carrying the supplies they would need for the black mass: the cast iron chamber pot, the brass Chinese gong, the cased ceremonial sword, black and white candles, and a rusty bucket filled with chicken blood. Weasel usually brought his Casio keyboard to the black masses they held at the scattering of abandoned houses they frequented, but Spencer assured him the church had a full-sized organ that was in working order.

Earl dumped the two struggling women on the stone floor, next to the altar, and said, "Can we do the small one first, Spence? Lookit her go! She's like a rabbit that knows what's coming for it. So can we, Spence, can we do her first?"

"I'm in the mood for the blonde," Jesse said. "See if she really *is* a blonde."

"I'm with Jess," Weasel said. "We haven't done a real blonde yet, have we?"

"Cleave?" Spencer said. "Your call."

"The fuck does it matter?" he grumbled. "We doing both of them, ain't we? So it don't matter two flying shits to me what order we do them in."

"The blonde it is then," Spencer said.

Jenny was nearly insane with fear. She didn't know how

anything could have been worse than lying beneath the bed in that house, knowing Noah and Steve were dead, knowing someone was coming for her. But this was. Because at least when she was beneath the bed she'd had an inkling of hope she might yet escape. Not now. Now she was strapped down on an altar, stripped naked, the number 666 painted across her breasts with what smelled like sour blood. Now... God, now she was being *sacrificed*. These men were going to sacrifice her to their dark lord. They were going to rape her. Then they were going to bury her in a hole somewhere.

How is this happening? her mind screamed hysterically. *I'm a second-year medical school student. I'm supposed to be attending microbiology and pathology on Monday. I'm supposed to be studying all week for Dr. Mann's exam on Friday. I'm supposed to be a doctor one day, helping people, saving lives. I'm certainly NOT supposed to be strapped to an altar and sacrificed to the devil.*

A gong rang, reverberating loudly. Then organ music began to play, what sounded like corrupted church hymns.

God, it's happening, it's started, it's really happening!

Jenny thrashed so violently that the rope securing her limbs sliced into her skin. Warm, syrupy blood spilled down her wrists, her ankles.

Abruptly two of the men appeared before her. One wore a black hooded robe that concealed his face, the other the habit and wimple of a nun.

Jenny shook her head from side to side, screaming, but the gag in her mouth turned the screams into muffled whimpers. Sobs wracked her body.

A third man appeared between the other two—the leader with the beard. He wore the same navy blazer, crisp white shirt, and red and yellow striped necktie he'd had on before.

The hooded man rang a bell nine times. The leader raised his hands, palms downward, and began chanting in Latin.

And right then something inside Jenny snapped with a dry, delicate *whick*, and she believed this to be the sound of one losing their mind.

◆ ◆ ◆

Cherry could close her eyes but she couldn't close her ears, and she was forced to listen to the horrible organ music and chanting and wild shrieks—and near the end of the ceremony, the grunts of pleasure from the men as they mounted Jenny one after the other.

And Cherry knew she was next. They were going to gang rape her like she was a piece of meat. The irony of the situation was not lost on her. She had spent her entire life following the Roman Catholic decree to abstain from sexual intercourse before marriage. She had upheld this edict even as she worked for a sleazy massage company with men propositioning her daily. Yet now she was going to be violated a half dozen times within minutes—all on the altar of a Roman Catholic church.

If God had a sense of humor, He would surely be laughing at this. And suddenly Cherry was furious. How could He sit by and let this happen to her? If He was so omniscient and omnipotent, how could He let horrible acts of savagery like this occur in His creation?

She knew the answer. The last several hours of horror had pulled back the curtain on life and shown her the cruel truth.

God was not sitting on His throne in heaven in all His glory, surrounded by His angels, beckoning for her to join Him at His side.

God didn't exist, He was dead, and very shortly she would be too.

After Spencer plunged the ceremonial sword into the blonde's chest to conclude the black mass, he turned to the assemblage and said, "I must admit, gentlemen, I have enjoyed myself thus far immensely."

"And we still got one more," Earl said excitedly.

"That we do." Spencer stroked his beard thoughtfully. "Cleave, what would you think about leading the next mass?"

"Me?" Cleavon said, surprised.

"You don't want to?"

"It ain't that. It's just…I don't know none of that Greek mumbo jumbo."

"Latin mumbo jumbo. And the mass doesn't have to be led in Latin. You can recall most of the English parts can't you?"

"Sure…probably." He shrugged. "I guess."

"Then you'll do fine."

Cleavon cocked an eye suspiciously. "Why you offering to let me lead the mass?"

"It seems in our excitement we forgot to post a sentry out front of the church." A brief uproar followed this announcement, which Spencer promptly cut off. "Calm down, gentlemen. Calm down. We simply won't make the same oversight twice."

"I'll go, Mr. Pratt," Jesse Gordon said. "I don't mind. The old pecker's not what it used to be, and I'm not sure I could get it up for another go anyway."

"Thank you, Jesse," Spencer replied, "but my libido isn't what it used to be either. Also, to be perfectly frank, without my robes and headgear I don't feel comfortable leading the mass. The psychodrama is not at the level it should be." He started walking toward the double front doors. "Collect yourselves, gentlemen," he added over his shoulder. "Take your time with her, enjoy her, for she will be our last sacrifice for some time."

"You holler you see that girl!" Cleavon called.

"You'll hear me."

Outside, beneath the black, weeping sky, Spencer went to the Volvo, popped the trunk, and retrieved the two lengths of half-inch chain and the two heavy-duty padlocks he'd kept there since deciding on Mother of Sorrows church as the venue for his contingency plan.

He secured the doors on the east side of the church first, looping one chain through the sturdy brass handles several times before attaching a padlock. He repeated this procedure with the front doors. Both times he tested his handiwork, tugging the handles quietly.

Spencer had always been curious as to how he would feel when the occasion inevitably arose when he would have to murder his brothers. They weren't nameless, random women. He had grown up with them, went to school with them, opened presents on Christmas day with them. They were blood. He had hoped he would feel regret or sadness—those would be the appropriate emotions one should feel in such a situation—but as it turned out he didn't feel anything. Their deaths would be meaningless to him.

Back at the Volvo's trunk Spencer withdrew the red jerrycan, unscrewed the cap, and walked the circumference of the church, splashing a line of gasoline behind him. When he met up with where he'd begun, he lit a match and dropped it in the gas. Flames whooshed to life and chased the flammable fluid around the wooden building like a line of falling dominoes.

A sense of accomplishment filled Spencer. It was done. Everyone inside the church would meet their fiery deaths shortly. There would be no one left who knew about the Mary Atwater incident. Moreover, they would take the fall not only for the murders this evening but for every murder over the past twenty-four months. The police would raid the House in the Woods and find eight skeletons buried out back. They might not be able to explain who was responsible for locking and burning the church to the ground, but they wouldn't have any reason to suspect Spencer. It would remain a mystery, which, in the big picture, wouldn't matter anyway—because the main culprits were dead, justice was served.

Spencer, of course, could not continue with the Satanic masses on his own, at least not in Boston Mills. This would be a shame. He had become comfortable with the arrangement he'd orchestrated. Nevertheless, a return to his old ways would be its own relief. He would no longer have to worry about other people talking, other people screwing up. He would once again be wholeheartedly in control of his fate.

"Goodbye, gentlemen," Spencer said as the heat from the quickly escalating fire rose against his face. "Be sure to give our fair Lucifer my salutations when you see him."

CHAPTER 26

*"It's been a funny sort
of day, hasn't it?"*
Shaun of the Dead (2004)

T he storm continued to strengthen, the torrent of driving
raindrops turning the surface of Stanford Road into
a furious boil. The first peal of thunder rumbled
ominously in the dark sky, almost directly overhead.

Greta, more skipping than walking, said, "How are you
feeling?"

Beetle rubbed rainwater from his eyes. "Wet."

Greta laughed, tilted her head to the heavens, and stuck out
her tongue, to catch the raindrops on it. "I love walking in the
rain."

"You're in the minority."

"Then you should have brought an umbrella, Herr Beetle."
She smiled crookedly at him. "Are you still drunk?"

Yeah, he was. Drunk and stoned and a bit squishy inside. But
walking amid a storm had a way of sobering you up. "I'm fine,"
he said.

"You don't talk much, do you?"

"We're talking right now."

"Because I'm talking to you. I think if I never said anything, you might not either."

Beetle wondered about that. He supposed she was right. He'd never been much of a talker, especially with strangers. And although Greta was no longer a stranger—more like the talkative girl at a party who wouldn't leave you alone—he was in no mood for chitchat. He was already beginning to second-guess his decision to come along on this witch hunt or whatever it was.

He hunched his shoulders against the rain and dug his fists deeper into his pant pockets.

"See!" Greta said.

"Huh?" he said, glancing sidelong at her. Her eyes were sparkling, her wet face glowing. She was really getting off being out in a storm.

"I didn't say anything, to see if you would say something, and you didn't."

"What do you want to talk about?"

Greta rolled her eyes. "Nothing. That isn't the point. Talking doesn't have to be about something. You can just talk to talk."

Beetle nodded, realized this didn't qualify as speaking, didn't want to get reprimanded again, and so said, "Got it."

"Do you have a girlfriend?"

The question surprised him—and angered him. "No."

"I don't either," she said. "A boyfriend, I mean. I'm too tall."

"To have a boyfriend?"

"No man wants to date a woman taller than themselves. Only movie stars don't seem to care. Unfortunately, I don't know any movie stars."

Beetle glanced at Greta again. She must have been six feet, maybe six-one—his height, though likely two-thirds his weight. She wore a red rain slicker over a white T-shirt. The slicker was unzipped, the tee soaked through. She wasn't wearing a bra.

"You know," she said, "it's nice walking next to someone as tall as I am. I don't feel like a freak."

"You're not a freak."

"I was at a zoo last week, the one in Toronto. There were these young children there with their teachers on a school field trip.

You should have seen how they all looked up at me, with these big, curious eyes, the same way they looked at the animals. I stick out like a blue thumb."

"A sore thumb."

"A blue thumb doesn't stick out?"

"I guess. But the saying is a sore thumb."

"I like blue thumb. I think a blue thumb sticks out more than a sore thumb."

"Why would you have a blue thumb?"

"Hey," she said, "do you think if we had babies, they would be tall too?" Her eyes shone with bright mischievousness. "Don't worry," she added, "I'm not proposing we have a baby. I don't even know you. And you're too quiet to be my husband. I'm just wondering if you think we would have tall babies."

Beetle shrugged. "Babies aren't tall."

"Some are."

"No, they're not—inherently not. The same way ice isn't warm."

"Are you making a joke?"

"I'm pointing out a truism."

"No, I think you made a joke." She clapped her hands. "I can't believe it! Herr Beetle has a sense of humor. Tell me something else funny."

"It wasn't a joke—" Beetle stopped abruptly. Aside from the machinegun-like-patter of rain he thought he could hear the sound of an approaching engine. "A car's coming," he said.

"So?" Greta said.

Headlights appeared from around a bend ahead of them. Beetle took Greta's arm and steered her into the vegetation lining the verge until they were concealed behind a large tree.

"Kinky, mister," she said.

"It's coming from the direction of the church."

"Oh!" she whispered. "You think...?"

The headlights merged into a blinding white light. For a moment Beetle felt unacceptably exposed. He pressed his body against Greta's, wanting to blend further into the shadows. The car roared past, the sound of the engine faded, then they were alone once more.

Beetle realized his lips were inches from Greta's, his chest pressed against hers. Embarrassed, he led her back to the road. Her cheeks were flushed. Her erect nipples pressed against the fabric of her drenched shirt. She noticed him notice this.

Beetle looked away. "Guess we missed it," he said.

"What do you mean?" she asked.

"The mass," he said. "If that was one of the Satanists, it seems the party's over."

"We don't know who that was. It could have been anyone."

"At this hour—?"

"*Sue dumm fuhrt!*" Greta said. "Don't give up so easy on things, Herr Beetle." She took his hand in hers. "Now come on! There still might be time."

CHAPTER 27

"Sometimes dead is better."
Pet Sematary (1989)

C leavon had been the first to smell the smoke. They had replaced the blonde with the Asian on the altar—she'd been a bitch to tie down, fighting as if she really did have a demon inside her—and as Cleavon stood in front of her, trying to think how to begin the black mass, he detected the unmistakable smell of smoke. For a moment he wondered if someone was burning leaves before remembering the nearest neighbor was the motel some two miles away. He said, "Can you smell that?"

"That ain't how you start the mass, Cleave!" Earl said. "First you gotta cross yourself backward, that's what you gotta do first —"

"Jess," he said, "you smell that?"

Jesse was sniffing the air. "Sure do, Cleave."

"Something's burning, I reckon," Weasel said.

"What the fuck's Spence doing?" Cleavon growled. "Starting a fuckin' signal fire for the girl?"

Tossing aside the little bell he'd been holding—it landed on the altar with a small *ding!*—he snatched the flashlight and marched up the aisle to the front doors. Jesse and Weasel followed close behind him, with Earl and Floyd bringing up the rear. He gripped the brass door handle and immediately released it, crying out in pain. He spun in a clumsy pirouette, flapping his scorched hand in the air. "*Jeeeeee-zus!*"

"What is it, what happened?" Earl asked, reaching for the handle next.

"Don't touch that!" Cleavon said, slapping Earl's hand clear. "It's hot!"

"Why the hell's it hot?" Jesse said.

Cleavon kicked the door hard with his right foot. It didn't budge.

"It's stuck?" Weasel said, kicking the door himself to no avail.

"Mr. Pratt?" Jesse called. "Hey-o! Mr. Pratt!"

There was no answer.

Understanding dawned on Cleavon, and a body-wide coldness slipped beneath his skin. "The motherfucker!" he mumbled.

"Who?" Jesse asked, staring at him with eyes expecting the worst.

Cleavon, however, barely heard him. He was numbed. His goddamn bastard of a brother had double-crossed them all! No wonder he hadn't given a damn about finding the bitch who'd gotten away. She'd never seen *him*.

"Cleave?" Earl said, worried. "What's happening, Cleave? *Cleave?*"

"Bust them down, Earl!" Cleavon told him, pointing at the doors. "Bust them hard as you can!"

Earl shoved Weasel aside and raised his massive boot and slammed it into the crack where the doors met. The doors shook but held.

"Again!" Cleavon shouted.

Earl kicked a second time, a third, and a fourth.

"It ain't working, Cleave!" he cried. "They're too strong!"

Cleavon's shock and anger were quickly giving way to blistering fear.

They were trapped.

They were going to roast alive.

Spencer wouldn't have attempted something like this had he not been convinced it would work.

My brother! he thought, his mind reeling. *My own fucking brother!*

Then again, was he really surprised Spencer could orchestrate something so heartless? Two years ago he would have been, back before Spencer showed up at the house with that Mary woman, both of them bloodied and smashed up. Because before then Spencer might still have been a holier-than-thou asshole, but that had been all. After that night, however—that's when Cleavon began to see his older brother in an entirely new light. It wasn't the revelation that Spencer was okay with killing. Hell, as it turned out, the whole merry lot of them were okay with killing. Life was a spiteful whore, and you had to do what you had to do sometimes to make yourself happy. So it wasn't that Spencer was okay with the killing; it was that he *enjoyed* it. Jesse and Weasel, Earl and Floyd, himself too, they were in this devil worship stuff for the sex. That first woman, that Mary, she got them hooked on the black masses like junkies on heroin. This was not so much the case with Spencer, who always seemed more interested when he was looking in the women's eyes in those last few seconds before they died as if he were seeing something there no one else could see.

So, no, maybe Cleavon wasn't surprised to discover Spencer had it in him to murder his brothers. Maybe he wasn't surprised at all.

Cleavon directed the flashlight beam around the church's sanctuary. Three stained-glass windows lined the east wall, three the west wall, each a dozen feet tall, two feet in diameter, tapering to pointed tips. Earl could boost Cleavon up to one, but it would do no good. They were all secured with steel mesh on the outside to protect against vandals and the elements.

"Well don't just stand there looking pretty, boys!" he quipped. "Get looking for another way out!"

They searched every dark corner of the church. The only other set of doors they found turned out to be locked as tightly as those at the front.

Think, Cleave! he told himself, turning in a circle, panicking. *Think!*

But how could he? The scene was chaos. Earl wailing like a little kid. Floyd holding his ears and making that retarded deaf sound he made. Weasel and Jesse both shouting for instructions.

"Shut up!" he exploded, wiping sweat from his brow. It was as hot as hell in summer. "The lot of you! Earl! Shut the fuck up!"

They went quiet.

Cleavon's eyes fell on the dead blonde. A great sadness welled inside him. Not for her. For himself. Because shortly he was going to be dead too. Dead and crisped so black the sheriff will be identifying him by his teeth.

And I just unloaded two hundred bills on a new carburetor for the Mustang in the garage, and I ain't even gonna get a chance to install it. Ain't that a bitch, ain't that just a goddamn, motherfucking bitch.

His eyes drifted to the pew the blonde was lying on, then the pew's clawed wooden feet.

They weren't bolted to the floor.

An idea forming in his mind, Cleavon rushed to the pew, shoved the woman's body to the floor, and gripped the pew beneath the seat. He managed to rock it back an inch. "Boys!" he rasped in the dry air. "Give me a hand here! We got ourselves a battering ram!"

With Cleavon and Earl on one side, Weasel and Jesse and Floyd on the other, they lifted the pew between them, swung it perpendicularly, and carried it up the aisle. On Cleavon's instruction they set it down still some distance from the front doors.

"This is it, boys!" he said, shaking his spaghetti arms. "On the count of three we charge those doors like it's nobody's business! Y'all ready? *Y'all fuckin' ready?*"

"Ready, Cleave!" Earl said.

The others concurred with equal enthusiasm.

"On the count of three!" Cleavon said. They lifted the pew

simultaneously. "One! Two! Three!"

They rushed toward the double doors, shouting like a pack of crazies.

The front of the pew crashed into the doors straight on—and came to a bone-jarring stop. Everyone's momentum caused them to release the pew and torpedo into the doors themselves. Cleavon and Earl bounced backward, lost their balance, and collapsed to the floor in a mix-up of limbs.

"Shoot, Cleave," Earl said after a dazed moment. "That didn't work real good, did it?"

CHAPTER 28

"We all go a little mad sometimes"
Psycho (1960)

B eetle and Greta stared in disbelief at the white wooden church with the upside-down crosses incorporated into its architecture. It was engulfed in a glowing red fire that blazed against the black night. The flames, undeterred by the downpour, licked as high as the overhanging soffits, crackling and popping as they consumed the buckling weatherboards. Clouds of thick, acrid smoke streamed upward into the sky.

Beetle and Greta had frozen at the sight of the inferno when they'd breasted the summit of the hill on which the church had been built. Now they rushed past the two parked cars toward the front doors, where they stopped and stared again at the chain wound through the door handles and cinched together by a large bronze padlock.

"What the hell?" Beetle said.

"Hey!" Greta shouted, cupping her mouth with her hands. "Hello in there! Hey! Can you hear me?"

A chorus of weak croaks erupted from the other side of the doors, followed quickly by an equal number of gut-wrenching coughs.

"We need to help them!" she said as thunder crashed

overhead, so loud it seemed to shake the ground. Forked lightning flashed moments later, searing the sky a blinding white.

Beetle was already reaching for the Beretta tucked into the waistband of his pants. "Step back," he told Greta, aiming the pistol at the padlock.

"You have a gun!" she exclaimed. "Why—?"

"Stand back!"

Greta backed up.

Beetle squeezed the trigger.

The first bullet ricocheted off the padlock, pock-mocking the metal but otherwise leaving the lock intact. He fired two more rounds—*pop, pop*—both direct hits. The second smashed the tumblers inside the lock to pieces and left the lock dangling by the hook.

He tucked the pistol away, snapped a branch off a nearby sapling, and poked it through the ribbon of flames, lifting the dangling padlock free of the chain. The padlock struck the cement pavers with a metal clack. He worked on the chain itself next, unraveling its length loop after loop until it was free from the handles and dropped in a slinky coil beside the lock.

"Try opening the door now!" he shouted to those trapped inside the burning structure.

For a long moment nobody replied, nothing happened, and Beetle feared he and Greta had arrived too late. Then, abruptly, the right door swung open. In the hazy gray smoke that filled the church a man stood hunched over, the hooded black robes he wore pulled up over his mouth and nose to form a crude mask so only his eyes were visible. He leaped through the flames, took several drunken steps as if he'd forgotten how to walk, doubled over, and vomited.

A second man clad in black robes—he must have been close to seven feet tall—followed the first. He carried two unconscious men as if they weighed nothing.

"Nuh...nuther..." the big man said between poleaxing coughs. The two men slipped from his grasp like ragdolls. One landed on his back, his arms spread out at his sides, the other on his chest, his arms folded beneath him.

"Another inside?" Beetle said.

The man's head bobbed.

"Help them," he told Greta, nodding to the unconscious men. Then he covered his mouth and nose with the crook of his elbow and ducked inside the burning church.

The heat hit him like a physical force. The cloying gray smoke stung his eyes, causing them to blur and water. He dropped to his knees, so he could see in the space where the smoke had risen off the floor. He spotted the last man. He was several feet to the right, lying motionless on his side.

Beetle seized him by the wrists and dragged him toward the door. At the threshold he scooped him into his arms, stood—and heard coughing from deep within the church.

"Shit!" he mumbled. Leaping through the flames, Beetle deposited the man next to Greta and returned to the church, thinking, *So this is what a firefighter feels like—only firefighters have fire retardant suits and oxygen masks and powerful water hoses.*

Crouched low, he scrambled on all fours down the main aisle, and discovered a woman atop a candle-lit altar. She was naked. Her wrists and ankles were bound with a rope secured to the eyelets of four iron stakes hammered into the floorboards.

Ignoring the questions banging around inside his head, he untied the ropes and carried the woman outside. He set her down on the ground, then collapsed next to her. His eyes itched maddeningly. His throat felt stripped raw. Each breath was equally glorious and excruciating.

"Greta..." he rasped. He might not know what happened here, but he didn't think it was an innocent sex game gone wrong. "Go..."

"Not so fast," the first man out of the church said, standing straight and wiping puke from his mouth. "No one's going nowhere."

◆ ◆ ◆

Still on his knees, squinting against the rain, Beetle whipped out the Beretta and aimed it at the man with the muttonchops and handlebar mustache. "Get back!" he said. "Now!"

The man, who had been approaching them, froze. "Whoa, hold up there, hoss." He raised his dripping hands. His hair was plastered to his head like a helmet.

"Get back!"

"Listen—"

"Get back!"

He took a single step backward.

Greta helped the naked woman into a sitting position. "Can you stand?" she asked her, taking off her jacket and draping it around the woman's shoulders.

Still coughing, the woman nodded. Greta eased her to her feet.

"Get behind me," Beetle told them.

"Now wait just a sec—" Muttonchops said, his words drowned out by an explosion of thunder. "You don't understand," he went on a moment later. "We weren't doing nothing wrong. The little lady there, she's here of her own free God-given will."

The woman shook her head vigorously. Lightning shattered the sky. The succession of brief flashes illuminated her face starkly, gouging deep shadows beneath her saucer-wide eyes. "He's...he's lying...he killed them...he killed everyone..." Her coughs turned into sobs that wracked her body.

"Who's everyone?" Beetle demanded.

"Everyone!" she blurted, fixing the man with a murderous glare. "Noah! Steve! Jeff! Austin! You fed Austin to a snake! *You fed my boyfriend to a snake!*"

"Listen to her!" Muttonchops said. "Too much smoke got into that tiny pinhead of hers—"

"It's true! I heard you! And Jenny..." She issued a low moan as if reliving some terrible moment inside her head. "I saw you... you raped her...all of you...she's in there...the church..." She devolved into inarticulate noises.

Beetle glanced at the church. His stomach sank. It was nothing but a gigantic fireball now. If anyone were still inside, they were dead. He didn't know what was going on, but even if half of what the woman was saying was true, it was something much bigger than either he or Greta had imagined or were prepared to deal with.

"Greta," he said without taking his eyes or pistol off Muttonchops, "take her back to the motel, call the police, get them out here."

The big man, who had been slowly getting his coughing fit under control, now wiped a meaty paw across his slobbering mouth and pushed himself to his feet. He glanced at Beetle's pistol, then at Muttonchops. Beetle didn't like the dumb, cruel look he saw in his eyes. It reminded him of a dangerous dog awaiting an order from its master.

"Greta," Beetle said. "Get going, now—"

Muttonchops tipped his head in a barely perceptible nod. The next moment he and the Goliath charged Beetle simultaneously. Beetle fired a round at Muttonchops, clipping him in the shoulder, sending him to the ground. He swung the pistol at Goliath and fired two more rounds, point blank into his chest. Goliath stiffened and slowed but didn't stop, and then he was right in front of Beetle. He batted the pistol into the flames. In what seemed like the same instant his huge hands were around Beetle's throat, lifting him clear off the ground. Beetle straight chopped him on either side of the neck. It was as effective as striking stone. He dug his thumbs into the brute's eyes. Goliath roared in pain and launched Beetle through the air. He landed on the wet gravel, the sharp pebbles tearing the skin off his chin and both elbows. He rolled over to find Goliath rushing toward him. Rage had transformed his ugly, blunt face into something inhuman.

Beetle scrambled backward, splashing through shallow

puddles, away from the impossibility barreling down on him—
I shot the fucking guy point blank—but he was too slow. Goliath
reached him in a few strides and lifted his booted foot as if to
squash him like a bug.

Beetle slipped his legs around the man's ankle, locked his
ankles, and corkscrewed his body. Goliath fell like a tree, stiffly
and inelegantly, issuing a strange womanly yelp when he struck
the ground.

Beetle climbed onto Goliath's back and locked his arms
around his neck in a chokehold. Despite Beetle's size and
strength, Goliath lumbered to his feet with monstrous ease.
Beetle squeezed his arms tighter, in an equal effort to subdue the
man and hold on. His feet dangled in the air.

Goliath reached a hand over his shoulder and swatted Beetle
with powerful blows. Then he staggered, and Beetle filled with
hope. Either the gunshot wounds to his chest were finally
exacting their toll, or the chokehold was cutting off sufficient
airflow to his brain.

Goliath spun left and right, trying to shake Beetle free. Beetle
felt like a cowboy, riding a maddened bull. He held on with all his
willpower and strength.

The blows became weaker. The spinning lessoned.

Then Goliath staggered again, this time dropping to one
knee.

His calloused fingers pried at Beetle's arm in a final, desperate
attempt to free himself. He was making a dry, wheezing sound
that was almost lost in the drumming rain.

Beetle wondered if he was trying to speak, to beg for his life.

Finally he shuddered, then collapsed to his chest, dead.

While the stranger wrestled with the giant, Cherry attacked
the man named Cleavon, shrieking like a woman possessed. She
had never wanted to kill another person in her life, but she
wanted to kill Cleavon right then. She would claw his eyes from

his face if she could, she would spit in their bloody sockets, and she would laugh while doing it.

The man lay on the ground, cupping his injured shoulder where he had been shot, trying to rock himself to his knees. He saw her coming and kicked. She dodged his foot and fell on top of him, unleashing a fury of blows.

"Bitch!" he growled, shoving his hand in her face.

She bit his fingers to the bone.

He wailed, tried to yank his fingers free. She bit harder and tasted coppery blood. She shook her head, trying to sever the digits.

"Cunt!" he gasped and walloped her in the face so hard he might have broken her jaw. She seemed to fall through space, seeing stars.

Greta had picked up the wet, slimy branch Beetle had used to work the chain free from the church doors. Now she stood indecisively with it raised in a threatening gesture, unsure whether to help Beetle or the naked woman. When the man with the muttonchops walloped the woman in the side of the head, Greta made up her mind, rushed to the woman's aide, and began striking the man with the stick. He shouted obscenities at her and tried to protect his face. She got three solid licks in before he grabbed hold of the end of the stick and tugged it free from her grasp. He struck her with it across the shins, flaying the bare skin below the hem of her dress. She cried out and fell as he rose to his feet. He whipped her several times before the stick snapped in two. He tossed what remained away, then started toward one of the vehicles.

Wiping blood and rain from her eyes—the stick had sliced a gash across her forehead—Greta staggered after the man. She didn't know what she was doing. He was obviously fleeing the scene, and maybe it would be for the best to let him do so. But she was filled with adrenaline and hate, and she grabbed his hair from behind, yanking it as hard as he could.

"Aiyeee!" he said, stumbling backward.

She released his hair and gripped his injured shoulder, digging her nails into the bloody bullet wound.

He shrieked louder.

Nevertheless, he was not only muscular and wiry, but resilient, and he didn't go down. Instead he grabbed a fistful of her hair, bending her sideways, and growled, "Eat this, bitch!" He dragged her to the nearest car and slammed her face against the hood, smashing teeth from her gums and knocking her senseless.

CHAPTER 29

*"Trust is a tough thing to
come by these days."*
The Thing (1982)

S pencer made a left onto Grandview Lane, an unpaved rural
road that switch-backed to the top of Eagle Bluff. The
posted speed limit was twenty miles an hour, but it was
wise to slow to half that when rounding the hairpin corners,
especially in a full-blown storm.

The Volvo's windshield wipers thumped back and forth like
a metronome, yet even on the fastest setting they barely cleared
the water gushing down the windshield. Inside the vehicle,
however, it was comfortable, with heat humming softly from
the dashboard vents, warming the chill air. Paul McCartney sang
of yesterdays on the tape cassette.

Spencer had been a fan of the Beatles since he saw them
on their 1965 North America tour at the Cow Palace in San
Francisco. This was a year before the official inauguration of
the Church of Satan. He had gone with Anton LaVey, who had
used his connections to get them backstage passes, and while
LaVey had been tripping out on acid with Ringo Starr and George
Harrison, Spencer had spent an hour speaking to Yoko Ono.
They'd been alone, sipping wine in a room with comfortable

sofas, but aside from this all he could recall of their time together was the nearly uncontrollable urge he'd had to strangle her to death. Although he had these urges often, the reason for the intensity of that particular urge, he suspected, was because she was famous—or at least famous by association to someone famous by merit—and he had never killed a famous woman before. But of course killing her had been out of the question. He would never have gotten away with it. So he parted her company with a pleasant farewell and a kiss on the cheek.

When John Lennon was murdered fifteen years later, Spencer liked to think he was indirectly responsible for the man's death. Because if he'd killed Yoko Ono that day in 1965, John Lennon's life would have followed a different path. He might never have purchased the apartment at The Dakota. He might never have returned from Record Plant Studio on that fateful night. And even had the delusional man who shot him tracked him down elsewhere, the bullet he fired might not have been fatal.

Time, Spencer thought, was like a coat with an infinite number of pockets containing an infinite number of futures: you never knew what lay hidden within each.

A reflective yellow road sign warned of an upcoming turn.

Spencer slowed to fifteen miles an hour and reminded himself to return the jerry cans to the shelf in the garage, and to wash his hands in the first-floor bathroom, to eliminate any trace smell of gasoline. He and Lynette no longer shared the same bed. He had taken to sleeping in the guest bedroom some years ago, so now it was no longer the guest bedroom, he supposed, but his bedroom. Even so, when the news of Mary of Sorrows church burning to the ground during the night reached her tomorrow, he didn't need her wondering if she could smell gasoline as she puttered about the house. She wouldn't be able to, of course, he was being paranoid, but being paranoid had served him well throughout the years.

At the summit of Eagle Bluff, Grandview Lane flattened out and continued for another half mile. He passed only two other residences, both impressive country estates with gated drives and three-car garages. Grandview Lane was the most desirable address in all of Summit County, offering sweeping views of Boston Mills Country Club far below.

Spencer's home sat on two lush acres at the end of the road. It was a modern design made of reinforced concrete and glass, oval in shape, the second-floor off-centered from the first in an avant-garde sort of way. He had designed it himself and had collaborated with the architects during the planning phase, then with the builders during the construction phase, making sure no corners were cut. It had been an expensive project, but money had not been an issue. He'd been investing in the local real estate market for nearly twenty years. He had a savvy knack for finding diamonds in the rough, and knowing when to cut his losses. Consequently he'd amassed an impressive portfolio of properties, all of which were occupied with long-lease renters, providing him a substantial cash flow on top of his regular income.

The Volvo's headlights fell upon a rain-whipped police cruiser parked in the roundabout driveway in front of his home. Lights burned behind the Levolor blinds in several of the first-floor windows.

Spencer was so surprised he almost slammed the brakes. His immediate impulse was to turn around and get the hell out of there. He didn't do this. His headlights might have already been spotted. Moreover, whatever business had brought the police to his home at this late hour couldn't be related to Mother of Sorrows church. He had set the fire all of ten minutes before. This had to be an unrelated visit—but concerning what?

Had something happened to Lynette?

Yes, that had to be it. She'd had a stroke or a heart attack.

Spencer wanted to believe this was the case. He wished fervently it were so. Yet he couldn't convince himself of it. The timing was too coincidental.

Spencer parked behind the black and white—"Sheriff" stenciled next to the police department shield—and cut the engine. He retrieved his briefcase from the passenger seat, climbed out, and hurried through the downpour to the front stoop. He took a moment to collect himself at the door, then swung it open and stepped into the marble foyer. The house was silent. "Hello?" he called.

Alan Humperdinck, the Summit County sheriff, and a young deputy, both wearing gray rain slickers over their uniforms, stepped from a doorway down the hall. They had been in the living room.

Humperdinck was in his sixties, on the cusp of retirement. He had a sun-weathered face and hard gray eyes, cop's eyes, suspicious, wary. Spencer had been introduced to him a half dozen times over the years at community gatherings and festivals. However, they'd never exchanged more than passing pleasantries. The deputy couldn't have been more than twenty. Beneath his wide-brimmed Stetson, his face was gaunt, white, anemic.

"Sheriff Humperdinck," Spencer said, allowing his genuine confusion to inform his tone. He took a step forward and extended his hand in greeting.

Humperdinck merely looked at it with an expression equal parts surprise and loathing, and right then Spencer knew Lynette was fine. They were here for him. Somehow they knew about the church. It was impossible, but there was no other explanation for the frosty—no, the downright rude—reception.

Spencer lowered his hand and adopted a concerned expression. "What's happened, Sheriff? Is it Lynette? Is my wife all right?"

"She's okay," Humperdinck said tightly. "She called us."

Spencer frowned. "She called you? Why? What's happened?"

"Where were you just now, Mr. Pratt?"

"I was at the hospital."

"At this hour?"

"I often stay late, to catch up on work. Now, Sheriff, I must demand to know what's happened."

Humperdinck reached a gnarled, liver-spotted hand into the back pocket of his trousers and withdrew a card. He began to read from it. It took Spencer a moment to realize he was citing a variation of the *Miranda* warning: "You are a suspect in several capital crimes. You will accompany us to the Boston Mills police barracks. You have the right to remain silent—"

"Now hold on a minute, Sheriff—"

"You have the right to legal counsel. If you cannot afford legal counsel, such will be provided for you—"

"I'm not going anywhere with you," Spencer interrupted more forcefully. "Not until you tell me what in God's name is going on."

"You're coming with us one way or the other, Mr. Pratt," Humperdinck said. "If you refuse to come willingly, Deputy Dawson will wake Judge Pardy and get a warrant for your arrest. Given what your wife has shown us, that would be very easy."

"Lynette? Where is she?" Spencer stepped forward.

The two officers blocked his path.

"Get out of my damn way," he snapped. "This is my bloody house, isn't it?"

For a moment Spencer didn't think Humperdinck was going to concede. His old body seemed to tremble with a barely constrained hostility. But then, reluctantly, he stepped aside. The deputy did so as well, his eyes downcast.

Spencer turned his bullish body sideways to slip between them in the narrow hallway. He stopped at the entrance to the living room, from where they had emerged. Lynette sat on the buffalo-hide chesterfield, staring up at him with wet eyes.

Dozens of Polaroid photographs were spread out on the coffee table before her. Spencer stiffened in surprise. This morphed into panic, then rage. The dumb whore had gone snooping when he was out! She had somehow gotten into his locked study. She had discovered the false top on the ottoman, what he kept *within* the ottoman, and she'd called the police on him.

Spencer's mind raced, searching for excuses, but there were no excuses to be found, there was no way to explain the photographs, nor his collection of Satanic paraphernalia, which alone would link him to the massacre at Mary of Sorrows church.

"Lynnette?" he said, stepping into the living room, his eyes searching for a weapon. "What's going on? What are these photographs? Why did you call these gentlemen?"

She didn't answer.

"Mr. Pratt," Humperdinck said. He and the deputy had stuck close behind him. "You need to come with us. Now."

Spencer whirled on him. "Not until you tell me what the bloody hell is going on here, Sheriff! What are these purported capital crimes of which I have been accused?"

"Murder," Humperdinck said coldly. He moved next to Spencer and pointed at the photographs on the coffee table. "These were discovered in your study."

"My study?" he repeated, though he was thinking: *A chair? No, too unwieldy. The bronze bookend on the bookshelf? But how did he reach it without drawing suspicion?* "Impossible," he added. "I've never seen these photos before in my life."

Humperdinck gripped Spencer's right biceps. "We'll continue this discussion at the barracks."

"Just a moment, Sheriff," Spencer said, reaching into the inside pocket of his blazer. "I need my eyeglasses."

"He doesn't wear—" Lynette began.

Spencer's fingers curled around the gold-plated ballpoint pen in the pocket. He plunged it into Humperdinck's right eyeball, driving the shaft three inches deep, into the man's brain. Humperdinck spasmed, almost as if he had been zapped by an electrical shock, then fell to the floor, where he continued to convulse.

Lynette screamed. The deputy cried out and faltered backward.

Already moving, Spencer tore open the buttoned clasp on Humperdinck's leather holster and withdrew the .357 Magnum. He swung the service revolver toward the deputy, who was fumbling with his own holstered weapon. He squeezed the trigger. The kickback rocked Spencer onto his rear. The hollow-point slug blew straight through the deputy's chest, punching him backward into the hallway. Spencer fired a second time. The bullet hit the already dying deputy in the gut. The kid slid to his ass, leaving two blood-splattered, plate-sized holes in the wall behind him.

Spencer leaped to his feet, shot Humperdinck in the chest to end his suffering, then aimed the gun at Lynette, who had turned white as a sheet.

"Spencer..." she whispered. "I'm your wife..."

"Not anymore," he said.

He blew her brains out the back of her skull.

Spencer went to his bedroom on the second floor, tugged his suitcase off the top of his bureau, and tossed it onto the queen bed. He unzipped the main pocket and filled it with his clothes, not bothering to remove the wire hangers. He selected items mostly from his summer wardrobe, shorts and golf shirts, given that the Yucatán Peninsula enjoyed a year-round tropical climate. Next he went to the master bathroom, retrieved his leather travel case from the cupboard beneath the sink, and filled it with toiletries. Back in the bedroom he upended the contents of the studded oak box that sat on the dresser—cufflinks, watches, rings—onto the clothes he had hastily packed. Finally he zipped the bulging suitcase closed and lugged it downstairs. He left it by the front door while he went to the basement gym. He glanced about the room, at all the Life Fitness exercise equipment which he had used every day for much of the last decade. Today his workout would have been chest and triceps and quads.

No matter, he thought. He would choose a hotel when he reached Kentucky tomorrow, or even Tennessee, that featured an exercise room. Perhaps one with a swimming pool as well... and maybe a heated hot tub. Yes, why not? If you're going to live life on the lam, you may as well do it as comfortably as you could.

Adjacent to the floor-to-ceiling mirror was a glass-and-steel fire ax case. Spencer depressed the two screw heads on the underside of it. The case with its false backing swung away from the wall on hidden hinges, revealing a safe. He swiveled the knob left and right, entering the correct number combination, then opened the thick door. He tugged a black duffel bag out. It dropped to the floor with the heavy thump of two hundred sixty-three thousand dollars.

Contingency plan two.

Spencer returned to the first floor. On the way to the front door he found he had a slight bounce in his step. He had wanted to leave the life he had become a slave to for a long time now: the hospital, Summit County, Lynette. But he always felt he had too much invested to simply pack up and leave. Nevertheless, necessity was not only the mother of invention but also of motivation. Getting ratted to the cops by his duplicitous wife was, ironically, the best thing that could have happened to him.

He had become untethered, unconditionally free.

In the living room, stepping over the sheriff's body to retrieve the Polaroids from the coffee table, Spencer's gaze fell on Lynette. Although slumped backward on the chesterfield, she had remained in an upright position. She could have been knitting, or watching television, except for the fact she was missing her head from her mandible up.

Had he ever loved her? he wondered. Yes, he thought he had. He had been lonely in those early years after being kicked out of the Church of Satan, he had needed companionship, and she had offered it to him. She was never a great conversationalist, and she didn't have many original ideas of her own, but she was a good listener. And he supposed that's what he'd wanted. Someone to listen to him, to agree with him, to admire him.

Spencer slipped the photographs into his blazer pocket and went to the front door. He paused on the front porch to watch a magnificent display of lightning, then he carried the suitcase and duffel bag to the Volvo, loading both onto the backseat. He was about to return to the house, to collect the contents of the ottoman from his study—the police might eventually piece together his role in all that happened this evening, but he saw no need to make it easy for them—when a voice said, "Not so fast, Spence."

Spencer whirled around. Squinting against the onslaught of rain, he made out a shape emerging from the nearby trees. Thunder boomed and lightning flared almost simultaneously, and in the brief heavenly illumination he recognized Cleavon. His brother held a long, thick branch in his hand.

"Cleave...?" Spencer said in disbelief.

How the hell had he gotten free of the church?

"Who blew the whistle on you, Spence?"

"My, er—my wife, Lynette, if you can believe that."

"So you killed her, did ya?"

Spencer cleared his throat. "There was no other choice."

"And the sheriff too?"

"Again, there was—"

"No choice." Cleavon nodded. "Just like there wasn't no choice but to burn everyone alive in the church, that right?"

"This was your mess, Cleave. Weasel, Jesse—they were your friends. They screwed up, not me. Someone had to take the fall."

"And Floyd and Earl? They were your *brothers*."

"It's...unfortunate, yes... I certainly didn't want to—"

"And me, Spence? What about me?"

"Christ, Cleave! Don't—" Thunder drowned out the rest of the sentence. "Don't get all maudlin on me," he repeated. "You left me no choice. You would never have agreed to—"

"That woman wasn't your first, was she? That Mary? How many people you killed, Spence?"

"What does it matter?"

"It don't. But I'm curious."

"Forty-one," he said. "Plus Mary and the eight you know about."

"What's that? Fifty?" Cleavon whistled. "You're slicker than greased goose shit, Spence. That's gotta be a record or something. And I didn't never suspect nothing. Not 'till that Mary anyhow."

"Yes, well, now you know," Spencer said impatiently. "Your older brother is a serial killer. And so are you. Now, I have a long drive ahead of me…" As he spoke he reached into the blazer pocket for the sheriff's revolver.

Cleavon was unexpectedly fast. He covered the distance between them almost instantaneously, swinging the branch in his hand as he came. The business end struck Spencer in the face with bone-shattering force, spinning him about. He landed on the macadam, on his chest, dazed. He rolled onto his back, blinking stars from his vision, wondering what happened to the revolver.

Cleavon loomed over him, backlit by a burst of lighting that electrified the black sky, turning it a deep-sea blue. He raised the branch with both hands.

Spencer opened his mouth but choked on the blood pooling inside it. Nothing came out but a garbled, incomprehensible plea.

Cleavon felt no pity as he brought the tree branch down with all his strength across the top of his brother's skull. He repeated this action again and again, payback for Earl, for Floyd, for Jesse, even for that dumb shit Weasel.

Then, panting hard with exertion, his eyes tearing from sweat and rain, he tossed the blood-covered tree branch aside and stared for a long moment at what remained of his brother's head. He spat on his lifeless body and turned to leave, to head back to the El Camino he'd parked up the road when his eyes fell on the Volvo. The back door was ajar. A suitcase and duffel bag rested on the seat. The duffel was unzipped, and a brick of cash wrapped in an elastic band poked out the top.

Cleavon blinked twice, then went to the car. He tugged the mouth of the bag open wider. "Judas Priest!" he whispered. "*Judas fuckin' Priest!*" Then he turned his face to the heavens and danced in the rain and laughed like he had rarely laughed in all his miserable life.

CHAPTER 30

"We came, we saw, we kicked its ass!"
Ghostbusters (1984)

Beetle discovered a set of car keys on Goliath's body, which turned out to be for the rusted old banger parked in front of the church. He set Greta gently in shotgun and the small woman across the backseat. They were both unconscious but breathing. Then he got behind the wheel and sped to town. Given the late hour, and the full-throttled tempest, the rain-slicked streets of Boston Mills were deserted. However, he came across a twenty-four-hour gas station, where a clerk told him directions to the hospital. He arrived at the emergency entrance of the Boston Mills Health Center a few minutes later. Medical staff wheeled the two injured women away on stretchers while Beetle remained behind in the reception to explain what happened. He was then led to a private room where he changed into a dry paper frock and was checked over by a grandfatherly doctor who, upon finding no serious injuries, advised him to rest until the police arrived to take his statement.

Exhausted and emptied, Beetle fell immediately asleep, waking some eight or nine hours later at eleven o'clock that same morning. He was surprised to find a pretty redhead in the previously empty bed opposite his. She was watching him with haunted green eyes.

"Hi," she said hesitantly.

"Hi," he said.

"The police were here for you."

"When?"

"Three hours ago? I was just admitted then. They questioned me. They wanted to question you too, but they weren't allowed to wake you up."

"They questioned you?" he said.

"My friends..." Her face dropped. She looked like someone who had just been told they had a week to live. "You saved one of them. Cherry. The doctor told me she's going to be okay."

"She was your friend?"

The woman nodded. "The police told me about you. What happened at the church. I told them I had never met you before."

"Who were those men at the church?"

"Crazies."

"Satanists?"

"I don't know. They attacked my friends and me in the woods. I got away and hid in a school bus. Then when it became light I found the road. I followed it out of the national park. I came to the church—or what was left of it. There were police and firefighters. They brought me here. They said they didn't know what happened to the rest of my friends. But I think...I think..." She rubbed tears from her eyes, shaking her head. "Where could they be?"

Suddenly Beetle remembered the small woman shouting off the names of three or four people who the man named Cleavon had murdered, along with something about a snake...feeding her boyfriend to a snake?

He decided it was not his place to break this news to the already distressed woman. Instead he said simply, "I'm sorry."

She nodded, still rubbing her eyes.

He said, "Did you hear anything about someone named Greta?"

"The doctor mentioned her. He thought she was my friend.

He said she was also in stable condition."

Beetle felt a bit of the tightness in his chest loosen. Then he wondered where the police were, when they would return to question him. And after they did, would they contact the army, tell them they had an AWOL soldier in their custody? Or would they release him, let him go…to where?

Beetle frowned. It was a valid question. Where was he going to go? Not back to Savannah. The recent events hadn't changed his relationship with Sarah; there was nothing left for him in Georgia. However, something else *had* changed. He found he no longer had a desire, a need, to kill himself. Although the night before he had been so sure it had been his only recourse, his only way out from the nightmare his life had become, he no longer felt that way. He didn't know why this was the case. He wasn't going to philosophize over it either. Because perhaps this feeling was only a reprieve, perhaps the darkness and despair would return in a week, or a month…perhaps…but he didn't think so. A switch had been flicked inside him. He felt different, not ebullient—not like he had as a kid on his birthdays, or on the day he wed Sarah—but different. Alive. He had almost forgotten how pleasing, how natural, a feeling that was.

The door to the room opened. A portly man with salt-and-pepper hair and a too-tight tweed jacket appeared. His eyes fell on the redhead, and his face lit up with joy.

"Mandy!" he said.

"Daddy!" she blurted.

The man rushed to her bedside and wrapped her in an embrace.

"They told me they called you…" she mumbled into his shoulder.

"I came as fast as I could."

The redhead said something more, though Beetle couldn't hear what, not that he was listening anyway, for he was suddenly thinking of his own parents, how nice it would be to see them again, and he knew he had a place to go to after all.

EPILOGUE

"Boy, the next word that comes out of your mouth better be some brilliant fuckin' Mark Twain shit. 'Cause it's definitely getting chiseled on your tombstone."
The Devil's Rejects (2005)

The school year had only finished one week before, but eight-year-old Danny Kalantzis was already anticipating the best summer of his life. Most past summers he stayed in Cincinnati and didn't do much of anything and then September came around and it was time to start school all over again. This year, however, his best friend Roy Egan had invited him to his family's cottage for a full week. Danny's family didn't have a cottage, and he had never been to one before, so he wasn't sure what to expect. But it was on a small lake in northeastern Ohio, and they could go swimming every day and take rides in the motor boat. He could even try water skiing if he wanted to. He wasn't sure he did. It sounded difficult. Roy told him there was also a rope hanging from one of the trees along the shore, and they could swing from it into the water. That was probably good enough for Danny.

Nevertheless, what made this week really great was the fact Roy's sister, Peggy, had come along as well. She was a year older than Danny and Roy, and Danny thought she was the prettiest girl in school. Originally she was supposed to attend summer camp for ballerinas, but then her friend backed out, so she did too.

Because Roy didn't want to sit beside her during the car trip, Danny got to, and he was fine with that arrangement. He had been thrilled every time his knee touched Peggy's, or his shoulder brushed hers.

Ten minutes ago they had pulled into a picnic spot in Cuyahoga Valley National Park. Roy's mother had packed a cooler full of egg-salad sandwiches. Roy had wolfed his down, along with a cold can of Pepsi, then told his parents he and Danny were going to go ahead to check out Brandywine Falls. Danny had wanted to stay behind, so he would be close to Peggy, but he couldn't say this, of course, and he obediently jogged after Roy, still finishing off his sandwich as he went.

Halfway to the falls, however, Roy left the trail and began making his way through the forest.

Danny hesitated. "Where are you going?"

"Come on!"

Danny followed.

When Roy found a glade suitable to his liking, he plopped down on his butt and took a sad, bent cigarette from the pocket of his shorts, along with a book of matches.

Danny's eyes widened. "Where'd you get that?"

"My dad. Don't worry. He doesn't know."

Roy stuck the cigarette expertly between his lips.

"You smoked before?" Danny said, impressed.

"A few times," Roy said proudly.

He lit the cigarette with a matchstick and sucked hard. His face turned gray, then he bent forward and began coughing up a lung.

Danny bust a gut laughing. Roy must have kept coughing for a full thirty seconds. He was holding the cigarette toward Danny, telling him to try it.

"No way," Danny said.

"Don't be a chicken!"

"Look what happened to you."

"Chicken!"

"I don't want it."

"You're such a wimp."

"*You're* a wimp."

"At least I tried it."

"Try it again."

Roy contemplated the cigarette, then tossed it away.

"Seriously, Danny," he said, "you're such a wimp."

"I know you are, but what am I?"

"Oh jeez." Roy rolled his eyes, then jumped to his feet. "I gotta take a dump."

"Right here?"

"No, not right here, you perv. What, you wanna watch?"

"Then where?"

"In the trees."

"I think there were toilets back at the picnic area."

"Those things are disgusting. You can get diseases from the seats."

"You don't even have toilet paper."

"You can lick my ass."

"You're so gross."

"I'll be back."

Danny watched Roy forge a path through the trees until he was out of sight. Then Danny lay down to get comfortable, folding his hands behind his head and staring up at the sky. Much of it was blocked by the canopy of branches overhead, but he could see bits and pieces, all bright blue, not a cloud anywhere.

He closed his eyes and wondered where he would be sleeping tonight. Would he have his own bedroom? Or would he share a room with Roy? That would be fun. They could stay up late, talking or reading comic books, like they did when they had sleepovers. Roy's parents were pretty cool with curfews and stuff like that. They let Roy do a lot of things Danny's parents would never let him do. And besides, it was summer break. It wasn't like they had school the next day.

And what about Peggy? he wondered. She was a girl, so she would have a private room, obviously. Danny wondered if he should try to kiss her at some point. He was a year younger after all. He was only going into grade six. She probably still thought of him as a little kid. Then again, she'd laughed at some of his jokes in the car. Didn't that mean she liked him? Maybe if he could keep making her laugh, *she* would kiss *him*. Maybe they would even get married one day. That would be pretty neat. Then Roy would be his brother or half-brother...

As Danny unwittingly drifted into a light sleep, his thoughts turned to what Roy's dad had told them about Helltown during the car ride. The place was right around here somewhere. Supposedly there had been a bunch of devil worshippers a few years back who lived in the woods and kidnapped people. But then some army guy, Special Forces or something like that, tracked them all down and burned them alive in some church. Roy's dad stopped there because Roy's mom told him he was going to give "the kids" nightmares. Roy and Danny protested, they wanted to hear more, but Roy's dad changed the topic. Sometimes it seemed to Danny that Roy's mom ruled Roy's family. It was true she was stricter than Roy's dad (who was still pretty lenient by Danny's parents' standards), and she could be scary sometimes when she got angry, but for the most part Danny liked her. He just better make sure he stayed out of her bad books for the next week...

The twenty-six-foot-long green anaconda slithered silently through the deadfall toward the sleeping boy, forked tongue flicking in and out of its lipless grimace, collecting the sleeping boy's scent particles from the air and the ground. It had devoured a similar creature years before, on the night it had escaped the House in the Woods, and like all the raccoons and deer and foxes and rodents it had subsisted on since, it knew the creature to be easy prey.

When the snake came within striking distance, it opened its mouth one hundred eighty degrees and sunk its rear-facing teeth into the boy's shoulder. The boy awoke, jerking then thrashing, trying to flee, but the snake was already coiling its body around its prey, constricting and wrapping, around and around and around, until the boy went still.

Then it ate.

ABOUT THE AUTHOR

Jeremy Bates

 USA TODAY and #1 AMAZON bestselling author Jeremy Bates has published more than twenty novels and novellas. They have sold more than one million copies, been translated into several languages, and been optioned for film and TV by major studios. Midwest Book Review compares his work to "Stephen King, Joe Lansdale, and other masters of the art." He has won both an Australian Shadows Award and a Canadian Arthur Ellis Award. He was also a finalist in the Goodreads Choice Awards, the only major book awards decided by readers.

Made in United States
North Haven, CT
25 June 2024

54070548R00164